LAST CHANCE

A FIRST BORN BOOK

FROM

THE GUARDIANS OF DARE CHRONICLES

Janelle Gabay

Copyright © 2022

Janelle Gabay Books LLC

All rights reserved.

ISBN: 978-0-9961588-4-8

FIRST BORN

FIRST AWAKENED

LAST CHANCE

BALEFIRE CITY

After the great Entente War, half of the world's cities collapsed, destroyed by a combination of horrific events including, but not limited to, the use of nuclear weapons, an infestation of autonomous artificial intelligence, and some nasty little fungi spores stirred up during the battles. The same aggressive political, civil, and religious unrest that had erupted before the war continued after it. This toxic soup birthed the Wastelands. It spread like a jagged edged cancer. Countries either got devoured or built walls to hide behind. One metropolis arose inside the Wastelands. It didn't rise with ease or by a lack of hard work. The Sannas family labored for decades to grow Balefire City—the light among shadows.

House Sanna 2122 comprises of Queen Priscella, Princess Marianne, Princess Lucianna, Prince Briggen, Prince Theo, and Princess Brianna.

ONE

The blows came one after the other, dynamic and painful, but Germaine kept her footing until a solid punch from the gang's leader, Jinx, knocked her to the ground. Germaine's winnings scattered around the street.

Xander, a thick, grubby street kid, picked up Germaine's most coveted prize, the magical spectacles. "Huh. Let's see what else she's got in those pockets."

Hands clawed and grabbed at Germaine's body. The street's gravel scraped her back and elbows as she squirmed to get away. She glimpsed Samantha's face amongst the gang, standing at a distance, and flashed her a silent plea.

Sam's eyes dropped.

Crow, the meanest girl in the group, landed a wicked kick to Germaine's stomach. A rib cracked, and blood hit the back of her throat. Anger raged through her, but the pain kept her from reacting. She rolled onto her side and curled into a ball. Her body braced for more abuse.

"That's all I got!" Germaine muttered.

She'd won all that stuff fair and square. They had no right to take it all back, but what had she expected walking away from their nightly game of Wack. No one was allowed to quit after a winning streak. She should've been smarter. She couldn't believe she'd let them sneak up on her like that. Walking home alone after dark was foolish.

Beaten, bloodied, friendless, and picked clean of her things, surrender seemed her only option. Then it happened. The gang quieted and the air stilled. Germaine dared to open her swollen eyes. Her attackers didn't move, didn't swing at her. She sat up. Their eyes glazed over as if entranced. She cautiously stood. Again, they didn't move, didn't speak.

Crow, the one that had landed the last and fiercest kick, stood as rigid as a stone pillar. Germaine staggered over to her. The girl didn't budge. Germaine spit in her face and laughed. She waltzed over to the brutish boy who held her spectacles. She pried open his dirty fingers and took back what she'd fairly won. She collected the coins but left the useless junk.

The strangeness of the scene began to sink in. She wanted to punch her spineless friend in the face, but the street's eeriness crept under her skin. She needed to get out of there.

Where's my knife?

She turned and ran smack into a ragged figure. "For Pall's sake," she cried out on instinct. Running into thieves and drug addicts who swung bats and fists was a problem that she, a Nerve spy, could handle. She'd been doing it for years. But colliding with a creature of the dark could be deadly.

Her feet moved slowly away from the short creature. She held her breath hoping whatever hid under those layers of cloth wouldn't hear her. Some creatures were blind others deaf. She'd heard about vampires that wouldn't strike unless triggered by stress hormones. She willed her body to be calm but had no idea how to control instinctive bodily functions.

"Stop." A youthful voice came from under the hood.

The word held Germaine still in some sort of invisible force-field, but she wasn't entranced like the others, which was even worse. If this creature wanted to do something horrific to her, she'd rather her mind be numb.

Slender, pale hands extended from floppy sleeves and pulled off the hood to expose the face of an extremely young child with shimmering skin.

"Who are you?" Germaine asked.

"Nichola."

The invisible hold let go. Germaine stumbled forward nearly toppling into Nichola. She had tensed each muscle fighting off the spell that its release felt like a rush of energy.

"Sorry," Germaine said. She didn't know where to look. She worried Nichola was some sort of siren and gazing into her lavender eyes would be dangerous. Instead, she focused on the scene around her. She spotted her knife but didn't dare go for it. Blood stains dotted the concrete. Her blood. Scrapes covered her face, arms, and legs. Her nose ached. She swiped under it then wiped the fresh blood on her pants.

"Go home." Nichola flicked her wrist and the street kids walked away.

Germaine watched in awe. Once again terror struck her core. Now she was alone after dark with a demon child. She clutched her magical spectacles, but her knife lay on the ground a yard away. What use would it be against a girl that could send kids like Jinx and Crow away with the flick of her wrist?

Her mind raced through all she'd read about the creatures of the Wastelands. Nichola was small and youthful and beautiful. Maybe she was fae—a fairy or sprite. Didn't that kind like to bargain?

The girl's head tilted as if she expected Germaine to offer something.

What? What did she want? Germaine was grateful to have her special glasses and her life. And she hadn't thanked the girl yet.

"Thank you."

Nichola smiled.

The two little words seemed small and petty. Germaine wanted to offer her something, but all she had were the spectacles that she desperately needed. She'd been told that with them she could see the Pall up close, while remaining miles away atop her tower. She would use them to study the Pall's foggy mist that devoured people. But not just the Pall, she could watch everything from a safe distance, gather her information without anyone knowing. As a spy, the spectacles would be a useful tool. And who knows what else they could do. They'd been crafted with magic.

She'd worked hard to win them and was nearly beaten to death to keep them. Her grip on the spectacles tightened.

"How can I ever repay you?" Germaine asked the horrible question. Being indebted to a creature could be an endless nightmare.

"I want you to have dinner with me once a week."

Germaine's mouth gaped. Had she heard her correctly? Rancid suspicion coated her throat. It couldn't be that simple.

"I live over there, one hundred sixty Rose Jardin, but the zero is missing so it's just Sixteen Rose Jardin." Nichola giggled. "Tomorrow. We eat at seven. Don't be late, Germaine." She drew her hood back over her head and skipped home.

I didn't tell her my name, or did I? Germaine inhaled deeply then let it out slowly. The oxygen didn't relieve her anxious confusion. Her heart still pounded, and her nerves continued to jump. She ran.

When she arrived at the Central Nerve outpost, Franny awaited. Her tall willowy body stood ghostly in the moonlight as her nightgown blew in the wind. She opened her arms and Germaine ran into them. "What happened child?"

"I got jumped by some street kids." Germaine swallowed down the fear and sorrow rising in her throat. She looked up into Franny's eyes, the same shade of lavender as the strange girl she'd just met. She'd heard others call Franny a Lavender Witch, maybe Nichola was one too. She almost told Franny about her. Instead, she laid her head against Franny's chest and exhaled all her exhaustion. It was almost as if she couldn't tell her. Maybe the little witch had spelled her silent.

"Do you need tending to?"

"No, just some soap and water and sleep."

"Okay child. Let's get you to your block then." Franny escorted her home.

Germaine walked inside then turned back to thank her and possibly tell her all that had happened. The heavy weight of it might go away if she confided in Franny.

"Franny?" Germaine stepped back outside and glanced around. The old witch who looked like a thirty-year-old woman had vanished. It was no secret Franny was capable of walking through time and space, but she rarely used her magical ability.

Something locked inside Germaine as she stood alone on the front steps of her concrete block home. Her heart cinched her new secret like a message in a bottle corked tightly, for now.

TWO

NORTH CASTLE — BALEFIRE CITY

APRIL 2122

PRINCESS BRIANNA

Brianna Sanna had scarcely two minutes of warning before the attack. She'd been walking the halls of her home, Eminence Castle. These were no ordinary hallways. They rose the height of two giants with lengths expanding into unseen distances. The extraordinary castle was wedged at the base of Eminence Mountain, hundreds of miles east of the true Wastelands, and only a few miles west of that ominous shadow void, the Pall.

The Eminence Mountain stood north of Balefire City, hence the affectionate nickname North Castle. The mountain's magnificent peaks provided a formidable backdrop for the architectural genius of the castle. Combined, they towered over the city's people below.

On several occasions, when Brianna was a little girl, she'd gotten lost inside the castle. Seriously lost. Not a silly girl playing a game of hide and seek, the kind of lost that a child's paranoia never forgets. She'd run breathlessly down a maze of corridors and galleries frightened by the antique art. Paintings of old dead queens from reigns long before the world fell to the waste and shadows. Their painted eyes followed her every turn. Fanged wolves leaped from painting to painting or seemed to.

Even the newer charcoal on canvases haunted her with tendrils of shadow smoke stretching past their boundaries to reach for her. She'd sworn one caught her long flowing gray hair and created her unique streaks of midnight blue. Every wastelander had gray hair. None had blue. She'd cut it short the next day to her mother's chagrin. But the blue remained. Now it hit slightly past her shoulders, but she rarely wore it unbound.

Then there were the albino rock statues. As a child, she'd feared they'd come to life and grab her, pull her out of reality and into another dimension. But for all its many rooms, scary paintings, and cold hard stone, she loved it. She grew older, became less imaginative, and gained a better sense of direction. Now this elaborate home felt natural, even cozy.

As she strolled seconds before catastrophe, the castle lived and breathed energy. So when a hulking man misted into solid form in front of her, she wasn't entirely surprised. After all, she was a witch, and this was obviously some magic trick set up by her twin brother, Theo, to tap into her childhood fears and scare her.

The man's giant hands clasped around her forearm and tugged. "Please. Come with me!"

"No! Who are you?" She stepped onto a black marble square on the chevron tile floor and cast a halting spell. He stumbled when she froze, and he didn't. Both of his bear-like hands grasped around her waist and yanked. The spell held, but either this man had inhuman strength, or squares didn't bind as well as circles—or both because he nearly dragged her away.

A violent storm brewed in his blue eyes, but his voice remained calm. "In one minute, the Grand Sorcerer Lautaro and his army will storm this castle to kill you and your siblings."

"Where are they?"

"They've each been assigned a Guardian or Elite. I'm sure they're safe."

She believed him for reasons she didn't know. He was a stranger. But she recognized the name Lautaro. She released the spell and ran.

He followed.

She reached the spiral tower stairs and began to climb.

"No, Princess. This way."

She glanced back. "I can't leave Grandmum's grimoire."

He scooped her up and despite his size, climbed faster than any silver fox she'd seen in the mountains or scorpion-tailed waste-monkey in the Wastelands.

"Here," she yelled before he blew past the twentieth floor. She hopped from his arms and rushed to the chest of drawers, thrusting open the last one. She grabbed the giant volume of spells then hopped back into his arms as if he was a stallion and not a man. "Let's go!"

He nodded a hint of a smile played on his massive face. But they didn't get far. Two Maldito Ministry Soldiers charged up the tower. He set her down and swung one soldier over the banister. She stabbed the second.

"Where was that hidden?" His brow cocked.

"It's one of many." She frowned at the blood staining her bone-blade. She sheathed it between her breasts.

His eyes followed the blade then darted back up.

All seven blades felt hot on her skin, as if they itched to fight. She carried a blade strapped to each thigh and ankle, one between her breasts, another at her waist, and lastly, the blade camouflaged as a hair clip pinned up the sides of her locks. And she wasn't a warrior princess like Lucianna, her sister. However, she'd been trained, as had her brothers and sisters.

Brianna wasn't dressed like a princess. Her black shirt clung to her curves. Her trousers fit loosely but cinched tightly at both the waist and ankles. She wore plain slip-on shoes each decorated with a shiny Pall stone, smoke trapped in smooth round crystals. Pall stones cuffed her wrists, hung from her ears, as well as from a chain around her neck. The crystals were the only pieces of clothing acknowledging her rank and status.

Her hero wore a uniform that molded to his immense body, the material clinging to an extravaganza of muscles. There were several pockets and compartments that held modern weapons, not ancient bone-blades. But the bones were surprisingly good at killing creatures.

They continued down the spiraling steps until shots fired up at them. They ducked into the third-floor arcade.

"The balcony." She pointed, and they raced to it.

Peering over, she swallowed. The daunting drop wrenched

her courage. Technically it was three stories, but physically it measured thrice that, due to the elevated height of the interior ceilings.

"Guardian?" she mumbled the question as the title twirled inside her mind searching for a definition. "You're immortal."

"Yes." He nodded. "Get on my back. I'll climb down."

She hesitated then jumped into place, clutching his waist with her legs, and the book with her arms, and murmuring all the protection spells she could remember. Plummeting to the rocky ground and being flattened by a beastly man wasn't the death she'd imagined for herself. She was a princess for Pall's sake. She would die with dignity and romance.

They landed, she sprang from his back cherishing the gritty gravel under her feet, but her reveling didn't last long. He dragged her back into the race for her life.

Sweat sheathed her back. She was ridiculously hot, burning from the inside out. The dusk's coolness whipped through the air providing minor relief to the bare skin of her chest but not cooling the rest of her clothed body. She stifled under its constraint and wanted more than anything to strip down to nothing. But for one, she couldn't risk the stop, and for two, she didn't undress in front of strange men even if he'd just saved her life.

Suddenly, he did stop. "Are you alright?"

Coughs and gasps escaped her before words. "Of course."

He cocked an eyebrow. "You're fire red."

That's when she noticed he had barely broken a sweat. Lucianna had warned her that she was out-of-shape, kept insisting she workout, train harder. Her sister was right. Brianna stood there panting, infuriated with her laziness. Once she caught her breath, she turned back to look at her home and screamed. She jolted toward the castle, but the man's giant arm slammed down pinning her back to his chest.

She sobbed.

In the distance, flames violently thrashed out of the windows, towers crumbled leaving gaping holes, shots and explosions echoed across the fields.

She shook under his hold, letting the rage and heartache surface.

He didn't let go.

Finally, she wilted.

He gently held her up and whispered into her hair, "I'm sorry."

Gulping down mouthfuls of tears, she said, "The staff. The orphans. What about the art? All those old pictures." Her limp body hiccupped against his hard chest. She wanted to save those awful paintings that had given her nightmares.

"I'm sure a lot of them were saved. Come. Let's get you to Umbra Castle."

She straightened. "Mum?"

He nodded.

"Theo, Lucianna, Briggen, and Marianne!" She stood firm, her feet burrowing into the soil.

"Yes. We got them all. Your family is safe." He tugged on her arm.

She didn't budge just looked around and saw only a falling sun and a fading sky and miles of forested trees. "How can you be sure?"

"I trust my fellow Guardians." He released his grip on her. A long exhale escaped his lips in surrender.

"What's your name?" she asked.

"Marcus, Guardian of Dare. At your service, milady." He mocked a bow and winked.

At last, she actually saw him, her mind calm enough to take in his features. She'd assumed from his monstrous size that he'd have an equally monstrous face. It wasn't the case. His face was kind with flushed cheeks and lazy eyes. A handsome face with the mischievous grin of a boy, but he was a man. Plump pink lips and tousled blonde curls that fell casually around his jawline completed the boyish charm.

She caught herself staring up at him, cleared her throat, and smothered the tingles creeping up her spine.

THREE

GUARDIAN VILLAGE — THE ENTENTE

MAY 2122

GUARDIAN SASHA

Josh Farmington twitched and glanced over his shoulder for the tenth time. His eyes darted from store to store, down alleyways and across the street.

"What is it?" Sasha Middleshire growled. He'd frayed her last nerve.

"Do you ever feel shadows following you in this village?" Josh twitched again.

"Not since the Wakers." She continued strolling the cobbled sidewalk of Rue de la Magie.

"No, this is different and strange. Shadows in the daylight." He shook his head. "It isn't normal."

Sasha halted as suspicion raced up her spine.

"Who's there?" Josh snapped his head around as if someone had tapped his shoulder.

"Marcus! Christopher!" Sasha ordered.

Soon Marcus, clad in a customized purple Guardian

uniform, shimmered into sight. Josh jumped and tripped nearly stumbling to the ground.

A mist frosted the air and soon Christopher was visible, guffawing alongside Marcus.

Sasha lit up with an uncharacteristic giddiness and bear hugged her friends. "How long?"

"Ay beg ya pardon," Marcus teased in an absurd cockney accent.

"How long have you guys been back?" She resisted the urge to punch his bulging bicep.

"Day before yesterday," Christopher said.

"What? And you didn't tell me!" Sasha shoved him.

"Too busy pranking your partner," Marcus said, accent gone, but not the teasing manner. He nudged Josh. "Come now, Josh, you're not mad, are you?"

Josh seemed startled anyone had included him in the conversation.

"Oh ... no ... It's fascinating. You two can go invisible?"

"Yep." Christopher nodded and smirked.

"Is that a common immortal gift?" Josh asked.

"No, it's rare." Christopher winked and landed an elbow blow to Josh's ribs.

Marcus added another nudge. "Only three of us."

"Who's the third?" Josh asked as he pinballed between them, never fully catching his balance.

Marcus and Sasha stilled as Josh stumbled into Christopher who placed two sturdy hands on his shoulders.

Children's giggles from the park at the top of the hill echoed off the air that froze between them. Even the rays from the sun could be heard whispering. And though surrounded by these pleasant things, as well as the scent of freshly baked bread from the Appleton's bakery, the three Guardians stared grimly at Josh.

"The traitor Gregory Lycott is the third Guardian with the gift of invisibility. He betrayed us all," Sasha said.

"How?" Josh asked.

"Long story best told over a pint." Marcus hung his mighty arm around Josh's neck and drew him inside the Blonde Dog Pub.

The pub was the old stomping ground for Marcus, Christopher, and Sasha. It thrived, as did many of the village vendors now that the boards had been lifted from the windows. A few months ago, being caught drunk in the streets after dark meant certain death at the hands of a Waker, but now, that fear was gone. The patrons drank, sang, ate, and celebrated.

They took a table in the back. A curvy brunette brought a round of ale over, gave Marcus a wink, and skipped away.

"Still a helpless flirt I see." Sasha lifted her glass and smiled.

"Can't help me love of women. Can't believe me little Audrey is gettin' married." Marcus clanged his glass with hers, took a swig, and sighed.

"Is that why you're back from assignment?" Sasha's voice hardened.

"Are you still vexing over that?" Christopher asked.

"I don't vex. I just felt I could've been an asset too."

"The High Council chose the squad, not us." Christopher gulped a large amount of beer.

"You're a fine Guardian, but ya' can't turn invisible." Marcus' brows lifted.

"Makes sense. It's a lot easier to spy when you can't be seen," Josh added. He had drunk only one fourth of his beer while the others ordered another round.

"See, the boy gets it. Smart one you got here." Marcus shoved his elbow into Josh's side again.

Josh huffed in agreement rubbing his bruised ribs.

Sasha planted her glass on the table. "So what's over there now?"

"Over where?" Christopher smirked, glints of teasing in his eyes.

Sasha shook her head and grunted. Both hands squeezed around her glass, her eyes never left Christopher's, even when she finally took a drink.

"Let's just say, I'm sure the horror you went through while the Wakers roamed the village equals the romance of the Wastelands." Christopher's tone dripped sarcasm. "Only it's still happenin' over there."

"That bad, huh?" Sasha's face sobered.

"Yeah." Christopher nodded. "And now that Lautaro's gone against the diplomatic agreement Audrey and Eleanor set up, it's gonna be war."

Silence fell over the group as they waited for Josh to finish his pint. The brunette brought over another round and a menu. Only Josh ordered food.

"So tell me more about this invisible traitor," Josh said.

"Remember I told you about Senator Zachary Eastwood and how he'd managed to clone an army of immortal offspring with Tarian's DNA?"

Josh's brows drew together in confusion.

"Since Tarian was the first immortal to be born in over 500 hundred years, Zachary thought his DNA held the answers to our immortality. And I guess it does since Zachary managed to clone immortals. When someone found out about his plan or got too suspicious of his treachery, he injected them with Death Serum." Sasha paused for a drink. "Well, Gregory Lycott was the one doing the actual injecting. He went invisible then snuck up on his victims. They were injected before they even knew what happened," she said, and Josh nodded in understanding.

"That's if you were a greenie," Marcus added.

"Non-gifted? The Guardians that wear green." Josh verified.

"Yep. Purple symbolizes extra talents," Marcus said, "Gifted immortals can see through the invisibility. We look like shadows to them, 'cept Tarian. He can see us outright. Sucks actually. I couldn't prank him. Your instincts are good, by the way."

"Thanks." Josh met Marcus' outreached beer with his own.

"Ya' kept Sasha safe right? You're a team."

"More like I saved his ass." Sasha frowned, but her eyes

softened with admiration. "We brought in only the best Entente Military Elites. Created a lethal Guardian/Elite task force to take down those Waker monsters."

Josh took two gulps, burped, then asked, "Where is Gregory Lycott? In prison?"

Sasha shook her head. "Burned up, with the rest of them. Zach realized the Death Serum's power to turn us into Wakers—Wakers that could kill Guardians. But Wakers die in fire so the joke's on him when we blew his warehouse of madness to the ground with him and his followers inside. Torched them all." Sasha cocked an eyebrow and took a swig.

Christopher's gaze fell. The emerald gleam of his eyes darkened and dulled to the green of a pine needle as he concentrated on the ale's effervescence.

"You're hiding something." Sasha leaned into him; her mouth so close to the side of his face she could feel her breath bounce off the stubble of his cheek.

"We never confirmed Gregory perished in that fire. We found proof of Zach and the others but Gregory—" Christopher shook his head. A lock of amber hair fell over his eye. He swept it away.

Sasha pulled away, swigged her beer then shrugged. "No one's seen him since."

Christopher and Marcus shared a glance.

A cold chill ran down Sasha's back as wild thoughts zoomed around her mind. She opened her mouth to speak but Marcus lifted his pint in a salute.

"Hey! We're here for a wedding! To Audrey and Tarian!"

"Hear, hear. To Audrey and Tarian," Christopher shouted, and soon the entire pub toasted the lover's happiness.

Sasha never got her answers as fellow Guardians and villagers began speeches praising the bravery of Tarian or the cleverness of Audrey even though the soon-to-be-newlyweds weren't in the pub. By the end of the afternoon, Josh's sentences slurred, and his stride tilted.

"This is your doing." Sasha wagged her finger at her two burly friends. "Help me get him home safely," she said, even though she was perfectly strong enough to carry him home on her own.

Marcus hoisted him over his shoulder and followed her back to the apartment inside Guardian Headquarters. Once Josh collapsed onto the couch the two men vanished.

Sasha threw up her arms. "Fine! Don't say goodbye."

The door opened and shut as if by a ghost's hand, their footsteps silent, but their chuckles loud.

She turned to see Josh plop over onto the sofa cushion and fall asleep. She sat on the opposite side, put her feet on the coffee table, and surrendered to mortal babysitting. "G.O.D. resume episode twenty-two." The personal robot switched on Sasha's favorite show, but it couldn't rid her mind of Gregory's ghost. What were Christopher and Marcus hiding? They'd found something in the Wastelands, and she wanted to know what.

FOUR

GUARDIAN VILLAGE — THE ENTENTE

GUARDIAN AUDREY

Audrey took the seat next to Tarian at the round rosewood table, the only resplendent thing in the dark, gloomy room. The mood forever somber around the four High Councilors as they paralyzed the air with a chill, but this gathering actually warranted the aura. If Eleanor couldn't convince them to enlist the Nerve Rebels' help, then House Sanna would fall and Lautaro would win, unless the Pall shadows killed them all.

Christopher and Marcus seemed to double in size adjacent to the frail Councilors. The men beamed life, warming everyone, and melting the chill. While the Councilors penned their papers, the two brutes kicked one another under the table and made rude hand gestures like rotten little boys stuck in detention at middle school.

Audrey huffed, but truly the silliness delighted her.

"So the wedding's off, aye?" Marcus asked.

Tarian replied *no* at the same time Audrey replied *yes*. They looked at one another.

Audrey sighed, "It's postponed."

Tarian crossed his arms and fell back in the chair with a thud.

Audrey refrained from rolling her eyes. *What did he expect?* They couldn't have an elaborate wedding while Lautaro invaded Balefire with the intention of enslaving the people of the Wastelands.

The Chancellor stepped through the door, Patrick trailing behind her. "My apologies." Eleanor glanced around. "I see everyone is in attendance. Good. Let's get started."

Councilor Harry cleared his throat. "This meeting will commence. We have gathered to hear Guardian Christopher's and Guardian Marcus' account of the Wasteland assignment they led. What say you?"

Marcus gave Christopher the floor with a wave of his hand.

"As predicted, Lautaro didn't adhere to the agreement set forth by Chancellor Eleanor and Guardian Audrey in alignment with the current Entente President. His army is mostly human. He must've sailed them across the ocean right under our noses."

Marcus interrupted, "He'd been planning this for months. Two armies—humans for groundwork and malditos for special missions."

Christopher nodded and went on, "He took the North Castle of Eminence Mountain, but we saved the royal family and managed to secure the South Castle of the Umbra Sea. Balefire is divided with set boundaries, for now. I'd feel more comfortable with a few thousand more Entente Elite Soldiers. However, Lautaro shows no signs of progression."

Audrey shifted in her seat. Lautaro's imperiousness still covered her entirety like a slick coat of black oil. The man couldn't be trusted. He would conquer the weak Wastelanders. Audrey's stare cut to Eleanor imploring her to convince the stubborn councilors.

Councilor Elizabeth's keen intuition must have sensed Audrey's plea as she turned to Eleanor. "Chancellor, I believe you have something to add."

Eleanor nodded. "Lautaro will invade further but not now. His resources are currently stressed with the Pall." She flicked her wrist summoning the prodigious map of the East. The dense, ominous shadow obscured a sizeable mass of land east of Balefire City.

"House Sanna is the people's future promise. Over the decades, they've become royalty. They honestly care for the people and want to build a better world. So far, Balefire is the most advanced city within thousands of miles. There are scattered villages, rebel outposts, and no one knows what's behind the Lì Xià wall, but Balefire is a jewel amongst …"

"Shit," Marcus said bluntly.

Eleanor grinned. "Well, yes. However, it's in its infancy and remains dangerous, but with the potential greatness worthy of the old cities. Therefore, it must be kept away from the Grand Sorcerer's evil enslavement, but it also has another enemy—the Pall." With a pointer, Eleanor struck the gray mass on the map.

"A deadly circle of black shadows just east of Balefire known as the Pall. We're studying the samples Christopher and Marcus brought back. The Entente military is extensively testing for acids and gases, all levels and combinations of oxygen. They've been able to recover some of the dead, if they don't tread too far into the fog. House Sanna and Lautaro have not been able to conquer it either. It's existed for as long as the Sanna family can remember. It's been spreading over the years and is close to infringing on the city." Eleanor slapped her hand with the pointing tool, her face taut with concern.

Patrick spoke in her silence. "It could be a by-product of the war's toxins, possibly, although there is no proof. Maybe it's a new variant caused by the war. And radiation levels are low. However, our tests revealed something none of the others had." He paused and glanced at his superior.

Eleanor gave a slight smile, then an exasperated sigh. "Traces of genesis magical properties."

Shock raced through Audrey. In all their recent meetings, Eleanor never mentioned these findings. She nearly growled under breath. Once again Eleanor and Patrick were hording mysteries in their laboratory. Her eyes studied her dear secretive friend, but Eleanor's eyes fell on Councilor Elizabeth.

"It will be discussed during Moon Cycle. The Esurients should have the answers we seek." Councilor Elizabeth's old, pale, yet smooth, face divulged nothing. However, a frost crossed her blue eyes.

It was just enough of a tell to secure Audrey's suspicions.

The High Council had known about the Pall all along, maybe even this genesis magic, and they feared it.

"We need to harness or conquer this force before Lautaro. I believe this may be raw origin energy but am not confident in the data yet. It should bend to the positive or to the negative depending on who masters it first. It's undoubtedly dangerous. Mortals and Guardians alike cannot enter more than a few feet without immediate death. Christopher and Marcus are the exceptions, but they can only enter while transparent, and even then, it slowly kills. Explain." Eleanor turned to Marcus.

"It's like walking through Haddock chowder. Pushin' against your every movement even though it appears to be nothing but shadows and air, it ain't. It feels like electric currents buzzing through your entire body. It's a mass, and we can collect it. But we've only been able to last ten, maybe fifteen, minutes. We begin to feel weak and have nearly passed out. So, we can't go venturin' far. The middle may be a completely different organism."

Eleanor continued. "I want more troops. The President is resistant. His excuse is that this is a creature problem but truthfully, it's an election year and he's scared. Sending troops to the Wastelands is not a popular idea among the voters who want to keep not only our people from harm, but also our resources from foreign powers. The Wasteland's technologies are outdated. Most Elites will have to be trained how to use them. The Guardians already know how, but we are few. We need to enlist the local rebels."

The Councilors leaned together and inaudibly

communicated, then resumed positions. Councilor William said, "Permission granted to engage with the rebels."

Those were the words Audrey longed to hear. The weight of a hundred horses had just lifted from her. She and Eleanor had secretly been communicating with the rebels through Christopher and Marcus. Coming into this meeting, Audrey felt confident they'd get the authority but sitting there learning more dreadful facts and watching the four councilors' sour faces without an ounce of compassion or hint of hope had slowly sucked the certainty out of her.

"Now what of Gregory Lycott?" Councilor William asked.

Tarian stiffened, his rigid anger evident when his knee brushed against Audrey's leg. She placed a hand on his thigh. It didn't relax under her touch, so she pulled away. Her heart skipped. She wished she possessed better caregiving skills. Why did she think a pat on the leg was sufficient compassion for Gregory's betrayal?

Christopher let out a long gruff. "There was a man in a market on the western side of the Wastelands. He resembled Gregory—"

"Looked like the crumpled bastard," Marcus growled.

Councilor Elizabeth cleared her throat.

"Sorry." Marcus' eyes fell to the floor.

Christopher continued, "As I was saying, he resembled Gregory, but this man had a child. A girl," he hesitated and glanced to Marcus for assurance, "The child was swathed in too many rags to make that definite. Again, the Nerve Rebels can assist us. They have spies. If we give them a description—"

"No!" Councilor George interrupted. "This is a Guardian's problem. No one outside of this room is to know about the possible Gregory siting. Go back and find out more."

Christopher and Marcus nodded.

"We must prepare for the Moon Cycle Summit." Councilor George stood. "Meeting adjourned."

The three sitting Councilors stood. All four retreated behind a lush velvet curtain. Awkward glances skipped around the table. Eleanor was the first to cordially dismiss and the rest followed bone-weary from the meeting.

Audrey's energy returned the second she stepped out of the room.

Eleanor caught her and Tarian before they reached the elevator. "I'm sending the two of you to the Wastelands today."

"It's imperative that we have *all* information, Eleanor," Audrey snapped.

Eleanor's lips thinned obviously feeling the bite in Audrey's tone. "Yes, all my findings were revealed to everyone in that room."

Tarian grunted. "Not exactly what I had in mind for a romantic honeymoon."

Audrey wished her heart would sink, show some remorse at this horrendous timing, but instead, magnetism ignited her blood as it raced through her veins enlivening her skin and pumping her heart. She wanted to be a wife, but she needed to be a soldier.

FIVE

BALEFIRE CITY

GUARDIAN TARIAN

Tarian stared at the woman he loved wishing they were lounging on a sunny beach instead of spying in a foreign land of toxic waste. An image of her in a tiny bikini flashed across his mind's eye, driving him mad. He should be living his happily ever after because she was his—Mrs. Tarian Prescott. He laughed. If she knew his thoughts, she'd pummel him.

"Why are you laughing?" She stabbed him with an icy stare.

"Just delirious with boredom."

They'd waited hours for the malditos to make a move and still nothing.

A warm breeze swept up the mountainside, cutting stripes of heat in the already uncomfortable late afternoon air. A tiny patch of blue hid behind the lace of gray haze.

"Blue sky is scarce here," he said.

"It is. This place was uninhabitable decades ago. And there's lots more to do before they catch up to the Entente." She sighed. "The Entente War took so much from this world."

He studied her as she remembered experiences during a time when he wasn't even born yet. His chest ached but not from jealousy, he'd gotten used to it, from a sense of loss. But he'd make new memories with her, better ones.

She held the glasses to her eyes then quickly lowered them. "They're on the move. Let's go."

He jumped up, eager to give his mind something to do other than wallow.

They packed up camp and rushed to catch the malditos' trail. The group of five marched around the city, hidden in the trees of the mountainous terrain. Tarian's excellent tracking skills worked overtime as he and Audrey kept a significant gap in distance.

"They're going to the Pall," Audrey whispered.

He met her intense stare with a reassuring nod. The Pall was a far cry from his honeymoon vision.

The wan malditos moved slow and tripped often. They coughed and grunted with each step and didn't seem at all aware of Tarian and Audrey's pursuit.

"They look sickly," Audrey said.

"Don't they all?"

"No. Lautaro's Maldito Apostólos are heartier, taller, more intimidating. These must be underlings. The disposable army ants."

The malditos trekked for miles. Their hunched appearance and limp gait abated Tarian's patience. Night fell. The scrape and thump of the malditos' footsteps became magnified in the quiet of the dark. Their moist, tacky skin glistened absurdly in the faint glow of the moon gossamered by pollution's haze. Their vacant eyes now black holes in the shade of night. One blink would forge nightmares in a mortal.

The temperature dipped, and Tarian's fatigued mind drifted to Audrey's warm body, envisioning it next to his under satin sheets in their honeymoon tropical paradise. He'd much rather be doing that instead of avoiding the uncanny notice of a cursed creature.

A humid fog set in as they drew nearer to the Pall. They risked a closer tail. They could use the special glasses that lanced through the mist, but it distorted distance. It was best to see things as they truly were and utilize their enhanced senses.

Audrey sniffed. "We must be close. Do you smell that?"

The sharp smell of chlorine burned his nose and eyes. He detected an underlying smokiness that might have eased the intensity of the more prominent pungent odor if not for the petroleum smell. The bouquet was nearly impossible to breath.

They'd reached the end of their forested protection and perched. Audrey slid her backpack off and took out the spectacles. The group of malditos ventured on.

Audrey muttered, "They're not going into that stuff. Are they?"

Suddenly a cloaked figure appeared, took two malditos by the hand and walked into the Pall. Slowly vanishing with each step.

"That was strange," Tarian said.

"Yes. Must be a special creature capable of walking into the mist. Hopefully, we'll get a better look when they come out,"

Audrey said.

The remainder of the group waited. They chatted, laughed, nibbled on snacks, appeared completely unconcerned about their fellow malditos.

Over an hour later, the vague shape of two persons materialized and slowly walked out of the Pall. The two malditos appeared unchanged. No burns, scars, marks of any kind, and no cloaked individual accompanying them.

Audrey sighed out her disappointment then perked up. "What's that?"

"It's a container, but I can't see what's inside because of the black mist encircling it."

The maldito dropped the mysterious container into a pouch.

"Did you see a golden shimmer?" Tarian asked.

"No." Audrey raised the spectacles to her eyes. "They're collecting samples." She lowered the glasses. "And not a simple surface sample. They were gone too long." Audrey bit her lip. Her face fell, worn out by their dauntless efforts.

It'd been twenty-four hours since he and Audrey had arrived at the designated stake-out point. He resisted the instinct to wrap her in his arms. He knew her boundaries while on the job but remaining professional proved more and more difficult now that she was his fiancée. The longing to protect her swelled in his heart. A debate raged inside him—reach out as her lover or hold back as her fellow soldier. But the malditos renewed their movement and the decision was made for him.

They retraced the path back to the ruined castle that Lautaro had invaded and overtaken last month. The malditos with their collected sample disappeared behind the heavily guarded doors.

Tarian fought the urge to storm inside, confront Lautaro, and tear him off his stolen throne.

Audrey grabbed his hand. "Come on. It's time to find transport to Central Nerve and report back to Eleanor."

SIX

This time Mike Lazaro followed the new kid. No one needed that many bathroom breaks. His hunch proved correct. The young male miner slipped under the caution barrier. Mike slid into the restricted area as well. Highly suspicious now, he kept a keen eye on the sneak, but the young man didn't do anything except look around. His hands roamed over the earth walls. When he turned to leave, he ran straight into Mike.

"What are you doing here?" Mike frowned.

The new kid lowered his head. "I'm sorry Supervisor."

"That doesn't answer the question. This is a restricted area."

He nodded. "I lost my friend from the … gold stuff, and I just needed to see it for myself."

"Why've you needed to see it more than once?"

The kid's eyes shot up. He looked at Mike in surprise. "I haven't."

Mike snarled. "You've been disappearing once an hour."

"No sir."

"Yes, you have."

"With all due respect sir, you must be mistaken."

The young man's eyes widened. He seemed so sincere that uncertainty flashed through Mike's mind. There were several new miners. They were all young, thin, and with the hard hats on looked similar. Had he been mistaken?

"Go on then. But don't let me catch you here again," Mike said.

The young man scurried past Mike and hustled around the corner.

Mike took off his hard hat and scratched his head. For a man of fifty-five, he still had a good head of black hair.

"¡Chin!" Mike swore as goosebumps raced across his skin. He'd been exploring these mysterious mines with their extraterrestrial elements for over three decades and still trepidation burrowed into his bones.

He inhaled deeply, filling his lungs with courage, then walked deeper into the prohibited cave. He searched for the dangerous golden lava. He knew now, since he'd been promoted to supervisor, what it truly was—ichor. In myth, ichor was the blood of the gods, so Mike had been sworn to secrecy by people far above his pay grade. He wouldn't have told his men anyway. Gossip and fear inside these caves didn't do anyone any good. All his men needed to know was the gold stuff killed people. Do not touch it.

He peered hard at the cave wall but saw only packed,

brownish gray earth. His hand passed through a shadowy mist. He quickly jerked it back. The strange fog disappeared. He strained his failing eyes and flashed his light up, down, and sideways. Everything looked as it always had.

The young man didn't show up to work the next day or the day after that. Mike returned to the restricted area of the cavern system to have another look and hopefully reassure himself that everything was fine.

An icy shiver ran through him, and he thought of his men's superstitions. They feared the *Cucuy* haunted the restricted area. But the new kid hadn't seemed frightened at all. In fact, Mike now questioned the look of sincerity he'd thought he'd read in the young sneak's eyes.

A shadowy figure caught Mike's attention. "Hey! I told you—"

No one stood there. Where Mike thought he saw a person only shadows existed. The misty darkness formed the shape of a person. Mike whipped around in all directions searching for the maker of this shadow. He was alone.

Up the lift and several winding passages away from the restricted area, the lunch pit buzzed with hungry miners. Mike set his lunchbox down on the picnic table next to his son, Carlos.

"Papa, you look awful," Carlos said.

"Do I?"

"Maybe you should go home."

"Nah." Mike took a large bite of sandwich then a swig of turmeric tea. "I just need food."

Carlos glanced sideways at his father throughout their lunch.

Mike swallowed the last sip of his tea then relented. "Come. I'll show you."

The cage squealed as it lowered them deeper into the cavern. Mike stepped off the metal floor and onto the solid ground then continued down the dip, Carlos following close behind. When they reached the caution tape, a scattering of shadowy clumps replaced the far more intimidating shadow figure.

"What are they?" Carlos slipped under the tape and swept a gray fog bubble with his hand. It melted away in curling wisps like smoke. "You know what the men will say?" He cocked a brow.

Mike grunted.

"The *Cucuy* and all that nonsense." Carlos continued to bat at the mist until it had almost disappeared. "It's probably nothing, but we should keep an eye on it."

"I plan to." A glint caught Mike's eye. He marched over to inspect. A tiny dot, a mere gold fleck lingered on the stone.

Carlos leaned over his dad.

"Do you see it?"

"It's barely dust, but yeah, unfortunately I see it." Carlos reached a finger out.

Mike yanked his son's hand back.

"Dad. Come on. That tiny spec won't kill me."

"Do you want to take that chance? Don't tell anyone about this. Not even your brothers."

Carlos frowned. "I won't lie."

"Just give me time to inspect further. Gossip is like fire. I don't need this place overrun with panic."

"Fine, Dad."

"Are any of the new hires with you?" Mike asked.

"Yeah, two."

"I don't trust them."

Carlos laughed soberly. "Me either. Can I fire them?"

"Maybe, but not yet. Just don't let them out of your sight."

Carlos rolled his eyes. "I got twenty miners."

"You only need to watch two."

"Alright, Dad."

A slice of shadowy mist fell across Carolos' face, darkening his brown eyes to black and deepening the purple circles to hallow out the eye sockets. Even his naturally rosy cheeks and lips drained of color as if stealing his youth.

Mike dragged his son across the restricted barrier and out of that horrid gray fog. Carlos' face regained color but his eyes remained sunken with a look of unease.

"I guess you won't tell Mama."

Mike's heart sank so fast he nearly stumbled. "No. I doubt I will."

SEVEN

ENERGY DISTRICT — THE ENTENTE

EMA CADET MARIA LAZARO

The small three-bedroom house seemed ample size with her brothers gone. Two of her brothers had their own homes and families now. The other two hadn't returned from work. Maria remembered growing up in this cramped house where she'd struggled to be heard, to be seen, to be important, and to eat. When she was young, she'd get up extra early to snag a piece of bacon or a chance to use the bathroom before her brothers peed on the toilet seat. Nevertheless, she missed all of it and wouldn't change any of those chaotic, uncomfortable moments.

Maria watched her mother brew coffee in a clay pot. She'd longed for a lot of things while at the Entente Military Academy, but Mama's cinnamon coffee was top of the list.

Mama limped to the table with two cups of coffee. She sat next to Maria and smiled.

Her dark eyes gleamed. "My Maria." She sipped then gestured roundly with her hand at the cluster of dirty boots by the front door and layers of large jackets slewed over the coat rack haphazardly. "Surrounded by all these boys." She laughed loudly. "Men now. Wait 'til you see them. No chicos. No more."

Maria smiled. "And how's Papa?"

Mama sighed and shook her head. "Tired. Anciano." She laughed. "The work is hard, but he won't stop."

"He's stubborn."

"And you're just like him."

Maria chuckled. She knew she resembled her father in more than appearance. Mama placed a leathered hand on hers and squeezed. Loving warmth shot up her arm and filled her heart.

"Tell me, mijita."

Maria huffed. That's another thing she missed, her mother's terms of endearment, her unconditional adoration for her only daughter. It brought joy to Maria, but it also spirited her competitive drive to provide a better life for her parents. Let them retire in comfort.

In the three years that Maria had been away, her mother had aged a lifetime. Farming the caverns was hard work. It took a toll on the entire household. Even though her mother didn't descend into the depths and dark of the cave halls, she did wash the mold from the clothes and worry after each explosion. She'd sit fidgeting her fingers unable to do any chores, waiting hours, eyes never leaving the door. She would only breathe when it opened, and her sons and husband walked through alive. And then she'd attend the funeral of someone else's son, daughter, brother, sister. Or bring food to a mother or father as they sat at an injured child's bedside.

"I'm going overseas." Maria winced, hating herself for adding yet another burden to her mother's long list of worries

Her mother said nothing, only patted Maria's hand. A smile formed on her face, but it couldn't stop the worry lines from accumulating on her forehead.

"It's dangerous. I know. But I fought for this assignment. I'll get paid and promoted."

Mama nodded still holding her tongue.

Maria stood and strolled over to the window.

Mama chuckled. "Blue hair."

Maria spun around. "You like it?"

"I love it. We need more color. Maybe I'll dye mine too." Mama lifted one shoulder and winked playfully.

Maria laughed as the image danced in her head. She glanced back to the scene outside the window—burnt lawns, desert sands, concrete sidewalks, asphalt roads, drab green cacti. Beige. How had she stood it for so long? And the Wastelands would be worse.

Her mother joined her and placed an arm around her shoulder. "Not much to look at, is it little dove?"

"Fly away."

They both smiled. Mama was the parent that spread Maria's wings. Papa would've wrapped her in a burrito and forced her to stay. She was strong enough to mine the elements and tough enough to survive the many unexplainable things they encountered down there. That's what he'd preached all the while her mother routed her escape, filling out EMA forms, enrolling her in schools with the appropriate testing for the academy, and lining her mind with destinations, places with lush forests, vast seas, grand mountains, and sands unlike the desert. Sands of fine white and pink crystals that didn't leave a chalky residue that itched.

Mama dropped her arm and returned to the sink. "Go. Walk to Jessica's or go see Clarisse at the shop."

Maria nodded. She left but she didn't walk to her old friend's house or the shop she'd bought candy from as a girl. Instead, she walked to the end of the street, past the caution barricades, and slipped through the gash in the wired fence.

"Will they ever fix that?" she muttered.

She strolled to the rock. It was as tall as she was now, and took some effort to hop upon, but as a child, it felt like climbing a mountain. Back then she knew Papa did important work mining the extraterrestrial pure elements that advanced their sustainable energy capabilities. She remembered peering from her rock mountain with pride and vigor. Now, thanks to having a Guardian for a best friend and being an Entente Elite, she knew exactly how deadly those caverns were.

The ichor had been sealed off after the deaths of the miners that had stumbled upon it. But that didn't mean it wouldn't appear at the end of another's drill. Since she knew what the golden fluid was capable of, she was far too aware of its value as an ingredient in the Guardian's Death Serum and Awakened Serum. Trouble attached itself to valuable things. Stuck to it like dog crap on boots.

She remained on the rock all afternoon, watching the

drones hover, studying the guards' actions, and inhaling the smell of sweat and metal. She stayed in the sun's heat, stealing its energy, until it began to descend. Desert sunsets were by far the prettiest she'd ever seen.

She wished she had Gabe's shoulder to lean on. He'd grown up here as well. They'd sat on this rock and watched the sunset probably half a dozen times together. They'd always been close friends, but never intimate until the second year at the academy. She had the memories of their shared sunsets as friends, but she longed for a new, lover's memory.

The sun swallowed the sky. First turning it as pink as berries then as orange as fire until finally devouring all color. She lumbered home in the dark. The little house was lit up and noisy. Her brothers' voices carried out the windows. Maria's step quickened. When she flung the door open, she was met with roars of laughter at her blue hair, followed by hugs and headlocks.

"Mi vida!" Papa shoved his sons out of the way. Tears pooled in his bloodshot eyes, but he smiled. He pulled Maria into him.

"Hi Papa." She felt his burdens and absorbed them. She could handle the weight and he needed to lighten his load.

"My soldier. You've no idea what a nice surprise you are." He caressed her hair and seemed lost in her embrace until he grabbed her shoulders and spun her toward her brothers. "Look at your hermana. So strong." He clasped her biceps.

"Papa," she drew out the word emphasizing her embarrassment.

"What? I'm a proud Papa. Nadia was right." His head twitched in Mama's direction.

She threw her hands up to the sky. "Oh. Dios mío. Mark the wall. I'm right!"

"Where's Gabe?" Papa asked.

"Only those of us that qualified for the assignment got a two-day leave."

Papa winked at Nadia. "Our girl. She's smarter than the academy boys. Ha." A mischievous grin stole his face.

"Miguel," Mama warned.

"What?" He shrugged innocently.

Nadia wagged her finger at him. "You know what."

"Ah!" He swatted the air. "What good's a best friend if you can't give him a hard time."

"I'm sure Gabe is upset enough already. He doesn't need you stirring up his father about it."

"Yeah Papa. Mama's right." Anxiety knotted Maria's stomach. When she'd left the academy, Gabe had barely spoken a word. He was happy for her but furious at himself for failing the test.

She didn't like the shared glance between Papa and her brothers. She glared at all of them.

"Fine. We won't say anything," Carlos said, and the rest huffed and murmured.

"Papa?" Maria asked.

He frowned. "I'll just remind Antonio that my daughter is smarter than his son."

Maria grunted. "You're impossible."

"Well, you are." He squeezed her some more and chuckled.

Maria couldn't help a little laugh at her boyfriend's expense. She loved making her parents proud but hated the doting attention.

A little girl hid behind her eldest brother's leg. Maria went to her and knelt. "What's your name?"

"Ava."

Wow. Time flies. She was an aunt. The tears invaded. The fire burned her lungs hoarse. The ache to return home or go back in time ravaged her bones. And this wasn't like her. She didn't have all these feelings. She was the tough Lazaro girl. She had a world to see and malditos to fight and battles to win. The urge to run back to the academy, board the jet for the Wastelands, and never look back consumed her. Then Ava stepped forward.

"Who are you?" Little Ava asked in a sugar-frosting voice.

And just like that, Maria's misgivings vanished, freed to enjoy her two-day leave with her family.

EIGHT

THE WASTELANDS

NERVE SPY GERMAINE

Germaine sat one thousand feet in the air with her magical spectacles spying on the Wastelands below. Nothing seemed out of the ordinary. Young thieves looted the city while the addicts slumped in the alleys binged out on Blue. *Typical.* Several Nerve camps stood guard as the Pall hovered over the lands far away. *Also, typical.*

From up high with her unique glasses, Germaine could see the vast spread of the eerie grayness. She'd seen many people swallowed by it. They walked in of their own freewill, but few walked out. The mist engulfed them, just as it engulfed the horizon. She'd spent many hours squinting to see the beyond. Nothing but shadows. One day she'd be an adventurer. She'd risk the beyond— beyond the seas, beyond the walls, beyond the Pall, beyond these Blue junkies. But for now, she'd just watch it, gather intel, and report back.

At ten years old, she'd wanted to help the Nerve. When they'd said no, she found a way to make them say yes. She became useful, and now, five years later, she'd become irreplaceable. She wasn't an immortal or any of the magical beings she knew of, but she worked for a lot of them. She was fast at climbing and running. Built for speed with a low center of gravity and lithe limbs. The Nerve Rebels nicknamed her Germ for her sneaky ability to remain unseen while gathering pertinent information.

It'd been eight years since her entire family had enlisted in the cause. Germaine had thought by now, there would've been progress. By now, she'd be in school learning math and science, and eating meat on a regular basis, but it seemed to her those dreams were just that—dreams.

Oh, they had schools, but nothing Germaine had any intention of attending—hard benches under wispy tents. They studied from books missing too many pages. She knew more than the Wastelander teachers just through reading, but she didn't know math and science as well as she'd have liked. The books she'd seen on those subjects confused her.

Balefire had managed development. She'd visited, actually spied, over there twice. Those kids went to a real school, a building built just for kids. She'd peered into the windows and seen science labs and cool machines that counted numbers and solved equations. Or so she thought, considering the short time she had to investigate.

In the Wastelands, zero progress had been made in children's schools, or in anything else for that matter—food supplies, living conditions, working environments. No that's not true, there'd been backward progress. They'd lost half their fleet and all their hope after the attack on the Entente of Nations. The failure was a huge setback. She wasn't privy to all the information. After all, she was just a girl, even though she was a valuable girl, a germ, the adults kept their secrets. But she'd gathered the basic knowledge. The Nerve had been hoodwinked by a double agent—a traitor. Someone they called the Guardian Senator. Supposedly, he was immortal but had somehow died. No one had answered her many questions about how he'd died, so she didn't know.

She'd been taught to distrust the immortals, the malditos, the unknown witches, and all the other creatures. But Germaine watched others unseen from high above. She bore witness to acts of kindness done by creatures she'd been told were evil and seen humans participate in deeds so vile that evil certainly dwelled in their mortal hearts. Germaine had long ago dismissed generalized stereotypes. Her strong, free mind judged for itself whom she'd trust, and whom she wouldn't. She did, however, believe all the rumors about the Pall, and she did fear those distant shadows.

"There you are," she said, her voice heard by a lone bird. Every few months a bird would appear, able to survive the sunless, toxic sky. It would arrive with colorful feathers, and she'd stare in admiration. She'd wonder where it came from, and if that place was just as colorful. She longed to live in a world of color.

Looking through the spectacles, the sheer man became visible. She'd met him at the first dinner she'd attended as part of her bargain with the little witch, Nichola. But he never introduced himself. Simply said hello and disappeared into a bedroom.

She hadn't trusted him, not one bit, but having observed

him for months and having grown fond of the child he takes care of, she'd changed her opinion. She didn't necessarily trust him, but she didn't believe him to be evil or someone against the cause. He seemed like a creature just trying to survive in an insurmountable environment.

The man paid for three small fish and a bundle of carrots. He pocketed a bulb of garlic and two potatoes.

"I guess I have to share a potato, little birdie." In answer, the bird flew away. "Rude."

When she put the spectacles back up to her eyes, the man had turned translucent again. He walked unseen among the market's shoppers. Without the magical spectacles, she couldn't see him either.

She worshiped her hard-won spectacles. Thanks to Nichola she'd pried them out of the brutish boy's grubby hands and Jinx's gang hadn't jumped her again. She was more than happy to attend her weekly dinners and share company with a powerful little witch and a weird creature that turned invisible.

The shadow man never joined them at the table, although she knew he was there. She'd hoped he busied himself behind the bedroom door, but always wondered if he just stood in the corner invisible. She thought it'd be rude to whip out her spectacles and look.

The climb down didn't take long. Germaine had mastered it. No one climbed as high as she did, but several kids and thieves made it about halfway up. Most stopped at the first landing. A lot of kids risked the second so as to sleep out of reach of the addicts.

The Blue did things to people. Made them desperate and angry and sometimes hungry enough to eat human flesh.

She scampered quickly to avoid the others. She didn't want to get stuck in conversation or acquire a tag-along she'd have to ditch on her way to Nichola's.

The man sat down at the dinner table. Nichola smiled wide, Germaine didn't. Like always, she'd politely helped Nichola set the table. Just as at past dinners, she had placed three forks, three knives, and three plates onto the tabletop. This was the first time the man hadn't disappeared into the bedroom.

They ate. No one spoke. But Germaine examined. His presence made Nichola very happy, but also very quiet. The man definitely adored her. Germaine saw the love in his eyes. They melted at her smile. He folded and softened when she touched him. He swiftly removed a fish bone from her fork before she ate it. He smiled when she called him daddy, but the word brought him pain too. The pain trampled his face like a hundred scorpion-tailed waste-monkeys.

Germaine tried not to stare at his eyes. The solid black orbs without the normal division of white background and gray color nauseated her stomach. Terrible horror stories about creatures with soulless eyes spread across the Wastelands as either sincere warnings or spooky tales told over a campfire. At first, she'd thought it was the tinge from the Blue. She could spot a Blue addict instantly by the jagged edges of their irises. The gray only ringed the pupil as the deep ocean blue invaded the iris and left its edges blurred like watercolor.

He also seemed to struggle with an inner demon. A tangible one, not the intangible paranoia from Blue. When his twitching got too much, and he stood up.

"Please excuse me. I need to rest. It was nice to see you Germaine," the man said.

Nichola only smiled at him, her cheeks soft, round, and shimmering.

"My pleasure. It was nice to meet you too Mr.—"

"Lycott." He nodded, and the bedroom door shut.

Germaine turned to the girl. "Your dad's nice." Nice was inaccurate, more like creepy, odd, or even scary, but she wanted to be polite. She liked Nichola and would never hurt her feelings.

"Thank you."

Germaine helped Nichola clean the table and kitchen. She didn't know Nichola's age, but the girl looked absurdly young. However, Nichola had the vocabulary and dexterity of a teenager. Nichola also seemed to grow at an astounding rate. She hadn't known Nichola long, four months give or take, but now that she looked closely, she'd swear the girl had aged a year. Nichola had definitely gained an inch or two in height since the night of Jinx's gang attack.

The girl wasn't human, Germaine had known that the day they'd met, but her nature remained a mystery. She'd suspected witch, but maybe fairy or siren. She had color in her eyes, hair, and cheeks. No Wastelander had true color, just shades of gray. The Royals of Balefire City within the Wasteland's borders had hints of color, but nothing like the prism of Nichola.

When it was time to leave, Germaine hugged her on the doorstep, glanced up and down the street for dangers, then told her, "See ya next week."

But this time the girl didn't nod and smile.

"Are you going somewhere?" Germaine asked.

"Maybe. There's someone … a relative, I need to talk with." Nichola's eyes glazed over as if she'd briefly left this dimension. "If I don't see you again, be safe." Nichola pulled her down and kissed her cheek.

Warmth bloomed on Germaine's cheek, and she wondered if the little witch had sprinkled her with shimmering color. A wonderful then terrifying idea. Being unseen was her livelihood. She stroked her cheek and forced her eyes not to harden and show her angst. Years of gambling on the game of Wack had given her a good deadpan.

Nichola just giggled.

Germaine descended the steps, walked a short distance, almost looked back but didn't, then she ran.

She hadn't wanted to befriend these people. It started out as an inconvenience, a debt, but now the thought of never seeing those big, amethyst eyes or cherub pink cheeks left her vacant and hollow. She stopped running and doubled over choking out stupid feelings.

"Just when I'd finally learned the man's name," she coughed, "Lycott." Maybe they wouldn't leave. *Maybe.*

She snorted back the clump of tears threatening to release, swiped her eyes and nose then sprinted. It wasn't safe to be slow. Scarier things than addicts came out after dark.

The next morning, Germaine stepped outside to find the Central Nerve camp swarming with men and women dressed in crisp gray and black uniforms. Anxiety flooded her chest. She recognized these uniforms and these types of people—people with healthy skin of all colors. Everyone born in the Wastelands, from the tower to Balefire, had dry, ashen skin.

"Good morning, Hun." Her mother drew up next to her on the front step, dressed and ready for work.

"They're back," Germaine grunted. She'd expected their arrival because the skies had been active lately. From her tower, she'd seen people jump out of strange aircraft then the crafts zoomed away. It was just like three years ago.

"Remember, I'd told you to expect them, but they're not the same as before."

"They're Entente soldiers, aren't they?" Germaine asked.

"Yes, but not Senator Eastwood's soldiers."

"You mean they're not going to tell us lies, make us promises, change our name to Prevaller, show us fancy machines, and then ditch us."

Esmay gave her daughter an exhausted smile. "Get some breakfast Germaine. Maybe it'll improve your attitude."

Her mom walked off to join her dad in meetings at the Cerveau headquarters, the building that housed the seven Nerve Rebel leaders known as the Cerveau. There had been thirteen Cerveau members before the Senator had tricked them into flying those weird crafts across the ocean. They'd never returned.

Germaine strolled toward the Pit-Stop to get food. She ignored the new soldiers clogging the camp's pathways, but her heart pounded. She couldn't believe it. After all they'd been through dealing with the Senator and his Entente double crossers. Had Axon Glial, the highest ranked Cerveau, forgiven them because there was no way he'd forgotten?

Germaine couldn't forgive them for raising her hopes for a better life. She'd been so excited to go to a real school with books and science stuff. And she'd never forgive them for all the deaths. Half the Central Nerve camp had been lost.

She tried not to think of it as she grabbed some juice and cereal at the Pit-Stop then found a table in the back away from the hustling newcomers.

Franny walked over. "How's the juice today?"

"Not horrible. Wish I had ice, but I guess the ice maker broke."

"Is that why you look so glum?"

Germaine rolled her eyes.

Franny wrapped an arm around Germaine and squeezed.

"Remember when I told you I knew the royal family and you called me a liar."

"I never called you a liar," Germaine said indignantly.

"As I recall, you didn't believe me."

"Well, that's not calling you a liar." Germaine's lips pursed as she studied her friend. What was she getting at? That was the trouble with old people. They spoke in riddles.

She figured Franny was eighty or so, but Lavender Witches aged slowly. Franny only looked about her parents' age, thirty-five. Franny was one of the seven Cerveau members.

"I left South America and the insurgency to come here and work in Balefire where I befriended Bethalda Sanna …"

"I know." Germain sighed. Franny told long tales.

Franny stiffened. "Well, I can see you're in a mood today, so I'll get to the point. I've helped orchestrate a visit from one of Bethalda's granddaughters, Princess Lucianna. I thought you might be interested in meeting her."

Germaine's mouth gaped and she nudged Franny. "You know I would."

Franny smiled. "Yes, I seemed to remember you coloring picture after picture of the princess and running around with a pot on your head and a stick in hand pretending to fight like the warrior princess."

"I was eight." The heat of embarrassment warmed Germaine's cheeks. That was another thing old people loved to do—bring up old embarrassing times.

"Don't worry." She tapped Germaine's nose. "That'll be

our secret." Franny stood. "Come. She should be arriving soon."

Germaine followed Franny toward the Cerveau headquarters.

Princess Lucianna and four soldiers entered the building. The woman Entente soldier had four gold stars pinned on her uniform and her male companion had three gold stars plus an eagle. She didn't recall the Senator's soldiers having gold accents. Christopher and Marcus were with them. The two giant-sized Guardians of Dare had been around for a while, traveling back and forth from Balefire City and constantly meeting with the Cerveau.

When she'd first met Christopher and Marcus, she knew they were creatures by their massive size, and she'd witness them turn invisible. She wasn't a fool, and knew these formidable beings were worth having on her side, so she befriended them. She snuck them snacks, and taught them the game of Wack, and made them promise her ten percent of all their winnings. She liked them.

As they walked by, they threw her a smile and a wink that she returned.

Princess Lucianna made sickly gray skin look divine. Her cheeks and eyelids shimmered silver, drawing Germaine's eye. But it wasn't just her beauty that captivated Germaine. Princess Lucianna was a force, a fiercely strong and competitive fighter that Germaine tried to imitate. She'd graduated from drawing pretty pictures of the princess to whipping her knife around as if it was Lucianna's magnificent sword. Alone on the tower, she'd smear flecks of iron on her cheeks and pretend her face shined silvery too.

Germaine caught up to her parents that were about to head into the meeting room.

"Wait here," her dad said.

"Roberto," her mom said, but to no avail. Dad shook his head.

Esmay glanced back with a shrug. "I tried."

Germaine's stomach knotted, and anger burned her cheeks. She shoved her hands in the pockets of her raggedy pants then plopped down on the single chair on the other side of the door. It might as well have been labeled *Germ's chair* because she was the only one that ever sat in it.

After waiting patiently for twenty minutes, Franny opened the door and winked. "Come inside, child."

Axon smiled wide and strode toward Germaine. His arm fell across her shoulders. "This is our Germaine, fondly known as Germ. She knows these streets better than anyone. Do not let her size or youth deceive you. She's stealth and cunning. You need any information she'll retrieve it. Of course, it must go through the Cerveau first. We won't send our best asset out on a fatal mission." He squeezed her shoulders. "I know all missions have the potential to be deadly, but you understand my point."

"Nice to meet you," Germaine said and awkwardly curtseyed to the princess.

Princess Lucianna's nod of approval sent Germaine's heart soaring. She tried to stand tall and accept such praise from a royal with dignity, but her knees buckled. She leaned against Franny for support.

Franny looped an arm around her elbow and drew her up. Germaine swallowed down the giddy teenage girl that so rarely broke through her tough skin.

The meeting adjourned and small talk broke out. Germaine noticed Cerveau member Jen Monahue rubbing her fingers together with such force she could start a fire. And her smile wasn't its usual clever grin as she spoke to her former countrymen. Germaine sensed definite tension. That was a story she wanted to know. She'd never understood why Jen had left the Entente to come here. She liked Jen, and Jen had proven herself devoted and useful to the Nerve. Her dad often said, *I don't know how we would've done that without Jen. Her connections and intelligence are a blessing.*

For a moment the princess stood unattended. Germaine strolled toward her but with each step her nerves sparked, her steps slowed and her breathing heightened. What should she say? She'd die a slow, miserable death of shame if she said something stupid. Then Cerveau member Zella intersected and said, "Nice to see you again, Lucianna."

"Zella." The word was a quick, curt sound out of Lucianna's mouth, not a warm greeting at all.

Germaine stood still as the air between the two women thickened. Germaine suddenly felt like the center of attention, which was odd since neither of them had acknowledged her presence.

"You look lovely," Zella said.

Lucianna smirked.

"How's Marianne."

"She's well." The princess' tone sharpened, and her lips thinned. Obviously, Lucianna didn't approve of Zella's relationship with her sister, Marianne.

"Please, can we talk?" Zella asked.

They strolled away, out of Germaine's earshot. She'd never seen Zella act nervous and unsure. Zella Dunn was one of the remaining few Prevallers. The Prevallers were a group of Wasteland rebels that had been recruited and fiercely trained by the Senator.

Esmay strolled up to her daughter. "Germaine let's go. We've got lots to do to prepare for our guest."

"What?"

"Honestly, Germaine. Why is it you can gather intricate details of information on spy missions and yet never hear a word I say."

Germain knew better than to answer. She just shook her head.

"We're housing one of the soldiers. Her name is Maria Lazaro."

Esmay handed Germaine the casserole dish. "Take this to the table please."

Germaine looked at the green mushy food and scowled.

"Remember Germaine, Maria had nothing to do with what

the Senator did to us. Don't be rude at the table."

"Fine. I won't talk."

Her mom sighed. "Of course, I want you to feel free to speak your mind just do it with grace."

"Okay." Germaine walked the casserole to the table, set it down, then sat in her usual spot. The guest soldier, Maria, waited for everyone to sit before taking a seat.

"Thanks for welcoming me into your home," Maria said.

"It's the least we could do. The Entente's support is necessary to turn the Wastelands into a decent world for our future children. And with this new threat—Lautaro." Esmay shook her head and frowned before scooping out a large portion of broccoli casserole. It plopped onto Maria's plate. "I'm sorry, but edible meat is scarce around here."

"Don't be sorry. It looks … delicious."

"It'll take more than mortals to win," Germaine mumbled.

"That's the truth." Maria nodded.

Germaine stiffened not realizing she'd said that loud enough for Maria to hear. Her eyes darted to her parents. Her father winked but her mom's gray eyes narrowed.

"We have Guardians, and more should be over soon, plus more Elite soldiers like me," Maria said.

"It's clear now why we've been collecting bone-blades," Roberto said.

"Are they blessed?" Maria asked.

"Don't have to be. Most of the blades come from large beasts in the forests. They're cured in a salt mixture. The minerals and cells inside the bone penetrate the malditos just like a blessed blade. Diamond works too but they are very rare. Unfortunately, our guns aren't blessed," Roberto said.

Esmay's eyes swept from her husband to Maria. "While those may stop these maldito creatures, what of the Pall?"

Maria shrugged.

"Are you bringing more weapons?" Germaine asked.

"Hopefully. Weapons, soldiers, transportation, and technology."

"Hopefully?" Germaine put her fork down. "Surely the Entente can spare some weaponry." Germaine glared. Her mom nudged her under the table.

"Politics." Maria took a sip of water then continued, "Grievances from many years ago. The Entente people are scared, and I hate to say it, but they have a reason to be."

"Ha. You've got it backwards. You screwed us over last time."

"Germaine! That's enough," Esmay scolded.

"But we need help. Real help." Germaine clucked her tongue. *Politics. Grievances. Screw that!* Sounded like excuses. The Entente soldiers were going to leave them again, just like the Senator had.

"It's complicated." Maria looked Germaine straight in the eye, making the pathetic excuse seem substantial.

"You're still in school, the Entente Military Academy, right?" Esmay asked, then tucked a wisp of hair behind her ear. Her head of hair rolled into a long braid. Germaine knew when her mom needed to wash it by the tendrils that extended wildly around her face and the nape of her neck.

"Yes. I'm a fourth year. Fourth years have the opportunity to study in the field." Maria took a long swig of water.

"In the Entente, not the Wastelands," Roberto chuckled. "You got a bad deal."

Maria laughed. "I'm sure it looks that way, but even inside the walls of the Entente there are poor communities. I come from a mining village. I lived with a lot of brothers in a very small house, so I'm used to roughing it. And I had to train hard for this assignment. Every cadet at the EMA wants to come over here where history will be made." She paused and frowned. "My boyfriend didn't make the cut."

"That's tough," Roberto said.

Maria nodded.

"You're sad he's not here in this hell?" Germaine's eyes bulged.

"That's no way to speak at the table," Esmay said.

Maria snorted as she held back a laugh. "Yes and no. I'm glad he's safe inside the Entente walls, but I know if it was me, I'd be pi—" she caught the foul word before it formed, "upset."

After dinner, Maria asked Germaine to show her around Central Nerve before dark.

They strolled, and Germaine explained, "Central is the largest base. It was the original. So just imagine seven smaller versions of this around the Wastelands and three inside Balefire," Germaine paused, "Well, there were three. I don't know now."

"I don't know the exact number either, but we've got use of the House Sanna Umbra Castle," Maria said.

"Really?"

"Yes."

"No one calls it that, by the way."

"Oh."

"Yeah. It's just South Castle."

"Well damn, it's a good thing I met you." Maria smiled. "You saw those two extremely large men, right?"

"Christopher and Marcus?"

"Yes. They organized a rescue and saved the royal family. Now the city is divided. Lautaro has the North Castle and House Sanna has the South Castle."

Germaine already knew that. She often pretended she knew less than she did, in order to find out what other people knew.

Germaine gestured, "That's Cerveau headquarters because it's where the leaders meet. The leaders are actually the Cerveau, not the building. If you need something to eat, go there." Germaine pointed to a group of empty tables. "They close around five, but they bring in fresh vegetables, fruit, and juice daily. All these small blocks are homes. That hut over there is a makeshift school."

"Your school?"

"Hell no. See that?" Germaine pointed to the tall tower far in the distance.

"Yeah."

"That's my school. I climb it and report what I see."

"And what do you see?" Maria asked.

Germaine turned around to head back to her blockhouse.

"It's cool. I get it. You don't know me."

Germaine bowed her head.

"Look, sorry. Don't feel bad. You're doing the right thing. We need to prove ourselves. I know what Senator Zachary Eastwood did, and that a lot of you don't trust us."

"I trust you," Germaine said, and in her gut it was true. A sense of calm had settled in her stomach in the last few seconds. "But you're right, a lot of the Nerve Rebels don't. You're mortal though, so they'll trust you first. Even though I've seen a lot of mortals do bad. But they trust mortals over creatures all the time."

They walked in silence for a while.

"Back home creatures are a secret," Maria said.

"Really?"

"Yep."

"Isn't it obvious?"

Maria laughed. "You know, it's so obvious once you're aware, but most Entente citizens go about their daily routine completely clueless." Maria bent to pick up a handful of dirt. She let it sift through her fingers. "Everything here is gray and dry and metal, isn't it?"

"Yes. Most of the Wasteland is, but Balefire has some green and brown. The sea is gray-blue."

"Where I come from, it's a lot like this."

"Really, but I've heard stories about the Entente. It's blue skies and twinkling stars and super green trees and grass, lots and lots of grass so soft you can sleep on it."

"Well, yeah. The Entente is large with different districts. My district just happens to be where the meteor hit and turned it all to dust."

Germaine's heart sank, her dreams dashed.

"No. Don't get me wrong. Many districts are beautiful. We have every color of the rainbow," Maria said as she stared off into the distant dullness.

Germaine furrowed her brow. "What's a rainbow?"

"Are you kidding me?" Maria's mouth gaped. "Does it rain here?"

"Hardly. But I do know what rain is." Germaine kicked the dirt as she strolled.

"Well, when it rains and the sun shines you get a rainbow in the sky. In the rainbow, there are lots of colors. Blues, purples, greens, reds."

"Cool. I hope one day I can visit the Entente and see this rainbow."

"Me too." Maria's face rounded with a wide smile making Germaine feel like they could possibly be friends.

That night Germaine set up her cot in the living room and slept next to Maria. She listened to Maria tell incredible stories of her adventures at the EMA and the missions she went on with her best friend who was a Guardians of Dare immortal.

Maria propped up on one elbow to face Germaine. "His name is Tarian, and he's the first immortal to be born in over five hundred years."

"Cool." Germaine imagined living for five hundred years. People in the Wastelands were lucky to get to fifty.

"And his fiancée, Audrey, is cool too. Just don't tell her I said that." Maria winked.

"What's your boyfriend's name?" Germaine asked.

"Gabe." Maria's smile wilted.

"You miss him?"

"Yeah." Maria laid back to stare at the ceiling. "We both put in for this assignment. We envisioned our fourth year together. Whenever we talked of what it'd be like to come over here, it was always *us*. You know? It's just weird to be here without him."

"Couldn't you have stayed behind?"

Maria's head whipped around. "Of course, but screw that." Maria's hand flew up to her mouth.

Germaine laughed. "Mom can't hear you."

"Good. Anyway, Gabe wouldn't have wanted me to stay behind. You get an opportunity, you jump on it. Right?"

"Right."

"And what about you? Any boyfriends?" Maria's warm smile returned.

Germaine's heart fluttered. The blood rushed to her cheeks. "No."

"Girl, you're not fooling me."

Germaine sat up in her cot. "I did have a crush on this one boy."

"What was he like?"

"He kept to himself. Probably an orphan or his parents were Blue addicts."

"That's the norm around here, isn't it?"

Germaine nodded.

"Was he cute?"

Germaine grinned. "Yes. Very. He probably never even noticed me."

"What? You're a beautiful young lady."

Germaine rolled her eyes. "Whatever. He's dead now anyways."

Maria jolted upright in her makeshift bed. "Jeez, I'm sorry."

Germaine shrugged off the reality, but her gut twisted and twisted making it difficult not to double over.

Before the sun came up the next morning, there was a knock on the door. The Entente Elite soldier with the three gold stars and one gold eagle from the Cerveau meeting waited outside. He'd come to retrieve Maria.

Maria dressed quickly and grabbed her backpack. "I'll be

back."

"I hope so." Germaine couldn't hide the disappointment in her voice.

Maria's shoulders slumped. "It sucks. I wish we had more time to talk, but I think you'll be meeting some of my friends soon. They're the good immortals we were talking about last night, Tarian and Audrey. Watch for them on that tall tower thing you climb."

"Okay. I will."

"And be careful way up there." Maria clasped her shoulder. "See you soon, Germ." Then she walked out the door.

NINE

CENTRAL NERVE — THE WASTELANDS

GUARDIAN TARIAN

After a long, rough ride across the Wastelands, Tarian and Audrey finally arrived at Central Nerve. The aroma of freshly brewed coffee wafted on a breeze that buzzed with productive activity. His stomach growled.

At the sight of familiar Entente and Guardian uniforms, he exhaled relieved that not only had they found the correct place, but everything seemed to be progressing as planned. He'd feared a breach in security or an unwillingness to negotiate and work together, but it looked as if he'd worried for nothing.

"Well, well, well. Hello, First Born." A woman with a familiar face in a Nerve Rebel uniform extended a hand.

Tarian cringed at the nickname then shook her hand confused.

"Audrey." The woman acknowledged.

"Hello, Jen." Audrey hesitated then removed her grip from her scabbard to shake Jen's hand.

Jen's gaze dropped to blades affixed to Audrey's baldric

belt. "Diamond weaponry. Only the best for the Guardians."

This was the horrible trainee from the Realm. The one that hated him because she'd blamed him for the Prevallers attack on the EMA. And she wasn't wrong. It had been the treacherous work of the Senator to distract from his true mission of cloning immortals to create his wicked army.

"Thought you'd never see me again, didn't you?" She grinned.

"Yes. Weren't you dishonorably discharged?" Audrey asked.

"Not exactly. After that strange insect bit me and almost falling to my death in the simulator, I needed some time off."

"But you found yourself over here, in the Wastelands, where there are a lot scarier things than a simulated bug." Audrey gave Tarian an uneasy glance.

"That's right. I made a lot of discoveries about myself in rehab because of that traumatic event. I knew I had a higher purpose. I couldn't just remain in our beautiful walled off Entente while people suffered over here," Jen said, with a wide smile that seemed genuine.

"That's wonderful," Tarian said.

"Thank you, Tarian. Your friend Maria just left," Jen said.

Tarian's heart hitched. He hadn't seen Maria in months and now she was out on a dangerous mission, but she was tough. If Jen was surviving and apparently thriving over here, Maria would certainly be fine. She had to be.

"We need to speak to Eleanor … the Chancellor of the

Guardians of Dare. You have communications here, correct?" Audrey asked with apparent discontentment at seeing Jen in her voice.

"Yes. They're nowhere near as reliable as back home, but we can get you in contact with the Chancellor. And we have a tent set up for you. Afterwards, you can refresh yourselves before the debriefing."

"Thank you, that would be nice," Audrey said.

"This way to the Cerveau."

Audrey and Tarian followed her to the largest building inside the Central Nerve camp.

As they entered the building a man and his daughter exited.

"Hello, Roberto." Jen nodded to the gentleman holding the door. He nodded back. Jen's eyes fell to the teenage girl. "Hi, Germ." They performed a special handshake.

"Hey, Jen," the girl dressed in dull black said.

Tarian paused, expecting Germ to say something given that she stared at him as if they'd met before. But she simply turned and strode away with her father.

"Roberto will be at the debriefing. You'll get properly introduced then. This way." Jen continued holding the door open, waiting for Tarian to enter, but he didn't. "Let's go. You have a long day ahead. Lots of important people to meet. And believe me, they've heard a lot about you, First Born."

The nickname drew his attention away from the teen girl and her wise eyes. "Is Germ part of the Nerve Rebels?"

Jen nodded. "She's our best spy."

"But she's young," Tarian thought of his younger sister, Teresa. Only seventeen but determined to be useful.

"We need all the help we can get. Senator Eastwood depleted us of our best fighters all because of you."

TEN

GUARDIAN VILLAGE — THE ENTENTE

IMMORTAL LAVENDER WITCH PIPER

Piper was tired from her strange dreams of gray fog, and she was bored. She missed wedding planning. The postponement of Audrey and Tarian's wedding meant no more twinkle lights. No more cupcake tasting. No more lace and tulle. No more fun! And it wasn't just that. Everyone had been sent overseas.

She took a stroll in the sunshine and the sun's warmth lifted her mood. She'd go visit Carolyn and the kids. Playing with Chloe and Joe Jr. would cheer her up. Surely, Tarian's family felt the loneliness too.

A whiff of cinnamon from the Appleton's Bakery detoured her. She entered the store, walked to the counter, and ordered. "I'll have a cup of coffee and an apple strudel. Oh … and a dozen cinnamon rolls to go. I'm going to visit Carolyn and the kids." She told Mrs. Appleton.

"Piper!"

She turned around to find Hope Appleton and Teresa,

Tarian's sister, sitting together at a table. Hope hopped off her stool to hug her. She squeezed Hope extra tightly. It had been almost a year since the Waker had attacked and nearly killed young Hope. Piper shook off the horrible memories.

"Hi Piper." Teresa sat sipping a cup of steaming coffee.

"Hey Teresa, do you stop in here often before going to work?" Piper pulled up a chair and sat next to them.

"Lately I have." Teresa glanced at Hope. "Patrick gets to the lab early and there's hardly anyone in the infirmary, so I have extra time to check in on Hope."

Piper smiled. Her mind drifted to wedding ideas for Teresa and Patrick but quickly snapped out of the fantasy. Teresa was much too young. "Getting ready for summer camp, Hope?" Piper asked.

"Yep, but I don't have to leave for another half an hour."

"Here you go Piper." Mrs. Appleton placed a cup of coffee and the apple strudel down on the table.

"Thank you." Piper leaned over her plate and inhaled the intoxicating aroma of spiced apples.

Hope gawked at the strudel. "Mom! Can I have one too?"

"Certainly, sweetie," Mrs. Appleton left and returned with another plate of scrumptious strudel. "Any for you dear?"

"No, thank you," Teresa said.

"Thanks, Mom."

"You're welcome hun." She kissed her daughter's forehead. Her eyes lingered a few seconds too long, the consequence of almost losing a child to a ravenous Waker beast.

After her mom walked away, Hope said, "Don't worry, the wedding will happen."

"What?" Piper sat half on and half off of the stool.

"The wedding. I dreamt about it. We dreamt about it." Hope sheepishly smiled at Teresa. "I know it's postponed, but we saw it, plain as day, in a vision."

"Vision?"

"Yep. Dream, uh, vision." Hope shrugged.

Teresa jumped off her stool. "I gotta run. Sorry. I didn't realize how late it was."

"Wait. Why is Hope having visions? She doesn't have any witch blood."

"Come by the lab later and we'll talk. Bye." Teresa waved and rushed out of the bakery.

"Hope, do you have a lot of these … visions?"

"A few. I keep seeing this man with a little girl, but I don't know who they are. She kind of looks like you, but she's really young."

"In the village?" Piper sat back in her seat.

"Definitely not. Wherever they are, it isn't nice. Everything's gray. A lot of trash everywhere. And it smells. At least, I assume is does. Not sure you can smell in dreams."

Piper nodded.

"Weird, right?" Hope took a large bite of her strudel.

Piper's stomach growled. She ate her own strudel then

asked, "How does she look like me?"

"The lavender eyes. But she's not cheerful like you. Teresa thinks she looks like you too, but the girl always seems serious and sad. And no matter what, the man and the girl have to stay together until the end."

"The end of what?"

Hope shrugged. "I don't know. It's always just blackness. But I know that's important."

"How?"

"I just know like you know the grass is green. It's like that."

Mrs. Appleton strode up to the table. She placed the box of cinnamon rolls down. "Here's your rolls. Hun, we need to leave. It's a ten-minute walk to day camp."

Hope rolled her eyes at Piper. "Mom still worries."

"I know those horrible things are dead and gone, thanks to Tarian," Mrs. Appleton patted the box of rolls destined for Tarian's mom's apartment, "but I still worry. Always will."

Piper grabbed Hope's arm as she stood to leave. "When did these strange dreams start?"

Hope thought for a minute. "They started in the infirmary right after the attack." She took a step toward the door then turned back. "But not with him or the girl, just the place. The trashy place. I keep seeing it when I sleep. It seems like the people there need help. It makes me sad. Oh and last night, I saw an explosion, but not in the trashy place." Hope frowned. "I think I saw people die."

"I'm so sorry."

"It's okay." Hope shrugged, but it was clear by the glisten in her eyes that the dream still haunted her. "Bye Piper, have a good day."

"You too." Piper waved and smiled as she watched Hope skip off to summer camp with her mom.

Anxiety bubbled in Piper's blood. She tapped her fingers and wiggled her toes trying to release it. It didn't work. She disappeared, vading out of the bakery. In her haste, she completely forgot the box of rolls.

Piper popped into the infirmary and sought out Teresa. She found her mixing something in a dimly lit backroom. The odor of vinegar and sulfur infused the air.

"Stay over there." Teresa held out a straight arm and firm hand.

Piper did as she was told. "So, these visions Hope has?"

"Yes," Teresa said still busy compounding her mixture. "At first, they seemed to be vivid dreams, but now I suspect she sees future or current events. When I check with the soldiers that have been overseas, her … our description is dead on. The place we keep seeing is the Wastelands."

"Interesting. You share the same visions?"

Teresa finished her job, took off her gloves, and washed her hands, then she gave Piper her full attention. "Only recently."

"So you saw an explosion too?"

"I did." Teresa's voice cracked. "I've told Eleanor but it's against a black backdrop so there's no hint of where or of what. Hope was very upset over it. The vision is troubling. It's haunting and unfinished like we're supposed to prevent it. Mrs. Appleton asked me to give her some guidance, but this is all so new to me too. I'm not much help. I guess it's just nice to know other people are just as confused as you are." Teresa chuckled nervously. "It's getting harder for me to hide my anxiety from Hope."

Piper squared her shoulders at Teresa. "You're not hiding it from yourself, are you?"

Teresa shook her head.

"Don't. It'll eat you up inside."

Teresa sighed. "I know, but I have to put on a brave face for Hope and the others."

"Do any of the other Waker victims have visions?"

"Lexy does, but hers don't match ours, thank goodness. Thomas' amputated leg is … healing."

"What?"

"Yeah. About two weeks ago, he woke up with a knee. Strangest thing. Of course, living here in the village I've seen a lot of strange things so—"

"But villagers are human."

"I'm human."

"You have witch blood. I meant villagers have never had any creature gifts. So it must have something to do with the Waker's bite or scratch."

"That's what Eleanor and I have concluded."

Piper nodded, her mind turning with ideas.

"It's only the children."

"What?" Edgy energy invaded Piper. She fidgeted with her hands.

"The adult victims don't have any of these peculiar side effects."

"How many children survived?" Piper asked.

"Only five." Teresa's caramel eyes dropped.

Piper frowned, her heart aching for Teresa who'd, at only seventeen, seen a lifetime of death in this place—the place of immortality.

"Are you okay?" Teresa asked.

Piper nodded.

Teresa stared at her friend. "Really? Because you're usually glowing with violet positive energy, but you're in a gray fog right now."

Piper perked up. "Fog! Trashy place. It's the same vision. Thank you, it's been bothering me." She scooped Teresa up in her arms. "Is that normal?" Smoke billowed up from the bowl Teresa had been using minutes earlier.

"No!"

Piper dropped Teresa back onto her feet.

"Damn." Teresa rushed to the small, sputtering fire. She pulled on gloves then stifled the fire with a hood and dropped the bowl into the sink. She whipped off her gloves, pulled Piper out of the room, and shut the door.

"What are you making?"

"I'm helping Patrick. He's trying to create a salve to compliment the Sanoxine."

"Why?"

"The soldiers are coming back with strange sores. It seems something is infecting the skin. A bacterium immune to the Sanoxine, but it's similar to the plague bacterium the Sanoxine attacks before it breeds other microbes." Teresa leaned against the door.

"You're exhausted," Piper said.

Teresa nodded.

"Get some rest."

"I will but first I need to find Patrick. See you later Piper." Teresa rushed down the hall.

Piper vaded into the library. She landed in her chair next to the window, perplexed. She gazed out at the wispy clouds and bright sky. Should she retrieve the box of cinnamon rolls and resume her stroll to Carolyn's?

A flock of birds distracted her. They flew in pairs twirling and spiraling, blissfully happy for the warmth of summer. She made a mental note to include birds at the wedding ceremony.

Below the birds on the street sat a processional of parked dark vehicles. Eleanor walked Entente President Henry Lloyd to one of vehicles where they shook hands and kissed cheeks. He slipped into his car and drove away. Eleanor's back faced Piper. She waved a gesture that appeared pleasant until she turned around and Piper caught the fire in her eyes. Her mouth immediately sunk into an exaggerated scowl.

"What are you up to Chancellor?" Piper murmured then vaded out of the library.

"Piper!" Eleanor gasped. They'd nearly collided when Piper appeared out of thin air.

"Good day." Piper smiled. "Did you come to an accord?"

Eleanor hesitated. "What?"

"I saw President Lloyd leaving." Piper waited in silence for Eleanor to expand on the President's visit, but she didn't.

Eleanor marched toward her office, high heels clicking rapidly.

Piper followed.

Eleanor got to her desk and said, "Please, excuse me. I must prepare for the High Council's departure."

"Oh, where are they going?" Piper asked.

Eleanor smiled, and Piper thought she might not get an answer. Finally, Eleanor said, "It's time they convene with the Esurients."

"Why?"

Eleanor fidgeted obviously annoyed with Piper's constant questions, and again, Piper assumed she'd be ignored, but Eleanor cleared her throat. "We need to stop Lautaro. We need more troops, more technology, and more scientists to figure out that ghastly Pall. I warned Henry he won't get reelected if he doesn't send more troops to the Wastelands." She sighed and leaned against the wall, the splitting image of Teresa's weariness. "He said I'm wrong. I'm out of touch with what the people want."

"He's scared."

"Hell, I'm scared, but doing nothing isn't the answer. Even the High Council agrees we need to interfere. It will spread, and when it does, it'll be catastrophic."

"Maybe that's the explosion."

Eleanor cocked an eyebrow. "What explosion?"

"Teresa and Hope saw an explosion in a dream/vision."

Eleanor sighed, "Right. Even more reason the Councilors need to convince the Esurients to help." Eleanor grabbed her cell off her desk. "We'll talk later Piper." She walked out of the office—her elegant heels clicking a little less and dragging a little more.

Piper slept alone in her apartment. In a dream, she drifted. Not exactly. It wasn't a dream nor was it vading. She relaxed and allowed whatever force held her to take control. Like the time-hop illusion of sleep, she opened her eyes and felt as if only seconds had passed, and yet, from the scenery she knew she was far from the village.

She stepped out of the mist that carried her and into the bedroom of a little girl. The girl panted with exhaustion. Long pale gold hair as fine as silk framed her face in perfect lines. Her skin faired next to her distressed eyes, big and pinned to her face like two giant amethyst gemstones. She sat cross-legged on top of a flowery bedspread in a faded pink nightgown trimmed in lace, both were clean but stained and ripped.

"Did you summon me?" Piper whispered for it was nighttime and the tiny room's door was shut. Piper assumed the house held more rooms with people sleeping. But when she peered out the window the sun rose as if it was morning. Had she drifted all through the night?

"I .. did," the child stuttered as she regained her breath from the hard work of magic.

"Are you okay?"

"I'll … be fine."

"How old are you?"

"Almost four human years."

Her voice and constitution seemed much older than four years, but Piper decided not to question it. "You're beautiful."

Her lips curled shyly. "You are, too."

"Who are you?"

"I'm Nichola Lycott."

Shock waves of horror shuddered through Piper. She looked over her shoulders fearing Gregory Lycott hid in the shadowy corners of the room. Vivid images of soulless eyes and the carnage of babies filled her mind. *Where is he?* She stared at the closed bedroom door. *Is he on the other side?*

Nichola continued to sit calmly on her bed. "Don't worry.

We're alone."

Piper's thoughts raced. Gregory Lycott was a deceitful traitor. He was Senator Zachary Eastwood's right-hand man. When the Guardians destroyed Zachary's warehouse of immortal offspring where he'd been breeding his immortal army, everyone inside had been destroyed, but Gregory's body was never found. The Guardians knew he'd escaped and wondered when he'd show his treacherous face again. He must have been raising this innocent child and feeding her lies this whole time.

"Why have you brought me here?"

"I need you. It took me a long time to find you," she paused. "They're after me. My father can no longer hide me." Terror grew in the little girl's voice just as it had in Piper's.

"Who's after you?"

"I don't know. But someone spies on us. And I feel something horrible will happen soon. Dad says I'm special. I'm supposed to help the immortals and stay away from Lavender Witches because they kill people like us."

"Us?" Piper softened and took a step toward the sweet girl. "You have the eyes." Piper's fingers brushed the curtain of hair away from her face.

"I know. I'm like you, tainted."

"Tainted?" Piper sat next to her, curious.

"We're not pure. I have the blood of a Lavender Witch and Guardian Immortal."

Piper froze. "No one in this century has been born of

Guardian blood except Tarian."

Nichola slammed her fist on the bed. "I'm telling the truth!"

A thumping and banging noise came from the other side of the door as if Gregory had stumbled into the kitchen for a midnight snack or breakfast. The exact time was still a mystery.

"You must go." Nichola jumped off the bed and tugged Piper to her feet. "Dad will check on me after he's had his coffee."

"I don't understand why you brought me here … Where exactly are we?"

"The Wastelands."

Piper nodded. That explained the time difference. It would be morning overseas.

"Get the others and search me out. And don't hurt Daddy." Nichola's anger had receded. She calmly yanked strands of her hair out and handed them to Piper for tracking. "Come back soon. We want to go home."

Her words were a warning and a threat, and Piper fully believed this child capable of wrathful magic.

Nichola brought her hands to her chest in prayer position, then thrust them outwards, palms up, arms outstretched and open. Her body shook as if it took great effort to cast Piper away. Like miniscule grains of sand into the cool mist Piper drifted back over the ocean, back to sleep inside Guardian Headquarters.

85

Piper shot up in bed, eyes wide. The bedsheets sodden with sweat. Her hand uncurled and she saw a tinsel strand of golden hair. Carefully she placed the hair inside a tiny locket then secured it around her neck for safekeeping. Could the man and girl that Hope had seen in her visions be Gregory Lycott and Nichola?

ELEVEN

CENTRAL NERVE — THE WASTELANDS

GUARDIAN TARIAN

The tent was anything but luxurious. A tiny space that barely fit two cots, no running water or bathroom facilities. Tarian and Audrey had to walk across the camp to use the common restrooms. Nonetheless, Tarian enjoyed the close quarters and slid his cot next to Audrey's. The metal divider made it difficult, but he managed to hold her as he fell into much needed sleep.

Something jolted Tarian upright. A dream perhaps. His elbow banged the bed's metal railing. A paralyzing ping of pain vibrated up his arm.

"What is it?" Audrey sat up in her bed.

"I don't know." He unfolded his hand to find a strand of hair far too blonde to be Audrey's.

Audrey lifted it for inspection. "You're lucky I knew where you were all night." She gave a wry grin, but her eyes hardened.

Uneasiness settled over Tarian like a scratchy blanket. "Something's wrong."

"You called out Piper's name just before jerking awake." Audrey handed the strand of hair back to him.

"I did?"

She nodded.

He hopped out of bed, pulled a container out of his backpack, placed the strand of hair inside, and sealed it. He glanced around the tent for any other signs but saw none. Then he stepped outside, but the camp seemed normal. Nerve Rebels carried on with their regular routine.

Audrey met him outside. "Think Tarian. What did you dream?"

He paced in front of the tent. The people walking by gave him strange glances. "I felt a mist, a drifting or pulling sensation."

"A mist like the Pall?"

"I don't know what the Pall feels like but it brought me back to the shadows of the Realm. The ones that were always watching, lingering. But that's it. That's all I remember, just misty shadows and Piper and someone I felt close to ... like a family member."

"Who?"

"I don't know."

"Charlie?"

Tarian shook his head. It wasn't his older brother, but the bond felt that strong.

TWELVE

GUARDIAN VILLAGE — THE ENTENTE

IMMORTAL LAVENDER WITCH PIPER

Piper raced through the maze of halls and stairs inside Guardian Headquarters to Eleanor's bedchamber. She knocked frantically until Eleanor opened the door.

She dashed into the apartment without a greeting.

"What are you doing here? It's the middle of the night." Eleanor blinked sleep away.

"Sorry," Piper hiccupped. "Sorry, sorry, sorry." Her jumpiness surged. "We have to go to the Wastelands." Piper's amethyst eyes nearly popped out of her head then she realized her rudeness and said, "Good morning."

"What?" Eleanor scratched her scalp.

"It's early morning."

"Too early. The moon is still out." Eleanor turned toward the kitchen. "I'm making tea."

Piper followed her into the kitchen. As the tea steeped,

Piper's angst eased a little. "Something's weird. There's a little girl. We have to find her." Piper paused trying to replay what she'd experienced in her mind before speaking it out loud. "I had a dream."

Eleanor stirred milk into her tea. "Would you like a cup?"

"No … thank you."

Eleanor closed her eyes and took two long sips. "Okay, tell me what you dreamt."

Piper twitched her nose and tapped her toes on the tiled floor as she retold the experience of drifting far, far away, to what she assumed was the Wastelands, and into the quaint house and pretty bedroom of Nichola.

"Well." Eleanor sighed. "This does match the information Christopher and Marcus relayed. They saw a man resembling Gregory with a small child." Eleanor's mouth thinned. "Can you find her again?"

Piper patted the locket around her neck. "Yes. I have a strand of her hair in here."

"Good. Let's get you to the Central Nerve with Audrey and Tarian." Eleanor set down her tea.

"Nichola said she was born of a Lavender Witch and Guardian Immortal. You don't think—" The question never fully formed on Piper's tongue.

"If she's the girl that Marcus and Christopher saw with Lycott, then yes. She could be an experiment whipped up by Zachary."

Piper bounced on her toes to release some pent-up energy. "We need more information."

"Hope and Teresa dreamed about it too." Piper waggled a pointed finger, as if that made her words more meaningful. "You do know she has visions? And the other child survivors have gifts too."

"Yes, but there's no sense getting worked up over any of this yet," Eleanor said, her black eyes full of assurance.

A shiver swept up Piper as her focus trained on those black eyes, the mark of an awakened.

In Piper's haste, she hadn't paid Eleanor's awakened eyes any attention. She'd never caught Eleanor out of her room before she'd had the chance to prep for the public. Piper knew Eleanor was an awakened but experiencing the phenomenon while still in her pajamas unnerved her. She'd never seen an awakened's eyes without the colored film over top and she couldn't stop staring.

Eleanor cleared her throat. "Anything else?"

Piper blinked and rubbed her nervous hands over her silky nightgown. "Hmm. Okay. Will you tell the High Council? I can't let that precious girl be used as some sort of pawn."

"And you said she was peaceful." Eleanor rose from her seat.

Piper nodded. "And with great power. Raw, untamed power. Dangerous. I felt it hum."

"The High Council has left. We have a little time to deal with this on our own." Eleanor strolled toward her bedchamber concluding their meeting.

Piper paced. "Oh … Yes … The Moon Cycle. Good!"

"Let yourself out." Eleanor turned and disappeared into the privacy of her bedroom.

Piper remained stationary for seconds. She glanced into the dregs of Eleanor's cup but saw only meaningless frayed specks. Frustration saturated her bones. For all her powers, she felt lost, answerless, heavy, yet in pieces.

She left the apartment, but the strange sensation stayed with her. She didn't understand how but she'd connected to Nichola, and she wouldn't feel whole until she was with the girl again. She had to get to Central Nerve immediately, find her friends, find this girl, and find out what bonded them so deeply.

THIRTEEN

Princess Brianna inspected the Pall sample as it swirled inside the glass container. It was full of life, personality, and shifting moods. One second red dashes aggressively zig-zagged up and down the cylinder, next it calmed to a boring gray fog, then it morphed into purple bouncing shadow balls.

Suddenly, the shadow balls exploded like firecrackers of brilliant light. Several tiny balls rebounded and glowed until finally stilling and spreading into a mist that expanded to fill the entire space. At that point the color shifted to the pale blue of a perfect sky Brianna had only seen in books. Finally, it transformed back to the gloomy gray of a Wasteland cloud.

"It's a dance," Brianna mused.

With renewed excitement, Brianna rushed to her grimoire and flipped the pages. She'd yet to find anything helpful, but she'd try again.

"Enhance clairvoyance with burning incense." She stopped

reading to grab a dash of cardamom and dried ancient dragon's blood. She sprinkled the fine powder mixture over lit charcoal.

"Hang a mirror by a thread over a fountain or pool of water." She retrieved her mirror and strung it above the pool of mist. It wasn't water—she was reaching—but the tiny droplets of mist would have to do since she'd tried everything else.

She read aloud, "Slowly lower the mirror until its base barely touches the surface of the water." She slid the top of the container off, exposing the shadows to the outside world. During the earlier tests nothing had exploded so she felt fairly confident. But this was witchcraft and science. One could never be too safe.

The unpleasant smell permeated her mask, but she tolerated it. Her heart pounded wildly as she felt the pull of the energy. She braced for it to spring to life and dart around the room destroying everything. Maybe, if it left a residue on objects that would be a clue to its makeup. If she knew what it was made of, maybe she could destroy it or at least control it.

However, it remained obedient, so she continued following the Grimoire's instructions. "Gaze within the mirror to receive information." She stared into the reflection glass for minutes. She saw gray mist, boring and uninformative, nothing more, nothing less.

She waited. And waited. Nothing. She set a timer and sat on the sofa. Three hours later she'd lost patience. She slammed the cap back onto the container. "For Pall's sake!" She chucked the mirror across the room. It shattered.

"That's seven years bad luck, milady," a deep rich voice crept into the room.

Brianna whirled around.

Marcus' brawn filled the doorway. Blonde curls touching the peak of the arch. He took one step past the threshold before she collided into him. She slammed every inch of her body on his. Her mouth hungered to taste his lips.

"I missed you," she said in between kisses.

He scooped her into his arms. "And I you."

Her body folded into his. She'd only known him for a short time, and he'd come and gone from South Castle repeatedly during that time, but in his absence her heart ached, food had no flavor, life had no spice. She threw all her energy into studying the Pall but had gotten nowhere, which only added intellectual frustration to her emotional angst and carnal longing.

"What did you learn? When are more Guardians coming?"

"Soon. I hope."

"You hope?"

"Alas, I've no news. And by the looks of that mirror, I'd say you're not doing any better."

"No!" She didn't want to think about the Pall and its wicked shadows that sneaked closer and closer to the city and people that she loved. He was here, and she wouldn't let the opportunity get away without satisfying her desire to kiss him. Her palms cupped his round cheeks. Her teeth nibbled the plumpness of his lower lip. She wanted to kiss him deep into the night.

"Uh-hum," Prince Theo cleared his throat. "Broken mirrors and kissing lovers. What in the Pall is going on young sis?"

"I'm older than you." Princess Brianna glared at her twin brother.

"I've come to tell you Mum requests your presence at midmeal." Prince Theo nodded to Marcus. "Good to see you."

Marcus clasped the prince's hand in a friendly shake.

Brianna's heart fluttered at their blooming friendship. She loved her twin and was happy he'd found a kindred spirit in Marcus. They both enjoyed life with no respect for death or consequences. Two men with generous smiles, raucous laughs, and cups brimming with ale, no matter the time of day or manner of business.

Theo strutted around the table where Brianna's experiment had gone awry. His long fingers trailed curiously over the glassware and instruments. "Hmmm."

Daggers shot from Brianna's eyes.

Theo clutched his chest as if hit by an actual blade. "Touchy. Touchy."

"As if you could do any better?" Brianna crossed her arms. He had no idea the work she'd put in. He couldn't possibly be more frustrated than her. She stormed off to fetch the broom and dustpan.

Marcus thumbed through the pages of the grimoire. "Pages are missing."

"I know." Brianna swept frantically. The sharp slivers of

mirrored glass peppered across her lab, gleaming proof of her failure and ridiculousness.

She discarded the mess and strolled over to Marcus. She glimpsed the frayed filaments of paper where the pages had been removed. Most of the it swallowed by the inner hinge. For closer inspection, she ducked under his arm to stand in front of his massive body. "Yes. Pages four hundred ninety to four hundred ninety-five have been missing for as long as I've had it."

Theo nodded. "We've wondered about those forever. It's a prophecy."

"How do you know that?" Marcus asked.

"It's torn from the prophecy's section. We figured Grandmum didn't want us to know the horrible fate of our miserable futures. Right sis?" Theo smirked.

"Well …" She sighed, totally miserable at yet another mystery that felt like a defeat.

"The question is *when* were they stolen?" Marcus asked.

Brianna turned in his arms to peer up at him. "Stolen?"

"Yeah. Think it's a coincidence these pages are missing?" Marcus ran a hand gently down her back.

"I've honestly never considered it. They've always been missing." She turned back to the book and gently stroked the edges of the frayed paper. Even with Marcus' protective body leaning over her shoulder, a shawl of dread fell down Brianna's back. She glanced to her brother.

"Maybe the rumors are true," Theo said.

"What rumors?" Marcus asked.

Brianna answered, "Grandmum died when we were only twelve. It seemed to happen quickly. Suddenly, she was very sick and then she died." Her voice broke as she fought the grief that clenched her throat.

"It's not exactly uncommon around here. There's lots to kill us," Theo said.

"Yes. Marianne liked to tease us that Grandmum had been poisoned by the devil, and if we weren't good, we'd get poisoned too. Grandmum had a sharp tongue and that was Marianne's line when our tongues got sharp too."

"It worked. We shut up fast. She's scary as Pall." Theo's eyes widened. "Have you seen Marianne before her gloss and shimmer? Ahhh." He mocked a shudder.

"Theo!" Brianna scolded, but she giggled just the same. Marianne was the fiercest looking Sanna sibling with her lips dyed red from insect venom and her hair naturally as black as night.

"Do you remember if they were missing while your grandmother had the book?" Marcus asked.

Brianna shook her head. "She never mentioned missing pages, but that doesn't mean anything. It's very old, passed down generations. It's survived many wars. Honestly, I'm surprised only four pages are missing."

"Well, those were ripped out carefully. They meant something."

"Yeah, like they didn't want us to notice," Theo said.

"Exactly."

"They could be anywhere." Brianna's heart dropped.

Lunch was a family affair with her mum, the queen, and all her brothers and sisters in attendance. Marcus, Zella, and Franny were their guests.

Franny's eyes found Brianna. A warm smile spread across the witch's face. After Father's death, Franny took over caring for her since Mum's time was devoted elsewhere. The vulnerable city had lost its king and needed a strong queen to rule.

Franny picked up the slack with the queen's youngest daughter. She'd enlightened Brianna in the ways of witchcraft and spell casting. She'd helped Brianna make sense of the grimoire when it was passed down to her. But time had changed many things.

Franny had been assisting the Nerve Rebels for a long time and hadn't been a staple in her life for years. She feared her love for her former caretaker lost. Maybe Marianne was right not to trust Franny.

Marcus grunted as he ate. The sound drew her attention from Franny.

Theo chuckled. "What is it, big man? Used to larger portion sizes and more blood?"

Marcus remained quiet. He smiled through the grimace as he chewed.

Brianna appreciated his attempt at good manners. He'd told her of the delicious food piled high atop his plate back home in the village. She wanted to reach under the table and hold his hand. But if Mum caught her, she'd ask too many questions that Brianna wasn't prepared to answer. She was too uncertain of her own feelings. And why did she need to be sure? She just wanted a little fun in this dreary city. Why did it have to be anything more than that?

Queen Priscella Sanna took a neat bite of her food and a delicate sip of her water then said, "So you feel that assistance from the Entente government looks to be unlikely."

Zella nodded. Her eyes flashed to Marianne but did not linger.

Marianne's face revealed nothing as she focused on Zella, but Brianna knew her sister still cared deeply for the Prevaller woman.

"It appears that way," Franny said.

Brianna startled when her sister, Lucianna, slammed a fork into the table, her face red with rage. Their brother seated next to Lucianna paled but appeared equally infuriated.

Mum sighed. "I understand your resistance, Lu. I share your concern over the children."

"Hold off their training just a little longer." Lucianna's voice trembled but not with weakness, with unwavering resolution.

"We still have time. Lautaro's army hasn't progressed."

Brianna's stomach twisted in disgust. Balefire was a young city with plenty of strong capable teenagers to enlist in the armed services. It was an idea that had been tossed around ever since Lautaro showed up and took over North Castle.

"Lots of young Wastelanders successfully fought for the Prevallers and continue to fight for the Nerve Rebels," Zella said, encouragingly.

"Yes, but many died. I don't care if they're big and strong or smart and crafty. They're children! They shouldn't be called upon to slaughter the enemy," Lucianna said.

"We don't have time," Zella said, focusing on the queen and ignoring Lucianna. "You might as well train your young. You don't have to use them. Fighting is a valuable skill that they can carry into adulthood. Whether they need it to fight a war or be safe on the dangerous city streets."

"No!" Lucianna threw down her napkin and stood. Rage flushed her skin. She cast one last fierce glare at Zella who remained stoic then she turned to Franny. "Do you agree?"

"I'm sorry to say … yes. We have many remarkable teenage rebels." Franny swallowed as if she disliked aligning with Zella. "They've proved invaluable."

"Thank you for a lovely lunch, Mum," Lucianna said through gritted teeth, then stormed out.

Briggen followed his sister saying nothing. His mouth such a thin line no words could pass, at least no kind words.

Marianne's stare fixed on Zella. "Don't let this witch fill your head with brutal ideas."

Franny bowed her head as if heavy with shame. "Child, the idea wasn't mine."

"Marianne, war isn't charitable. We will all suffer." Zella finally cast her full attention toward her ex-girlfriend.

Marianne's head whipped around with such force her black hair spun wildly. "Mum! There must be another way!"

"Go check on Lu and Brig, please." The queen smiled without a hint of scorn for her eldest daughter's rudeness.

Marianne's shoulders fell. Before she exited, she glanced briefly at Brianna with sorrowful eyes.

Brianna leaned toward Marcus absorbing the heat from his closeness, wishing she could lay her head against his shoulder.

The queen twitched almost imperceptivity, but Brianna noticed. Her mum had grown so old since Father's death. Brianna understood the concern in Zella's face. She was a good woman. She had hoped she and Marianne would reunite, but they'd always disagreed. They'd shared a tumultuous, unhealthy romance. This fight further proof they were not meant to be even if their love was strong.

Brianna's heart grew brave, and she gripped Marcus' hand under the table—its warmth a touchstone of reverie that she wanted to wrap up in. He squeezed, making her desire for him come alive, making her task of conquering the Pall more meaningful, and therefore, more daunting. None of what they'd discussed over lunch even mattered if she couldn't solve the shadow secrets.

FOURTEEN

CENTRAL NERVE — THE WASTELANDS

IMMORTAL LAVENDER WITCH PIPER

Piper arrived in Central Nerve in her usual graceless fashion. Her sudden appearance in the middle of the dirt road caused Germaine to spit water all over the place.

"Oh. I'm sorry." Piper reached out a hand. "Let me get you some more drink."

Germaine pulled away. "Who are you?"

"I'm Piper. Who are you?"

"Germaine. What are you doing here?"

"I was sent from the Guardian Chancellor to find Audrey and Tarian."

Germaine let out a long exhalation.

Puzzled, Piper asked, "Do you know them?"

"Not really, but I know where they are. Follow me." Germaine pivoted and marched toward a building.

"Thank you." Piper followed. "I didn't mean to scare you. You've probably never seen someone like me."

"Actually, I know your kind."

"Oh." Then the realization of what *her kind* meant hit Piper like a falling brick. "Ooooh! I'm not with the Lavender Witch coven. I'm a Guardian."

"Yeah. You said that."

The twiggy girl with knives in her belt made Piper uncomfortable. She kept glancing back, staring at her with those gray pearl eyes, and not smiling or talking. Piper licked each of her teeth, front and back. She didn't feel any remnants of lunch so what was the girl staring at?

The girl took her through a set of doors into an old, concrete building. It was stark and humid, the complete opposite of Guardian Headquarters. The ancient furniture lacked the charm of Eleanor's glorious desk or the rosewood table in the High Council room. This was an insufferable place. She hoped she wouldn't have to stay long.

"They're in there." Germaine pointed to a closed door.

Piper hesitated. She looked at the girl for verification.

"Go in."

Piper stiffened at her rudeness then cautiously opened the door and stepped inside to find several people gathered around a table in conversation.

"Piper," Audrey announced warmly.

Piper let out a long breath. She glanced back to thank the teenager, but she was gone.

Audrey strolled over and ushered her into the meeting.

"Let me introduce you."

Piper shook hands with the Cerveau's leader Axon, who proceeded with introductions. "Come meet Chess, Ralph, and Jen, three out of our seven Cerveau members. Franny and Zella should be arriving soon."

"Hello."

They all focused on her as if expecting a speech. Feeling extremely uneasy, she waded over to the safety of a familiar face. Tarian smiled and put a protective arm around her but something still felt off. The hairs on her arm rose as shivers ran through her. She sensed a disturbance in the corner of the room.

Suddenly, two women appeared. A witch with lavender eyes and a soldier. The witch pulled a weapon, a crazed look turning the lavender of her eyes to stormy purple.

Axon drew his gun. "Whoa, Franny. It's just us."

Franny's brows drew taut as her weapon trained on Piper. "Who's this?"

"She's a Guardian. Sent by the Chancellor," Axon said, then turned to face Piper. "Piper this is Franny and Zella, members of our Cerveau. They're just vading in from a meeting with the royal family."

Franny lowered the weapon. The features of her face slowly relaxing. "My apologies. I thought you were a Lavender Witch."

"Half," Piper said. "I'm a Guardian."

Franny fidgeted confused.

"My mother was a Lavender Witch. She died centuries ago. How old are you?"

"Not centuries. And what of your father?" Franny asked.

"Believed to have had immortal blood but I never knew him. Mother shipped me off to the new world with a Spanish expedition."

Ralph shook his head. "Why is she here?"

"She's here to help just as we all are," Tarian snapped.

"Be specific. She doesn't look like she can fight." Ralph squinted his wolfish eyes.

Piper stared at him in defiance. She could fight but didn't like to. That wasn't the point. What would Audrey tell them? The High Council had been adamant about keeping all Lycott information on a Guardian-only confidential level.

Audrey placed a calming hand on Piper's shoulder. "She can vade just like Franny. She'll be useful in transferring information to South Castle."

Piper's heart skipped at the bent truth. She'd been sent to find Lycott, not help these strangers. For all she knew, these were the spies Nichola spoke of. The ones that frightened her. Even though Nichola was a stranger too, Piper had a connection to the little girl. Piper looked at the floor hoping to avoid any more conversation about her intentions.

"Speaking of," Christopher butted in, "Has Princess Brianna made any progress with the Pall?"

"No." Zella shook her head. "And they're all highly

concerned about the Entente's resistance to send more soldiers."

"Eleanor's working on that. The President may change his mind now that we know Lautaro's malditos are wandering into the mist unharmed and with suspicious intent." Audrey shifted her weight uneasily.

Piper rocked from her toes to her heels. Boardrooms and meetings unnerved her, especially this one. Their invasive stares made her skin crawl. If only she knew where the coffee maker was, she'd escape and brew a pot. But soon, Audrey and Tarian rushed her out of there and into the privacy of their tent.

"Vade us to the girl." Tarian gave Piper the strand of blonde hair that had appeared in his hand after his dream.

Piper retrieved the matching strand from her locket and gripped both pieces together. "Grab my arm and hold on tightly."

FIFTEEN

THE WASTELAND

NERVE SPY GERMAINE

The two giant Guardians had been coming and going from Central Nerve for weeks. Never taking root but always friendly and kind, especially to Germaine. She knew they'd employ her skills sooner or later, but she never expected they'd want information on Nichola's dad. As far as she knew, no one knew about the little girl and her strange dad. She hadn't told anyone.

When the big guys had asked her early that morning, they'd emphasized the need for secrecy. Little did they know, she was already keeping that secret. She'd said she'd sleep on it, but by the afternoon Piper materialized from the dust. The foreign witch's sudden appearance had scared her not only because Piper had nearly knocked her over but also the resemblance to Nichola was uncanny.

Germaine had left camp, blended with a group of thieving allies, and kept her eyes sharp. Now she strolled next to Sam, wondering how she could break away from the group unnoticed.

"Damn," she muttered, realizing she'd passed Nichola's street.

"What is it?" Sam asked.

Germaine wide eyed her companion. She didn't trust her. She didn't trust any of these kids she was hanging with. They were survivors. They had to be. Like Sam, most of them didn't have parents or their parents were addicted to Blue, and therefore, not much of parents at all. The ransom from a magical witch-child like Nichola would fetch them either wealth or death. Germaine didn't want the latter on her conscience.

She searched her mind for an excuse to separate from Sam and the group. "Uh. I just forgot to look for a … battery. Yeah. Dad needs some, and I was supposed to be looking so I'd better start."

"Batteries aren't hard to find. I cross 'em all the time. I'll keep watch."

"Thanks."

Sam nodded and smiled.

Germaine feared that if Sam knew Nichola was special, she wouldn't hesitate to cash in. And could Germaine really blame her? Sam didn't look well. She'd lost another tooth and her belt pulled a little tighter.

Panic layered in Germaine's brain as they strolled farther away from Nichola's house, but she had to keep her cover. She was just there to scavenge and thieve, not spy for two oversized Guardian immortals.

The gang stopped in front of a group of strung-out addicts lying in a heap. The wind blew their foul stench into Germaine's face.

"Scum," Jinx snarled then hit a rock into the pile of human bodies with his bat. Jinx was gutter thin and lamppost tall, looked sixteen but was only thirteen, with the blondest hair Germaine had ever seen on a boy Wastelander. His parents had died last month from a Blue overdose.

Two kids she didn't know flanked either side of Jinx—a skinny boy with dancing evil eyes and a very large girl with hands the size of frying pans. This girl might even take out Crow in a fight.

Germaine didn't like newcomers. Newcomers equaled new problems. They brought new habits and ideas that didn't always gel with the rest of the gang and their old ways. She might not trust kids like Jinx or Crow, but at least she knew where they'd draw the line—that they had a line, some sense of honor.

The new boy caught her stare with those eyes like shiny, hard river stones. His grin spread slow and with purpose. It sent icy shivers racing up her spine. The chill crested her shoulders. He seemed to notice her dread and winked. It took all her courage, but she stood strong and didn't look away. It felt like peering into the mind of boy that tortured animals. He'd probably drowned kittens for fun.

His girlfriend nudged him, and he lost interest in taunting Germaine. The girl had a shard of glass and chucked it at the lump of people. Her laugh echoed and infected the group, including Jinx who had originated this sick game.

The people squirmed. Their movement only highlighted the smell. Sulfuric and sour. This group didn't have much time left on this planet. Their skin rotted. Open sores oozed yellow discharge. The two that opened their mouths to protest the abuse revealed blood filled gums and few gray teeth.

Germaine had little sympathy for these weaklings. Everyone in the Wastelands suffered. Why did these people deserve her kindness? Her family had fought and worked to rebuild this world. They still fought and worked day in and day out. None of the Nerve succumbed to such disgusting helplessness. But she saw the rage build in Jinx's eyes.

Her heart heard the same call to rage. A part of her desired the release it could bring. She understood the want to rip junkies apart. She sympathized with the street kids that had lost everything, never having had much in the first place, because of this drug and the people who succumb to it. It was a cruel world, and like Jinx, it could easily suck her in to its brutality, turn her into a monster. Unlike Jinx, she had a community, she had the Nerve, and she wouldn't allow the anger to breed inside her.

Jinx heaved a larger rock. The guy it hit stumbled forward. Jinx hit the addict's head with the bat. Blood and brain splattered everywhere. The addict dropped dead.

Everyone, except Germaine, laughed. Bile rose in her throat.

"Don't you think it's funny?" The newcomer boy stared straight at Germaine.

"No, not really." Germaine held his gaze.

"Too good for us, are you?" His girlfriend with the extra-large hands asked.

Germaine picked up a rock and chucked it at the lot of junkies. The stone hit no one.

The two newcomers laughed. "Can't you do better than that?"

If she'd wanted, her rock would've pegged one of the addicts square between the eyes, but she didn't want to. She wanted to leave without a scene, so she swallowed her pride and took the verbal bullying.

She turned to walk away.

"Who does she think she is?" The newcomer girl asked Jinx.

"Leave her be. She's part of the rebellion."

The strange boy stepped as if he might go after Germaine. "Is she now? Does she have connections?"

"She's with the Nerve so like I said before leave her be." Jinx raised his tone.

Germaine kept walking. She didn't glance back. Her breath lightened after Jinx stood his ground, and she could hear no more protesting from the newcomers. She'd never known Jinx to care about the rebels, so his tone of respect surprised her. Maybe he was just keeping the order, keeping his rank as leader. Maybe he remembered the night Nichola's magic froze him and saved her. Whatever it was, she planned to capitalize on it and get the hell out of there.

Sam followed her. "Where you goin'?"

"I don't have time for this." She faked toughness to hide her nerves. "I'm gonna climb."

Sam looked from Jinx's group of thieves to Germaine. "Yeah. I'm not in the mood to fight either."

Germaine rolled her eyes, but Sam didn't witness it. Germaine needed to be alone. She had a job to do. How could she ditch Sam? Nichola's house could be on the way to the climbing tower if she took a few detours. She could do it unnoticed by Sam possibly loose her during the winding stroll.

Germaine turned down Francis Street and Sam said nothing.

Good.

Sam's too busy scavenging for metals.

"Do you know those two new kids?" Germaine asked.

"No. Thought you might, then realized the rumors were shit."

"What?"

"Yeah. I thought they had some Nerve connection."

"Why?"

"Someone said so. Said they'd seen 'em with a Nerve Rebel," Sam said.

"That's a lie," she said with conviction as her stomach

twisted with apprehension.

There'd been a lot of strange newcomers at Central Nerve. Had someone met with the scary guy and girl? Street kids knew things and were always hot to make a trade. It could explain their sudden appearance hanging with Jinx's gang. She'd wished Jinx hadn't called her out as part of the rebels. Only Sam and Jinx knew she was a Nerve Rebel, but they didn't know she spied for them. When Jinx found out, he'd promised to keep that bit of sensitive information to himself.

Germaine shook her head. *Can't trust anyone in this place.*

SIXTEEN

Audrey, Tarian, and Piper landed with a thud. The sky gloomed a milky dark gray, dense with uncomfortable moisture and thick with an acrid odor. Piles of debris lined the beat of pavement they stood on. The six-lane boulevard looked familiar, but now the cracks, pocks, and potholes deformed it. Dirt, oil, and trash scattered as far as Audrey could see. *Was this the remnants of the Champs-Élysées?*

"We must be close." Piper unfurled her hand. There was no trace of the blonde strands. "Nichola's taken her hair back."

"Or you lost it during the travel." Tarian smirked.

"Hmph. This way." Piper rushed off leaving Tarian and Audrey to catch up.

They turned off the boulevard to venture down a two-lane street. Deteriorated old buildings framed the narrow road of broken windows, missing doors, cracked bricks, chipped corbels, and collapsed archways. This broken city made Balefire look pristine. It was the true Wastelands, and it felt more ruined and hopeless than Audrey had imagined. She'd seen Paris after World Wars I and II and this was worse.

Although Central Nerve was also considered the Wastelands, it had order and purpose. It may be a grouping of tents and run-down buildings, but it was clean, safe, and warm. These were the real streets where most of the survivors lived. The mortal struggle evident in the dispersing of needles, spoiled food, and soiled clothes. This was the Wastelands the Entente government wanted no part of.

Tarian's hand wrapped around her arm. He yanked her and Piper behind a stack of crumbled stone. He shoved their heads down and brought his index finger to his lips. A gang of vagrants strutted in the distance but close enough to catch Tarian's immortal eye.

As they gained, Audrey heard them, bored kids looking for trouble. They kicked everything that got in their way. Two carried baseball bats, hitting whatever they felt like. Youthful voices with a carefree cadence, but a sharp tongue, spoke in English with an occasional French word and some foreign slang.

Once they passed, Tarian turned to Audrey. "You okay?"

She was but her gut crimped with sadness. "Let's get out of here before they see us. I don't want to fight a bunch of kids just trying to survive and don't know any better."

Piper marched on, Audrey on her heels, and Tarian in the rear avidly looking over his shoulder. They came to a row of decent looking city homes, all connected and uniform with steps leading to entranceways. They were horribly decayed by any average Entente comparison, but for this place, they looked like gold.

"This is it." Piper jumped and landed at the foot of a staircase.

The address above the archway missed numbers, and the arch itself drooped, but the intricate frieze of lounging angels remained in pristine condition.

"Is anyone here?" Tarian asked.

"Doesn't look like it, but then again, I'm sure no one wants to draw attention to themselves around here." Audrey scanned the area. It was an ideal hideout for a traitor like Gregory holed up with a kidnapped girl.

"I don't sense her presence. I think the place is empty." Piper tilted her head and sniffed the air.

"Or maybe that's what she wants you to think." Audrey ascended the stairs.

The door swung open, and the little girl stood in the doorway, eyes fixed on Audrey.

SEVENTEEN

THE WASTELANDS

NERVE SPY GERMAINE

As Audrey, Tarian, and Piper, slipped though Nichola's front door, Germaine and Sam neared the house. *Why are they here? Did Marcus and Christopher know?*

Germaine took two steps closer. She definitely heard raised voices but couldn't see inside the row house since the curtains were drawn.

"Look at this! Freakin' gold."

Germaine jumped.

Sam sprung from the backseat of a beat-up car, her arm outstretched. "This is a gold necklace, right? I mean. I've never seen it for reals. I mean, people told me, and I seen pictures. Tell me it's gold." Sam shoved her hand in Germaine's face.

Germaine touched the thin chain. She rubbed a couple links with the end of her shirt. It left grayish streaks on the fabric and the necklace's dullness lifted slightly. "Yep, that's gold. If you polish it, it'll shine bright."

"But that will attract attention. No. No. I'll leave it like this for now. I'm trading this at Sully's."

Sully's was a good day's walk and Germaine knew Sam wouldn't leave for the trading outpost until daybreak. She'd return to the first level of the tower to sleep. She'd have to hide this valuable, or she could get killed.

"Or—" Sam leaned toward Germaine. Her face so close, Germaine smelled the tang of decayed teeth on her breath.

Germaine took a step back. "What?"

"I been thinkin'. You got a safe place with all the necessities. Maybe I trade with you … I want to join the Nerve—"

"What? No." Germaine's dad had warned her never to bring one of those *thievin' hoodlums* home.

"Why not?" Sam's voice grew louder.

Germaine glanced at the house.

Sam's worn gray eyes slid to the house just as one curtain opened. "What's in there?"

Germaine shrugged. "I don't know. I just heard voices." This was getting annoying. She had to ditch Sam. "You'd have to prove yourself to the Nerve."

"How?" Sam's eyes locked on Germaine.

"Well, they wouldn't trust you at first. You'd be kept locked up at night. Free during the day, but at night, when we all slept—well most of us—you'd be locked up. Your bed would be in a cell."

"For how long?"

"For as long as it took to trust you."

"Won't you vouch for me?"

"You let Jinx's gang nearly beat me to death. If not for—" Germaine stopped, clenching her jaw and grinding her teeth silent.

Sam's expression turned from pleading to puzzlement. "You didn't die, and I did nothing."

"Exactly." Germaine shook her head. "I can't make excuses just because you're my …" What was she to Germaine anyway? Sam had been the closest thing she had to a friend— someone her own age that knew the horrors of growing up in the Wastelands. They'd had fun playing Wack together and scavenging for treasurers. But Sam was a coward. Germaine wasn't.

"You're a thief and a killer. Sorry to be so blunt but that's what I've seen you do, and that's how the Nerve will look at you no matter what I say. If you really want to join the cause, you'd have to prove it."

"How?"

"Give up that necklace for nothing in return. Rebels don't fight for the glory; we fight to make a better life."

Sam's grubby fingers clutched the chain, then she shoved Germaine, knocking her to the ground. Germaine got up fast. The two girls stared long and hard at each other. Anger and fear brewed in Sam's eyes. Germaine readied for a punch that never came.

"I don't need you or your stupid rebel camp." Sam turned away and stalked toward the tower.

Germaine stood still, watching Sam's back shrink in the

distance, overcome with a sensation inside her chest as if her ribs and heart were breaking then mending back together harder and tougher.

She was done with liars. She removed the small tracking device from a pocket and hit the button pinging her father and alerting him to her location.

EIGHTEEN

THE WASTELANDS

GUARDIAN AUDREY

Once inside the small row house, Tarian slipped out of the living room to survey the upstairs. Nichola watched him keenly then her eyes shifted to survey Audrey. The girl trembled and bit her bottom lip. Audrey decided to give her some space and wander into the kitchen area. Maybe Piper could set the girl at ease with their intrusion.

The home seemed quite ordinary. There were dishes in the sink. Remnants of food smeared the stovetop. The refrigerator was surprisingly well stocked. If it was the traitor Gregory Lycott taking care of this little girl, he obviously cared enough to keep her well-fed.

Audrey walked the stairs to the bedroom. It was just as pink and girly as Piper had described. She noticed there were no electronics or communicators, modern or antique. Audrey returned to Piper and Nichola. They'd moved to the couch.

Audrey asked, "You have electricity?"

"Yes. I destroyed all of the communicators. I didn't mean to. I drew on the power source without understanding. I'm better now, but Daddy's sick of having to buy new stuff. I read books, and I like it better anyway."

"Who's Daddy?" Audrey needed to hear his name.

"My Daddy ..." Nichola glanced to Piper who nodded in assurance. "Gregory Lycott."

Even though Audrey wasn't surprised by the name, hearing the obvious adoration in the girl's voice sent shockwaves rolling over her skin. Nichola loved him—a treacherous, deceitful man.

Nichola's round cheeks sunk as she frowned with realization. "You didn't come to rescue us. Why? Why can't we leave now? We must leave!" Her sharp words sliced through the air. Tears pooled in her eyes and her shimmering aura power reddened.

Audrey vexed at the thought of what Nichola might do when provoked and scared. She'd need to tread delicately as if cajoling a cornered and frightened animal. "No, not originally. But we will. Please don't worry."

Nichola's halo of glittery mist faded, but her tears spilled. "It's not me I'm worried about. Daddy's in trouble. It's getting worse."

"What's getting worse?" Tarian said as he strolled back into the room.

"I don't know. He's always covered in bruises and cuts.

He's angry now." Her eyes fell to the floor.

"He hasn't hurt you, has he?" Tarian asked.

"No," she paused as if rolling her words around in her mouth. "He can control it. For now."

Audrey bent down to her eye level. "Are his eyes black?"

Nichola nodded.

Audrey stood and glanced from Piper to Tarian. They all knew what her daddy was. "It's too risky to leave her here with …" She didn't dare speak Gregory Lycott's name aloud.

Nichola left the couch, went to the window, and peered out. "He wants to go home, to the place he calls the village."

"Why? Why does he want to go there?" Audrey's voice hardened. Gregory would never step foot inside the village again. Not if she could help it.

Nichola wrapped her arms around herself. She sniffled and swiped her nose with the back of her hand.

Piper shot Audrey the stink-eye then dashed over to Nichola and hugged her. "Everything's going to be okay. Don't worry."

Nichola melted into Piper's arms.

Audrey dug deep and found a calm, sweet voice inside herself. "Can you read minds?"

Nichola nodded.

"What do you see inside your daddy's mind when he speaks of going home?"

"I read emotions and sense things. In Daddy, I see

snowflakes and the color yellow. I smell cinnamon and feel happy and at peace. I want to go to this village."

"Why didn't you just vade the both of you there?" Tarian asked.

Audrey knew the answer before Nichola gave it.

"I can't find it." Her head dropped.

"It's spellbound," Audrey told Tarian.

"I let Daddy down. I tried so many times." Her sweet frosting voice lamented.

"But why stay here in the awful Wastelands? You could have vaded anywhere into the Entente or Balefire," Piper asked as she caressed the girl's pale golden hair.

Nichola shrugged.

"You *can* vade?" Piper asked.

Again, the girl shrugged.

"Maybe Lycott doesn't want to leave. He fits in well here," Tarian said.

Nichola clutched Piper tighter.

Audrey shook her head at Tarian then called up her calm, level voice again. "Does your dad know you called Piper? Does he want us to bring you both back?"

"Maybe. We've talked. He thinks I spoke to Piper in a dream. He doesn't know I can summon. I scare him, and I don't want to scare him away. I don't want to be all alone."

Coward, Audrey thought. He'd always been a snake for as long as she'd known him.

Nichola glared at Audrey, and she winced. *Sorry*, she thought, then tried to will her mind clean. This reminded her of Ana-Clara, the Bruja Blanca back home in the Entente that could read her thoughts. She'd helped them awaken the sleepers.

Audrey didn't like people tearing off her veil. It had taken centuries of fighting and spying to perfect her mask of indifference. To have it shredded by a tiny child was maddening.

Audrey joined Tarian's pacing. It helped defuse the nervous energy stirring inside her blood.

Piper brought Nichola back to the comfortable couch and rocked her. "What do you want us to do? Do you want us to take you to the village now?"

"Not without Daddy!"

Audrey stopped pacing. "Sweetie your dad is a danger to our kind. I'm not sure we should bring him home."

"I'm not leaving a Waker that can kill Guardians roaming the Earth," Tarian said.

"They have to stay together," Piper said.

"What? Who?" Tarian asked.

"Gregory and Nichola. Hope and Teresa both saw this in their visions. It's imperative that they stay together."

Tarian scowled.

"Maybe we can get him into the chamber where Joe can keep him and us safe," Piper said.

"We—" Audrey gestured that *we* meant her and Tarian. "—can't vanish from our post at Central Nerve. We'll lose their trust … again.”

“You go back to Central Nerve while I help Piper get Nichola and Lycott safely inside the village,” Tarian said.

Audrey resumed her pacing. “No one's going anywhere until I talk to Eleanor.”

The doorknob rotated. All heads turned to see who or what would step over the threshold.

Audrey and Tarian readied weapons but neither of them had a Death Serum needle, the only thing capable of stopping a Waker. They were at the mercy of a little sorceress and a degenerate Waker.

“He won't hurt you.” Nichola tilted her head. She looked sweet, but Audrey knew better than to be deceived by innocent eyes and rosy cheeks.

“Well, I'm not taking any chances.” Tarian gripped his gun tighter.

Gregory Lycott stepped into the foyer, glanced at everyone staring at him, and went invisible.

“That won't work Lycott.” Tarian aimed the weapon at his head.

“It's okay Daddy. I asked them to come.”

Slowly his body materialized. He held a large toolbox.

“Steal that?” Audrey didn't hide the edge in her question.

“No … well … yes. I mean you steal everything here. There're no … well … not many stores. What you find, you keep.”

“What about all the food in the fridge?” She gestured to

the refrigerator.

"There's a market."

"And there's electricity." Again, she motioned to the fridge.

"Yes. I hacked into the Nerve's. A lot of people do. No one pays us any attention in the Wastelands. No one important that is."

Lycott twitched and his eyes darted like a trapped cat.

"Please stop pointing those things at Daddy." Terror draped over Nichola's face.

Tarian and Audrey didn't budge.

Piper stood up. "We need to work together. Put them down."

The weapons were stowed.

"He can be saved. I know it," Nichola pleaded. She had moved to her dad's side. They held hands, united.

"Maybe Ana Clara," Tarian muttered. "If anything can help his lost soul, it's her mix of magic muds and potions."

Audrey slowly nodded. "It's worth a try. We'd need to get Joe there and some guards to guarantee Gregory doesn't hurt anyone."

Tarian pitched him a deadly stare.

Lycott bowed his head. He didn't look like much of a threat—skinny, pale, and weak. Tired of living on the run. Tired of fighting down the Waker inside of him.

"We have no way of warning Ana-Clara that we're coming.

Do you think her dog will be a problem?" Audrey asked.

"Wolfgang will be fine. I'm sure she has some sort of voodoo magic detector. Her colored rocks will glow or something." Tarian smiled at his joke.

Audrey's nerves were too riddled with anxiety to enjoy the humor. She didn't like not planning the many details of a mission this critical, but they didn't have a choice. The Wastelands seemed to be closing in around them. Bands of teenagers, like the one Audrey had seen earlier, passed outside the windows on a regular basis. It was only a matter of time before one of them came upon Nichola. Her extraordinariness shimmered an effervescent energy. Unlike Piper's pastel glow, Nichola's illuminated hints of red. It could be mistaken for pink but not the soft hue of children's toys, a bolder color that could flip to a furious scarlet in the snap of a finger.

Audrey paced. It didn't feel right. She was a soldier that believed in the line of command, but on so many occasions she'd relied on her gut instinct. "You all stay here. I'll go back to Central Nerve and contact Eleanor."

"No. You stay here. I'll go." Tarian took a step toward the door.

Audrey's cold eyes zipped to Lycott silently communicating her thoughts on his instability.

Tarian huffed then glanced to Lycott. "You *can* control yourself, right?"

"Yes," Lycott said.

"I'm faster, Audrey." Tarian played his hand.

That was true but surrender had never come easy for her. Finally, she nodded.

Tarian kissed her then moved to leave but stopped. "Did you hear that?"

The front door burst open. Soldiers with shields and guns rushed in. The little room became loud and chaotic.

Audrey charged then stopped upon recognizing the uniforms. "Don't shoot. We're on the same side."

Cerveau members Chess, Jen, and Ralph shoved through the soldiers to greet them.

"What's going on?" Chess asked.

"I thought we were working together, First Born." Jen boldly confronted Tarian.

Tarian grunted. "We are."

"Really? I didn't realize working together meant sneaking away at dusk." Jen cocked an eyebrow.

"Our apologies," Audrey said. "This is creature business. And we had sparse intel."

"You're in the Wastelands now. It's *all* creature business," Chess said, his voice firm, his lips drawn tight over clenched teeth.

"How'd you find us?" Audrey asked.

At that moment, Roberto made his way into the house. "All's clear outside."

Audrey remembered the teenage girl, his daughter. Jen called her Germ. Audrey's mind flashed to the thieving kids she'd seen all evening.

Spy.

Piper yelped. Her face twisted in pain.

"What's wrong?" Breath caught in Audrey's throat along with her heart at the sight of her friend's agony.

"They've done something to this place. I can't vade." The purple in Piper's eyes stormed as she glanced at each soldier blocking the exit.

Audrey went to her side. She placed a hand on Piper's shoulder. "It's okay, Piper."

Piper's magic remained a mystery, and Audrey wasn't confident she'd hold her calm. For all Audrey knew, Piper would attack or stop time or something, ending all diplomatic relations in a blink. The Guardians had worked too hard to establish an accord to risk that.

When Tarian placed his hand on Nichola, Audrey assumed it a kind gesture until she interpreted the strain in his face. He was trying to read the little girl. He shared Audrey's distrust of the two witches' equanimity. Unfortunately, his hand recoiled and his brows furrowed. He shook his head.

Audrey inhaled deeply. This little girl certainly was a riddle. "This girl and her father need protection. Let's get them to Central Nerve then I'll arrange to transport them back to the Entente."

Perplexed, Chess, Jen and Ralph swept the room with their eyes.

Lycott materialized. His appearance revealed a man barely

holding it together. Audrey hoped he could, at least until she could get him safely into Joe's chamber. Nichola left Piper's side to comfort her father.

"We're not going anywhere until you tell us who these creatures are in relationship to the Guardians and the Nerve and what they're capable of." Ralph stepped in front of Jen.

Ralph was the youngest. She'd assumed Jen and Chess outranked him, but now she wasn't so sure.

Audrey huffed. Her truths too thick to spill out all at once. "Of course. I will if you will." She froze his wolfish gray eyes with her icy blues.

Ralph cocked his head. "The members of the Cerveau hold equal rank. Under us we have a typical chain of command. We want to trust you. Our goal is to secure Balefire and improve the Wastelands. To help all the creatures that live here. We hide nothing and we've told you everything. Covert operations are not acceptable."

Audrey resisted her instinct to conceal or fabricate. For as much as she wanted to unify, she'd been a secret keeper for so long, the disciplined glass was hard to break. But she kicked it and it shattered. She told the long story of Zachary's plan, his demented offspring, Lycott's escape that eventually led to the Wastelands, the sickness that grew inside him, and the enchanted, mystery girl who called him father.

All attention turned on Nichola.

Ralph asked, "So her power is unknown? It could be

dangerous?" He stood ready with hands locked on his weapon.

"Yes." Audrey relaxed. Here was a man that understood. He'd seen enough to not be fooled by cherub cheeks and tiny bodies.

Nichola tucked her arm around Lycott's. Her calm hinged to his security. With a look and a nod to the rebels, she concurred they all understood this.

Piper had been quiet throughout the discussions. She strayed from the group, circling the house in a daze, then returned with a question. "How did you seal the house?"

Jen walked to a window and drew back a curtain. Audrey peered out the glass. Outside on the street, Franny chanted a spell. The Lavender Witch caught Audrey's stare and smiled. She'd stifled Piper's abilities.

They were trapped.

NINETEEN

Eleanor sat in the back of the evergreen sedan as it sped down the highway toward the Government District. With each mile, the worry concreted her bones to her muscles. She stretched her neck, gaining some relief as the vertebrae snapped and popped back into place. Her refusal of Audrey's request to accept Gregory Lycott and Nichola into the village had taken its toll. She'd made centuries of difficult decisions, but this one was different. Something was different—worse.

Once again, she clenched her jaw and steeled her mind. She'd made the only choice she could make. The beloved mortals inside the Guardian village simply could not be put in danger again, let alone, the people of the Entente of Nations. A magical child of unknown ability unconditionally devoted to a treacherous Waker was too unstable and therefore unwelcomed, but Eleanor would help. That was the reason for this trip.

"Eleanor, are you alright?" Vice Chancellor Margaret

asked. She sat next to Eleanor continually declining correspondence requests since Eleanor didn't have the patience to speak to anyone until after she'd met with the President.

"I'm fine, Margaret." The curt response shut down any more prodding questions. She knew her old friend and confident meant well but she just needed her space, her quiet inner reflection. Her splayed nerves brought on a sense of helplessness that she hadn't felt in a long time. Not since she'd discovered her immortality and the fear of being trapped in Elizabeth's London.

Eleanor released a sigh as the sedan pulled onto the familiar street of the Capitol Building and the President's Estate House. Maybe Henry wouldn't refuse her proposal in person. Her coming to him, facing him on his territory meant she was serious. He'd have to know that. But all her silent encouraging faded when she saw the angry mob.

Police battled hundreds of protestors blocking the roads. The car was eventually forced to stop. The demonstrators raised their fists, sneered, and yelled. They couldn't possibly know who sat behind the dark, weapon-proof windows, but the vehicle matched the description of most government issued models.

"Margaret, how in the world are we expected to reach President Lloyd's office?" Eleanor turned an exhausted gaze on her Vice Chancellor.

"Oh dear, I'd suspected it would be difficult, but this is downright unacceptable." Margaret began working on her communicator. Under her breath she mumbled, "I told you to wait and let him come to us."

As Margaret worked to solve the issue, Eleanor read the words the protesters waved about. *Keep our troops at home. Save our children—we lost too many before.*

Blood red words glowed across black signs. *They don't deserve our help. Keep up the barrier wall—keep Wasteland filth out. The East is best left alone. Don't bring the Wastelands' problems here.*

Eleanor nodded to herself. She knew these feelings well. She'd agreed with these strangers a month ago, but now, with the threat of those deadly shadows, her feelings had changed. They didn't have the luxury to ignore the East any longer.

The people chanted, sometimes a clear united voice, other times divided speeches cutting jaggedly through the air. But the message was unambiguous. *Remember the past—REMEMBER THE ENTENTE WAR!*

Oh, I remember, she thought.

Margaret sighed. "They haven't forgotten."

Eleanor tried to shake her head in reply, but the angst in her neck returned, seizing it up again. How could she ask her dear friend Henry for another ten thousand Elite soldiers? How could she ask the Entente to protect a creature child and a monstrosity? Maybe she was asking the wrong man. She shouldn't be asking a human.

Margaret gave orders to the driver. "Back up and turn around. Go down Broward Street. We'll foot it through the tunnels."

A large group overtook the police and surrounded the vehicle making a quick three-point turn impossible. The protestors thumped the roof with their hands and signs.

"Oh goodness," Margaret gasped.

The driver looked back at them through the rearview mirror. His eyes wide in panic.

"Take your time. It'll be alright," Eleanor told him. She'd faced many a mob before inside this reliable car. At least she wasn't worried about their safety just concerned for all outside the vehicle. She understood their anger and fear because it pressed hard upon her too.

The driver nodded. An hour later they'd cleared the chaos and parked in front of the secret entrance.

"Wait here," Margaret instructed the driver.

Inside the tunnels, Margaret took three zippy steps for each graceful stride of Eleanor's. The loud tapping of Margaret's shoes needled Eleanor's nerves, so she walked faster. Margaret would catch up.

The tunnels were built during the reconstruction period after the Entente War when the capital city was moved, districts formed, and states abolished. The secret routes were erected to sneak Guardians in and out of the Capitol and the Estate unnoticed. At one point, plans were developed to run a tunnel directly into Guardian Village, but Eleanor voted it down. She wouldn't have her village, her sanctuary, easily accessed, even if it was the President of the Entente of Nations. A decision she'd never regretted.

Eleanor reached the end of the passage and moved on into the halls of the President's private estate. She'd had enough damp, moldy air, and snappy foot pedaling. Plus, the urgency to confront her friend and get this over with heated her blood. Even so, she took a moment to calm down. She fluffed her brown waves and smoothed her eggplant blazer. As she stood there waiting for Margaret to catch up, she decided to go it alone.

She nodded to the serviceman standing guard who was expecting her arrival. "Please inform my Vice Chancellor to wait for me out here."

"Certainly, Chancellor," he said.

She stepped inside the President's private office. The Entente of Nations' President greeted the Chancellor of the Guardians of Dare with a firm handshake followed by a more familiar cheek kiss. "How do you do Eleanor?"

She met his pleasantry with thin lips and stern eyes.

"Oh. Well, your day is going about as well as mine then." His smile faded.

Eleanor sighed. "My apologies. I don't mean to be rude, but I must press your hand."

Henry shook his head. "I'm not budging on my stance. I simply can't send more soldiers. The election's a week away and I'm already down in the polls. Lord, help us, if the people elect that twit Noah Aveyard. You can forget about diplomatic relations with House Sanna or that rebel Axon Glial."

"You don't know that. Things change when mortals get in office and learn the truth."

Henry chuckled. "Truer words never spoken."

Eleanor didn't wait to be invited to sit. She sat and dove into her dire circumstances leaving no detail untold—the Pall, Lautaro, Nichola, Gregory.

The President's face paled and he rubbed the bridge of his nose. "I appreciate your problem."

"*Our* problem. If we don't stop Lautaro and the Pall while they're still in the East, they will come over here. That will be much worse."

"I will give you what you ask just as soon as the last vote is cast, whether I'm reelected or not. That will at least give you a few weeks. Should Aveyard be sitting here after that … well … we'll just have to hope he understands the urgency of the situation."

"And that's your final word?" Eleanor asked.

"I'm afraid so. But do keep me abreast of all happenings. I don't like mysteries, whether they're little girls or giant shadows. And should something change … well … I may be forced to act sooner."

"Very well." Eleanor's green-film covered eyes bore into him.

Henry cleared his throat. "And another thing, I received word this morning that the soldiers returning from the Wastelands are experiencing a viral infection."

"Is it serious?"

"It's far more serious than the skin sores. I'd like your help on this."

"Of course," she sighed. An infectious disease changed the game. The horrors of past epidemics sprung to the forefront of the mind. She wouldn't let another one slip inside and spread across her nation.

Eleanor stood, gave Henry's hand a ruthless tug to remind him of her immortal strength, then strode out the door. Her mind was set. She'd have to play the only hand she had left, revisit the past no matter how much it would torture her heart, and plane walk to see an old friend.

TWENTY

CENTRAL NERVE — THE WASTELANDS

GUARDIAN TARIAN

A day had passed with no orders from Eleanor as to how to proceed with a Waker and an immortal witch child. Twenty-four hours of Piper's nervous doting over Nichola had decimated Tarian's patience. On the other hand, Lycott had earned some of his respect. It was a microscopic droplet of respect, but it was something. He'd behaved honorably and hadn't tarnished the name of the Guardians in the presence of the Nerve Rebels. Tarian wasn't sure how Lycott had managed to keep the beast within under control, but he'd showed no signs of Waker tendencies. Maybe, the little girl calmed him.

Everyone claimed she had magical abilities and tiptoed around her in forbearance. Despite the implication that his blood ran through her veins, he felt no affinity toward her. Piper obviously did. She wouldn't leave her side. At the moment, she braided Nichola's long golden hair with the care of a mother.

Why did the girl irritate him so much? Why didn't he

instantly love her as Piper did?

Tarian couldn't face the scene any longer and stormed out of the tent for some fresh air. He'd gone yards before Audrey caught up. Her fingers laced in his, but she didn't force him to stop. Instead, she fell into step. They strolled along the edge of Central Nerve, stopping atop a hill.

"That's a pathetic sunset," Tarian grunted.

"It's not the sunset that's bothering you. It's Nichola," Audrey said.

Tarian said nothing. He wanted to have this conversation, but his thoughts tangled. Where would he start? What would he say? Would Audrey be disappointed in him?

She sat on the ground but everything inside him begged to flee. She nodded in understanding. They knew each other so well.

"Go on." She smiled. "Work off the frustration. I'll be here when you're ready."

He descended the hill and raced across the dusty fields never glancing back. He didn't need to. He knew she was there, supporting him. The wind hit his face like prickly needles. The sting felt good, an ecstatic sensation that gave him life. After a few miles, his shirt soaked through, and his mind cleared. He felt young and carefree as he had during his EMA cadet years running trails along the Hudson. He pivoted and sprinted back.

He saw her on the hill and smiled.

She patted the ground next to her.

He sat and immediately began to confide in her. "I'll never

be rid of Zachary. We killed him, Audrey."

She nodded.

"He shouldn't still be in our lives and yet because he bioengineered Nichola with my … whatever … Now he'll haunt me forever."

"I know," she said.

"I feared it after the dream. After Piper told us she was a leftover from Zachary's experiments. I didn't want it to be true because I can't look at her without thinking of him." Tarian grabbed a fistful of his sweat drenched hair and pulled. His head throbbed from the truth, and he needed relief.

Audrey scooted behind him to rub his neck and shoulders. "You're entitled to feel that way."

As her hands worked the ache out of his muscles, he tried to work the bitterness out of his mind. "I want to feel something for her. Anything but resentment. And I know I'm just feeling sorry for myself. I know that." He turned to face her, certain he'd let her down, but only warmth shown in her crystal blue eyes.

"We won't know for sure until we run tests." Audrey caressed his cheeks with her fingers.

How wonderful was she? She'd made it so easy to confess. She'd understood without judgment and now she tried to bury his pain. He loved her more than he'd ever loved her before if that was possible.

"She's mine," he sighed. "She has my blood."

"How do you know that absolutely?" Her eyes glinted with

mischief, as if her question was a challenge.

"I just know."

"Because you couldn't read her when you touched her?"

He nodded.

"That's when I knew too," she said in agreement. "She has power. And although I don't doubt Gregory's love for her, I think it's an affection that grew over time. He didn't intend to be her father. He snatched her from the lab and ran. I figure, she was Zachary's first trial and since she was older than the newborns we saw in that place, she was probably already showing signs of magical abilities."

"What I don't understand is the other babies—the ones we found when we'd discovered Zachary's warehouse of immortal clones—they told me their story when I touched them. With Nichola, I see nothing but myself. It's like she puts it all back on me."

"She's a direct offspring. The others weren't."

"You think he had a sperm sample?" As soon as the words crossed his lips, shivers coursed through him. The idea of his identity being stolen via blood and seminal fluid horrified his conscience. A violation beyond the imaginable, and Nichola was the living embodiment of that infraction.

"The others were clones. For as much as Zachary in his delusional state tried to convince us they were more, some sort of special offspring, they weren't. They were immortal clones. I don't think she's a clone. She is a direct offspring of you and Piper."

"All the more reason I should have loving feelings for her."

"You're not a robot, Tarian."

The soft understanding of her voice, the way his name formed on her lips, carried his guilt away.

"I want to get her out of here. She doesn't belong in this horrible place." He frowned.

"We will. When the time is right. For now, we just have to keep her safe." She leaned in and gently kissed his grimace away. A sweet, short kiss that meant the world.

The good news arrived the following day. Tarian's father, Joe, was on his way from the Entente to Balefire City and House Sanna had agreed to accept Lycott and Nicola into Umbra Castle.

"Joe and Patrick will work alongside Princess Brianna and hopefully discover a cure for Gregory and an explanation for the Pall. Unfortunately, we have no extra soldiers, so we'll go unescorted to South Castle, and it's getting late," Audrey said.

"Do you feel it?" Piper questioned.

The air cracked and popped.

"Stay here," Tarian ordered Piper, Nichola, and Lycott.

He stepped outside with Audrey. A sound like a hundred champagne bottles bursting open snapped through the air, but this was no celebration. A flood of malditos riding cycles charged over the hills filling the streets. Rebels and soldiers sprung from their posts to protect the camp.

Audrey whipped out her diamond blades and joined the battle erupting on the dirt roads. Tarian ducked back into the tent to secure Nichola. "Hide her," Tarian demanded of Lycott.

Lycott threw a blanket over Nichola then he alone disappeared leaving the lumpy blanket in plain sight.

Tarian's chest clenched at the pathetic display but there was nothing more that could be done. "Piper stay here and guard them. If anyone steps inside do what you do and freeze them."

"I will," Piper said.

Tarian stepped back outside to fight. His eyes searched for Audrey. Relief coursed through him once he caught sight of her then terror struck his core. Blood ran down her face. She wiped it away and he realized it wasn't her blood. He could breathe again. She fought off the enemy with brilliant, determined rage.

Chaos filled the pathways within Central Nerve. Fire burned on all sides. Gunshots blasted the late afternoon air. Booted feet trampled the ground. Fifty? Maybe a hundred of the cursed creatures had rode in.

Tarian's head whipped side to side as he sliced his diamond blade through the malditos. He searched for the source. *Would Lautaro dare show his face here?* The Grand Sorcerer definitely possessed enough arrogance. Tarian glanced toward the Cerveau. Surely, that was the target. He needed to get inside to protect the only source of communication, but there were so many malditos clashing with rebels in his way.

"Christopher!" Tarian called out glad to find a familiar ally along the line to his destination. He rushed to his friend's side. "I need to get inside the Cerveau."

They fought back-to-back inching their way to the building. Dodging bullets. Swords slayed. He heard the woosh of the blade—too close.

"Jesus. They appeared out of nowhere," Christopher said.

Dust whirled high and wide blurring uniforms and faces, making it difficult to distinguish the rebels from the malditos.

"Have you seen Lautaro?" Tarian asked, as the keen point of his blade stabbed. Blood gushed. A maldito fell at his feet.

"No," Christopher said.

"Did we have any warning of this attack?" Tarian jabbed the blade into a liver then stepped back in position. His back returned to the security of his friend.

"No," Christopher replied in an exasperated breath.

They spun a lethal dance. He saw Axon and Audrey in his peripheral. She yelled something at him.

He concentrated his immortal hearing, fading out the rumble of engines and clang of swords.

"He wants the girl. Nichola!" Audrey yelled again.

Of course! Tarian should have known this. Why didn't he share a connection to his own daughter? The sting of his own self-loathing intensified his rage to fight.

Audrey had moved closer, but she still needed to holler. "We need to vade her out now!"

A maldito's booted foot flung high, aimed at Audrey's back. Tarian lunged but Axon got to her first. His blade whirled just in time to save Audrey from a devasting blow to the head.

"Go! Do it!" Axon called out just as Lautaro rode in on his massive beast-horse.

Before Tarian ran toward the tent housing Nichola, he yelled to Axon, "Order everyone to take cover."

Many heard Tarian and started for safety before Axon announced the official order, but Ralph hesitated. Tarian noticed the young man's his eyes locked on Axon emoting something powerful. Axon only glared back. Ralph rushed out.

Tarian shared a glance with Audrey, she'd noted the interaction too, but he didn't have time to ask what that was all about. She raced back to the tent, as he gathered as many rebels as he could and shoved them into whatever shelter he found. Then he caught a glimpse of a gangly girl battling worthily with a maldito.

Germaine wielded a sword that was as long as her body. She sliced up its groin.

Tarian winced, impressed.

She slid the blade from its residence, flung it over her head, and plunged it into another. But there was a third she didn't see aiming a gun straight at her.

Tarian pounced, caught the third mid-leap with his blade and with a kick propelled Germaine to the ground. She fell hard.

He scooped her up and ran for cover. Bullets rained as he dove into the tent. He tucked her lanky body into his and rolled. They somersaulted almost into Lycott's lap where Nichola sat clinging to him. Piper knelt beside them pleading with the girl to let go of her father and vade out of there with her.

"Germaine!" Nichola wailed.

Germaine reached out a hand and squeezed the little girl's arm.

A cyclone hit the tent. The wooden rods crumbled, and the flimsy fabric blew away. Everyone inside stood exposed. A brawny dark-skinned Lautaro sat atop his massive, beastly horse. The beasts' forelegs raised, kicking the air, fire flaring from its nostrils.

Germaine dodged left, nearly trampled. Tarian tackled Nichola determined to save her, to keep Lautaro from his prize.

A guttural, demonic laugh escaped the Grand Sorcerer. "You fool."

Tarian registered the words an instant too late. He lunged for Lycott, the true prize, but his arms grabbed nothing. Lautaro had already flung Lycott onto the horse.

They vanished. The horse, Lautaro, and Lycott. Gone. All went silent. No more rumbling cycles, clanging blades, or gunshots. Somehow the chaos left with Lautaro.

"How can Lautaro vade?" Tarian circled fierce, questioning eyes on Piper.

"He's plane walking or using a wormhole or duality of

some sort," Audrey answered.

Nichola wailed. Tears welled in her eyes, and a whimper formed in the back of her throat. She shimmered scarlet, and the air encircling her buzzed like a short circuit about to catch fire.

"We have to get him back. Hope told me, no matter what, they have to stay together until the end," Piper said.

"What?" Audrey asked.

"Hope and Teresa both foresaw this, and they warned that Nichola and Gregory have to be together. I think our lives depend on it," Piper warned.

TWENTY-ONE

ESURIENT DHAUMRA'S LAIR

GUARDIAN CHANCELLOR ELEANOR

Eleanor hadn't descended the silvery-white steps of the hollow mountain in almost two centuries, yet it felt as if she'd just returned from a trip to the store. *Honey, I'm home*, she wanted to call out, but humor wasn't her strong suit and often lost on an Esurient's isolated mind. Although, she did recall Dhaumra had a musical laugh.

Mirrors lined the stairwell, and she peeked into one. She smoothed her unruly curls and frowned at her pale lips. She whipped out a chic red lipstick then discarded it feeling foolish. She settled for a sheer shimmer slightly blackberry in hue. As she applied the lipstick, she focused on the face gazing back at her. She'd been an immortal for centuries but seeing herself so young yet feeling so old, was simply flabbergasting. She didn't feel the years in her muscles. She was perfectly fit. She felt them in her bones.

"Silliness," she said to her reflection.

She continued down the long descent, heels clicking. She'd missed Dhaumra, but she hadn't missed these bloody steps. "God in heaven, I'll never again complain about Headquarters' steps."

For all the silver and white, nickel and diamonds, mirror and glass, the stairwell breathed warmth. Its cold appearance charmed Eleanor. She and this place were alike in that regard. Cool and warm juxtaposed.

The clock struck midnight when her toe touched the last step. She studied the mysterious place that had stolen her heart—a cave of iron glass extraneous to time and position. She'd found it decades ago after much struggling. A tricky little hop through the planes, but one only a skilled creature could master. It helped that Dhaumra had wanted her to find him. He'd lured her with clues and a hidden talisman.

Once she'd finally crossed the threshold, had spent several days within the hollow mountain, and after they'd become close friends, she'd finally asked for a tangible explanation. He had grinned and pulled a figurine out of her pocket. She hadn't known it was there—a tiny nickel dragon.

He had laughed at her surprise and placed the figurine on a map, within the map lines of the Soviet Ukraine. He told her if his home existed on this Earth, it would be there. But all the former countries had been destroyed. The rich land turned to dust. Only the bravest of Wastelanders dared to tread past the Pall to gather property and build cities.

Eleanor fondled the miniscule dragon in her pocket. *Where*

would my clever friend place you now, little beast?

Eleanor didn't venture past the parlor. She sat in a lovely chair embroidered with fine silk and waited. It wasn't long before the man in the smoke coat glided down the hall, a reflection in the mirror. She didn't glance back. Instead, she let him come to her.

His sigh echoed through the halls. He took her hands, kissed one then the other. "I've missed you, stubborn woman."

Eleanor laughed. "How are you Dhaumra?"

"How do you think?" His golden cat eyes narrowed. "You know how these LMCI's are."

She smiled with sympathy. The Life-Magical, Cursed, Immortal conferences were long, torturous events. Which was why she avoided them.

"I hope our High Councilors are not bullying you too badly."

He drew her into him. He held the embrace in silence for minutes. If he never let go, she wouldn't care. The comfort of his strong arms nearly collapsed her. *Why couldn't she give in, be his mistress, and never leave, never live in the chaos and destruction of the mortal world?* That's what he'd promised so long ago. But he released her and took a hand. They strolled as old lovers do, down the hall, and out into the garden of stones.

The tomb had light, not from the Earth's sun, but light nonetheless. It pushed through a velvet haze and spun around the exterior garden path. The mind path meandered for many turns, but the last step remained invariable. She'd cut that clever path a hundred times and gotten nowhere and everywhere—a path of the mind not of the body.

"Your Guardian Councilors are hideous creatures," he said, picking up on their previous conversation.

"My goodness," she chuckled, "and you've got the rest of the Moon Cycle to deal with them." Eleanor brushed aside glistening pebbles with her feet as she strolled, admiring their brilliance.

"You, my dear, are a welcome distraction." He stopped walking and forced her to halt. He peered deep into her eyes. "I know what troubles you."

"I assumed you would. And the High Council? Has the meeting reached that point?"

"Actually, no. The High Council seems content to stall the meeting and dwell on my failures with the Pall." A smirk crossed his sharp, creature teeth. "I was going to mention the girl, today in fact, then you held the little dragon."

She smiled. "It isn't just Nichola that's puzzling me. There's been strange happenings in the Entente caverns."

He stepped closer.

Her breath hitched as she swam in the depths of his bottomless pools of swirling molten gold eyes and long lush lashes. His face framed by white hair but unlike the coarse hair of an old man, it fell into delicate curls that licked his shoulders.

To her, he was just a man like any other, but completely unlike any other. He was neither tall nor short, thin nor fat, earthly nor celestial. His attractiveness didn't come from angled cheekbones or broad shoulders. His skin radiated light through bronze flesh, as if he'd been sun-kissed from the inside. Her chest bridled from his beauty.

His hands found her neck. He massaged and cradled the base of her head. His lips pressed soft on her mouth. Eleanor's burdened heart ached to lie down. He granted her wish. They fell onto silken sheets. She'd forgotten how time bent inside this mountain. Magnificent pleasure stirred her entirety. She couldn't resist him.

TWENTY-TWO

CENTRAL NERVE — THE WASTELANDS

GUARDIAN TARIAN

Nichola darted around screaming, "Daddy! Daddy!"

Tarian ran to her. "He's gone."

"Why didn't you protect him?" Her lips snarled, morphing her appearance from angel to demon.

Tarian stepped back. "I didn't know Lautaro knew about Lycott."

"You hate him. You wanted this!" She bared her teeth.

"No," Tarian pleaded.

Nichola screamed. She hit Tarian. Little fists striking him over and over. Each punch like an electric current zipping through his skin to his bones pushing him back.

Piper grabbed a kicking and screaming Nichola, then glared at Tarian. His heart plummeted to his stomach. "What did I do?" He shrugged in complete confusion. Hadn't he tried his best under extreme circumstances. The girl was out-of-control.

Tarian turned to Germaine and asked, "Can we take her

to your home?"

Germaine nodded.

Dread thundered in Tarian's heart as they stepped outside. Bodies lay strewn across the camp, mostly malditos.

"Cover her eyes," Tarian instructed Piper then studied Germaine. The teenager's face remained stoic. She'd obviously seen this kind of gore before. He shivered at the thought. This was no place for a child and a teenager.

Germaine walked up the steps to her home. Tarian released a sigh. He'd feared there'd be no home but thankfully, it was still there. He didn't follow them inside, just watched as Germaine's mother took them in with loving affection.

Destruction spread across the Nerve base, a tangled matrix of debris. Some of the concrete houses had crumbled, but most had not. Collapsed tents blew like linen in the breeze. The huts heaped as if nothing but sticks and twigs. Lifeless bodies splayed across the grid. A surprise attack that decimated Central Nerve. All for a Waker. It made no sense. Then it made perfect sense. Wakers could kill Guardians. But the Pall could also kill Guardians. The Pall! Was Lycott somehow valuable to the Pall?

Tarian searched out Audrey. She was just where he'd expected, helping piece this place back together. She was the strongest, fiercest woman he'd ever known. He found her gathering the dead, separating the rebels from the malditos. She assisted the injured. She carried a limping Jen into the infirmary building. Tarian followed. With each step he saw the corpses, the blood, the ruin. There were so many.

Tarian aided Audrey with the injured. The questions and horror reeled inside him, but the task at hand gave him purpose and a little refuge. It took all night. When daylight hinted at the gray sky, he stood hand in hand with Audrey. Neither knew what Lautaro would do with Lycott, but they were certain it wasn't good.

"We need to get everyone to South Castle immediately," Tarian said.

Audrey nodded then said in a faraway voice. "He's stronger." She soberly watched the lightness sweep the night away.

The sky wasn't full of fiery color like back home, but it had its unique magnificence. The dull gray mist came alive with a silvery sparkle. The sun rose behind the dense clouds creating a halo like the small circle of a flashlight seen through a thick wool blanket.

He didn't know if it was exhaustion that stole her spirit or fear. "I agree. Do you think it's the Pall? Lautaro's harnessed its power."

"Yes," she said.

"He lost just as many soldiers as we did in this fight. He must've wanted Lycott badly." That familiar dread spread into his veins and throughout his body like poisonous spiders. "How did he know Lycott was here?"

Audrey turned away from the horizon and looked up at him. "We have a spy among us."

TWENTY-THREE

SOUTH CASTLE — BALEFIRE CITY

GUARDIAN AUDREY

The caravan followed the bloodless sun eastward to South Castle. By the time they'd arrived and set up their injured in the sick bay, it was too late for formal meetings with the queen. The eldest daughter, Marianne, showed Audrey and Tarian to their quarters.

The next morning, after meeting with the queen, Audrey, Tarian, and Marianne climbed what felt like a thousand steps but was probably only ten stories to get to the lab. Of course, Audrey's immortal body wouldn't collapse from exhaustion, but she was irritatingly uncomfortable. She grew even more peeved at the sight of Marcus lounged on a cozy sofa sipping ale with a young man whose cheeks shined like mercury against ashen skin.

Germaine waved hello. She was perched on the arm of the sofa.

Princess Brianna's impressive laboratory matched Joe's in all aspects except location. Hers inhabited the top of a tower in South Castle dark from an angry sky, whereas his dwelled in the dungeons of Guardian Headquarters dark under layers of rock.

Marianne cleared her throat. "We've just come from council. Joe told us you've made progress with the mist." Marianne charged farther into the room leaving Audrey and Tarian to introduce themselves to her youngest brother, Prince Theo, twin to Princess Brianna, lad with cheeks blushed silver.

Marianne leaned over her youngest sister's shoulder. "Bri you're brilliant."

The two sisters had their backs to Audrey. Curiosity invaded her skin like a raid of ants whose nest had just been stirred. However, before she had the chance to stroll over to see the experiment they were so keenly gawking at, it exploded in a loud pop.

"For Pall's sake! You put too much quicksilver." Marianne clucked her tongue.

"No, I didn't." Brianna lifted the giant book, and nearly lost her balance from the weight of it. She shoved it in her sister's face, which was tinged black from the smoke. She jabbed a finger on the list of ingredients. "You see. Right there. It says four drops. Four! That's what I did." She slammed the grimoire back down and screamed in frustration.

Joe had just made it up the stairs and into the room when the Pall sample exploded again. His face drooped.

Brianna's face wilted and her eyes filled with tears at the sight of him. "Je suis désolé."

"It's okay. It's not your fault. We'll just keep trying." Joe smiled but his eyes couldn't hide the hope that had been slain by the explosion.

Brianna sighed, swiped the sweat from her brow, and the smoke dust from her cheeks. "Yes. I suppose we will. Can you fetch more, please?"

"Of course." Joe used his shifting abilities and morphed into his hawk form, grabbing an empty glass container in his beak then journeyed out the window.

"Safe trip pigeon." Marcus waved.

Joe squawked piercingly through gritted beak so as to not drop the glass. He pulled his wings tight and dove as fast as a bullet.

Marcus chuckled. "He hates that nickname."

"You're such a jerk." Germaine shoved the big guy. She'd been sitting with him and Prince Theo drinking what Audrey hoped wasn't ale.

Tarian went to the window and watched his father soar. "Where's he going?"

"To the Pall, to get another sample since I ruined this one." Brianna walked over to Theo, plopped on the sofa, and laid her head on her twin's shoulder.

He put an arm around her. "Don't worry. You're going to figure it out. Grandmum gave *you* the book. She knew you were the one the book called to."

Brianna nodded but remained in the comforting arms of her brother.

Marianne stayed in the back of the room flipping the pages of the grimoire.

Audrey stood awkwardly. Words of encouragement rose in her throat, but they all seemed petty fragments for a situation that warranted poetry.

Marcus broke the silence. "What's the news from the queen?" He asked Audrey, reaching over and caressing Brianna's hair, trailing the midnight blue streaks that divided her gray strands. Her eyes softened and her body tilted from her brother to Marcus.

"First, the queen was disappointed that the Entente won't provide more troops. She reluctantly authorized children as young as fourteen to fight. Princess Lucianna, Prince Briggen, and Guardian Christopher will lead the training."

"Poor Lu," Brianna sighed.

Theo nodded.

The news proved too heavy for Brianna as she broke free from Marcus and marched back to the grimoire. She squeezed out her sister who'd been browsing the pages. Marianne was once more reduced to hovering over Brianna's shoulder.

Audrey understood the sisters' motivation. Worry had churned her stomach since the order crossed the queen's lips over an hour ago. Casualties of war were awful. Dead children were the worst kind of awful.

Audrey exhaled. "We'd hoped to have Patrick's help, but he's stayed behind to deal with a new crisis."

Marcus cocked an eyebrow.

"It seems Elite soldiers returning home have been infected by not just the bacterium resistant to Sanoxine but also a deadly virus. Another reason President Lloyd is refusing to send over more soldiers."

"What about the ones that are already here?" Marcus asked.

"They won't be allowed home until we find a cure. Strangely, symptoms didn't surface until they got back to the Entente."

"Why?" Germaine asked.

"We don't know that yet, but I'm confident Patrick will find a solution." Audrey wished she had a better answer to give the teenager. Germaine looked up at her with such curiosity and disappointment that Audrey felt an unworthy advisor. She forced a smile and switched the topic. "Prince Theo."

He nodded and gave her his undivided attention.

"You're a blood weaver, correct?"

"I am."

"We need Nichola bound. She's just a child, but an extremely powerful one. Her magic is wild, and she's thrown a couple temper tantrums since Gregory was taken. She may do something horribly destructive soon."

"I'll see what I can do," Theo said.

"Thank you."

"Certainly. Can you get her father back?" Theo asked.

"We're going to try," Tarian said. "Marcus and I will go

and find out why Lycott holds value to Lautaro. If we can retrieve him, we will."

"I hope you can turn invisible like your big friend." Theo chuckled.

"No, but we have Marianne." Tarian smiled.

"My sister?" Theo stiffened suddenly serious.

"Yes brother." Marianne strolled over and leaned over the couch on which he sat. "Finally, I can be of some use." She glanced back at Brianna and the grimoire.

Lines of anxiety crossed Brianna's brow as she looked at her oldest sister.

"Well good for you." Theo fidgeted and took a long swig of ale. "Be careful."

Marianne kissed the top of his head. "I will. You stay out of trouble."

Theo's chuckle lacked confidence.

"When do we leave?" Marcus asked.

"Now," Tarian said.

Immortal speed moved Marcus to Brianna's side in a breath. "Goodbye, milady." Marcus flashed a boyish grin.

Brianna hugged him. "Goodbye, Marcus."

Everyone except Theo and Brianna strolled toward the exit.

"Come along Germ. We'll deposit you in the kitchen for a snack on our way out." Marcus gathered her up.

"What? No! You said we're a team. I'm an excellent spy."

"I know you are. Next time." Marcus tightened his grip on her.

She fought all the way down until the fragrance of freshly baked chocolate cookies wafted up the stairwell. "What's that smell?"

Tarian sniffed. "I think that's homemade chocolate chip cookies."

"Chocolate! Why didn't you say that?" Germaine punched Marcus in the bicep.

"Now I know your weakness." Marcus tapped her nose with his finger.

"I've only had chocolate twice in my entire life, and it's amazing. Do you have lots of it in the Entente?"

"As much as you want." Marcus winked.

Germaine sighed. "I wish I could go there."

Audrey's heart sank. Not just sank, it gasped, bubbled, choked, filled with suffocating pain, then drowned, but she hid her anxiety. The last thing Germaine would want or expect from a hardened Guardian soldier was pity.

A boy who looked about Germaine's age gobbled down cookies in the kitchen.

"Christian this is Germaine. Show her around won't cha?" Marcus asked.

"Sure," the boy said. "They're still warm. Want one?"

Germaine hesitated, looking from Marcus to Tarian to Audrey to Marianne before turning back to Christian and the cookie. She wandered into the kitchen where she sat at the table next to the boy with the plate full of cookies who talked a lot. Germaine quietly listened gobbling up five cookies as he explained that a shipment of spectacular food had come from the Entente.

Audrey grinned at the little information gatherer, glad to have deposited Germaine in a safe place, at least, for now.

TWENTY-FOUR

ENERGY DISTRICT — THE ENTENTE

CAVERN SUPERVISOR MICHAEL LAZARO

Mike found the little woman strange and her green suit odd, but there'd been a lot of odd and strange things happening in the caves since he'd stumbled upon the ownerless shadows. He'd gone home that night and coughed a lot. His son had complained of the same cough. The next day he'd made several inquiries. Some had seen the shadows and felt ill, but not many. The mist seemed to dwell in the restricted area. The area where the ichor began to ooze again.

The woman was some sort of government official, and hopefully here to extricate the shadow demons and golden trouble so Mike's men would come back to work. Flanked on either side of her were two men. One was the Secretary of Energy. Mike recognized him from the news, and he'd visited the caverns before, but at that time, Mike hadn't been the supervisor. The other man wore a suit the same shade of green as the woman's.

"After you, Margaret." The Secretary of Energy held the elevator shaft door open.

"Thank you, Reginald." Her voice too sugary sweet for such a dark, grim place.

The shaft dropped drastically. The four held tight to the handholds. Impressively, Margaret kept her smile the entire descent.

Mike exited. "Wait here." He needed to check the sector's safety. It was a secured area rarely visited, at least until recently.

Without permission, Margaret pedaled her short legs into the heart of the darkness.

"Stop!" Mike called out but she only walked faster. "Be Careful."

"Don't worry about me, dear," the honey voice assured. She'd almost gone invisible in the blackness.

Mike followed with a flashlight. He halted when he saw her handle the ichor ungloved. He lunged to stop her then retreated once he saw that she was unharmed. "That stuff kills people," he stuttered. "This isn't supposed to be exposed. We had that packed into the rock."

"And how did you come to realize it'd been tampered with?" Reginald inquired.

"I'm not sure it has. It just happened." Mike shrugged his wide shoulders and felt foolish as the three officials stared at him, so he continued, "We've had a lot of new hires. Some of them just didn't seem right. I took to doing more inspections and came across weird shadows. A sort of misty fog. And then my men started getting sick. Started fearing the Cucuy." His feelings of foolishness tripled.

"A mythical monster?" Margaret asked, but she didn't mock, in fact, she seemed sincere.

"Yes," Mike said.

"And is that what your people said before, when the miners first found this and died?"

"Yes." Mike's chest weighed heavy as memories resurfaced. He'd lost friends. The community had lost children.

Margaret's fingers squeezed her chin as her face turned pensive. She pivoted and peered closely at the scrape marks on the rock. "Do you think anyone took some of this ichor?"

"I don't know why anyone would risk excavating it." Mike shuffled his feet, the unease needing an escape. He worried they'd blame him. The previous supervisor had been fired and accused of negligence. Mike needed this job. He had a wife, four children, and one granddaughter. He'd promised his beloved a vacation.

"So this isn't normal?" Margaret pointed to the fog hovering around.

"No." True terror, not the silly fear of bogeyman stories, eclipsed Mike's heart. "This gray mist started seeping from the cave walls a little over a week ago."

"Hmm." Margaret bit her lip and looked to her green suited partner. "You don't suppose it's cousin to the Pall."

"We'll take a sample." The green suited man said then turned to ask Mike, "What has happened to the men who've come in contact with this shadowy fog?"

"Coughing … feeling ill in general. Maybe a little anxious," Mike said.

That evening Nadia hobbled over to Mike at the table with two glasses of mulled wine. She set one in front of him, but he didn't drink it. His food and drink went untouched. His eyes glazed, mind wandered, and gut twisted.

Nadia fell into her chair. She took a sip of wine and bite of chicken. "Miguel?"

"Yes." His usual gruff voice only a faint whisper.

"Are you alright?" Nadia reached across the table and gently rested a hand on his forearm.

"Of course. It's late." He smiled. What could he say? He had no answers and wouldn't worry her over suspicions. His sons that worked the mines didn't seem to share his trepidation. At least, they hadn't mentioned it. He'd make a point to ask their opinion of the shadows tomorrow. Tonight, he just wanted to hold the hand of the woman he loved and marvel at her natural beauty, faded by time's cruel hand.

TWENTY-FIVE

GUARDIAN VILLAGE — THE ENTENTE

HEALER TERESA

Teresa entered the lab. She snuck up behind Patrick as he peered through the microscope and wrapped her hands around his waist, feeling the points of his hips. He couldn't stop her with his work gloves on. She'd trapped him on purpose ignoring the many warnings he'd doled upon her in the past. Safety first! He was such a Boy Scout.

"Hello, baby," Patrick said.

She pulled away and sat in a chair a respectable distance away from his work. "Is that the cavern mist sample?"

"Yes."

"Is it the same as the Pall?"

"Yes."

"Weird."

"It's terribly weird. It's not a good sign. If that stuff is spreading or somehow found a portal to our hemisphere, it's a huge problem." Patrick finally turned away from his work, tugged off his gloves, and walked over to her.

When their lips met, fire burned inside her. Her hands roamed under his lab coat to the soft shirt warmed by his skin. She pulled him closer. His mouth found her neck and she moaned then laughed.

He pulled back. "What's so funny?"

"We always make-out in the lab. It's not exactly romantic." *And I want to do more than kiss*, she wanted to add, but she didn't. She didn't dare reveal the true reason for her sense of urgency. Let him think it's as it was before, just her teenage hormones. But it was more so much more now. Each dream of impending doom that snaked its way into her conscience weakened her. These visions infested her daily thoughts. She needed to see and touch Patrick to escape the depression festering inside.

"I'm sorry, baby." He sighed and glanced at his table of flasks and beakers.

"What?"

"Nothing. Let's go to dinner."

"Really?" True happiness grew in her, and it felt magnificent.

"Sure. I'm sure. The plague ransacking our Elites overseas can wait."

Teresa's excitement collapsed. "You suck."

Patrick shook his head. "No! You're right. This can wait. I mean I haven't solved it yet, what's a couple of hours going to hurt anyway."

A sly grin crossed Teresa's lips. She'd finally broken him. She wouldn't let this opportunity slip away. After all, she happened to have her lacey underwear on. She'd done little things like that lately, in an attempt to reverse her sense of dread.

"I don't like the look in your eyes."

"Don't be silly." She hopped off the chair, took his hand, and pranced him out of the lab. She hadn't felt this light in days.

They ended up at The Flying Spoon, the most modern restaurant in the village. A new establishment opened after the Wakers. New things were rare and resisted in the village, but the delicious food drew a crowd.

After the appetizer, Patrick finally seemed relaxed. "This was a good idea."

"Thank you."

"I have a theory I want to run past you." Patrick's face lit up with a scientist's enthusiasm.

His glee engulfed her. There was no truer bliss than when his ideas encompassed her. Their minds melded almost more perfectly than their lips and just as seductively.

"What is it?" she asked.

He contemplated before answering. The anticipation sent bolts of euphoric fervor through her blood. His eyes widened and breath quickened in response to her adrenaline. She relished in the attraction that bounced between them just as their theories did.

"The Waker victims—the children. I want to run their DNA again. I think it could be a useful tool in the vaccine."

"How?"

"The virus brought back by the Elites contains a protein that I believe is similar to, if not the same as, the one created by the Waker bite in the children. If they sequence together and stabilize, it could work."

"Really!"

He nodded.

Neither spoke another word. The seed of arousal grew with each bite of delicacy, with each theoretical ponder of the possibility of a cure. He had no way of knowing just how much she'd needed this bit of hope.

Their meals came and went. She'd eaten but couldn't recall doing so. Her eyes had been transfixed on his mouth, his perfect lips. Every morsel he chewed, the bob of his throat when he swallowed sent shivers through her. They rejected dessert and tipped the server generously then ended up in Patrick's apartment.

She ripped off his jacket then snapped all the buttons of his shirt, and he let her. He stood still and watched as her hunger for him raged. She couldn't stop. She wouldn't. He couldn't have a moment to think. His mind was too conservative and respectful. She didn't want that. She'd waited so long. He had had so many excuses. She had none. Of course, she had no idea what she was doing. He'd probably had hundreds of lovers over his centuries of life.

Her lips never stopped kissing him. He didn't need air anyways, right? But she sucked in gasps of air then sealed her lips around his again.

"I love you," he whispered.

"I love you," she said.

He pulled away and stared at her.

"What?"

He smiled.

"What am I doing wrong?"

"Nothing. You're perfect and beautiful. And I'm not going anywhere."

She let out an enormous breath, needing to slow down, to enjoy and remember the moment. She saw the path of destruction she'd caused. Their clothes shredded on his floor. At the rate she'd been going her most precious night would've been a blur.

He pressed his mouth to her ear. Her body trembled. His kiss soft and yearning. His lips never left her skin. All of her nightmarish visions vanished. Everything she'd ever wanted from him, all of him, fell upon her like luscious liquid silk.

Teresa jumped in her sleep. She'd been a twitchy deer all night. She pulled the covers up to her neck as cruel tears rolled down her cheeks.

Patrick hugged her to him. "What's wrong?"

The dream couldn't be back. It wouldn't ruin her

wondrous moment. She was supposed to be awakened by Patrick's kisses. They were to roll around in bed entwined in satin sheets. Their toes would playfully tangle. That was how it was supposed to happen. That's how she'd always envisioned it.

"I don't know. There's going to be an explosion, but I don't know when or where. I'm afraid we're going to die." The sobs took over her entire body. Only his arms protected her and kept her from seizing.

"Shhhh, baby. Shhhh." He rocked her until the anxiety ghosted out of her chest, and she lay against him exhausted.

TWENTY-SIX

BALEFIRE CITY

GUARDIAN TARIAN

Tarian, Marcus, and Princess Marianne reached the long, grim string of Balefire recruits and Nerve Rebels that sliced the city in half. Hatred so vile for a sorcerer and love so strong for a monarchy bound these men and women. They would shed this life to protect Balefire and the Sanna royal family.

Entente Elite soldiers peppered the line. Their gray uniforms, though crisp, did nothing to add brightness. Nonetheless, they stood out in size and well-being, but their determined faces blended. The Elites may have had better fortunes, but they too were ready to die by the sword to protect freedom.

Across the makeshift border a similar thread bound the north side. Maldito and human soldiers dressed in finer clothes of red and black. The humans stood out, tanned and healthy, travelers from a southern distant continent, willing to fight for their strong sorcerer leader who promised them riches from this victory should they survive.

The malditos waned like anemic pirates. A parade of different faces sharing the same scars and disfigurement of the cursed. No set determination glowed behind their dead eyes. Why the cursed cared to live on this earth was a mystery. They had no family to love, no soul to care. But Tarian had felt the strength in their punch and fear in their grip, smelled the liquor on their breath and seen the endless depths of their vacant eyes. Only a fool would doubt their want to win.

Tarian couldn't study the opposing line for too long without feeling the weight of its strangeness. They seemed like robots awaiting a reboot that could come at any time. He supposed that time would be once Lautaro figured out how best to utilize Lycott. Tarian relished a fight but dreaded a standoff and found himself riddled with jumpiness.

His impatient eyes found nothing new in the malditos so he set his gaze on his allies. He searched for Maria but didn't see his best friend. He hoped that meant she was safe, far away from here. He wondered who stood guard on this front. He could see its length but couldn't identify a person's features in the far distance. He wished he had time to walk the line.

Tarian spotted the shiny black leather among the trail of gray rags. The tall woman, all lean muscle set on a spindly frame with long spidery limbs, stalked toward him. An eight-spiked mohawk shot up from her head. Her eyes and lips lined black with makeup.

Tarian smiled at his friend. "Hello Jun."

Jun was a predator, a Xia Preta that fed on the energy of others. She'd been cursed into this existence one hundred and eighty-two years ago.

"Hey Tarian." Jun pulled him in for a hug and patted his back. "Good to see ya again."

"You as well." Tarian soaked in the comforting warmth of seeing an old friend. "Thank you for doing this."

"Of course, we want the bastard stopped as much as you do."

Jun acknowledged Marcus and Marianne with a handshake and nod.

Tarian looked for the tall Asian or his fierce tiger shape-shift alter ego, but he found neither. "Where's Hu?"

"My brother walks the Pall," Jun said.

"How's that going?"

"Fine. We must rotate the mortals. It sucks the spirit right out of them more so than a hungry ghost," she laughed at her pun. "And the smell … it stinks to high hell. Hu can enter it as a Tiger but not as a man."

"Why does he enter it at all?" Marcus asked.

"To get the soldiers back."

Marcus harrumphed.

"It has a pull. The soldiers are supposed to stay ten feet from it at all times, but one millimeter past that, and it gets 'em. I don't know. Some describe it as a whisper. Others have no idea why they step into the mist. If they get too far, poof, dead. My brother has to always stay on guard. He's exhausted."

"I'll give him some relief after this mission," Marcus said.

Jun sighed. "I doubt you can. You must move fast inside that stuff to save the lives. As the cat, he cuts quick through the shadows."

Marcus frowned. "We're lucky to have him."

Jun nodded. "I let him cat nap," she grinned at yet another pun, "as it has no lure for me. But as soon as a soldier is in danger, he's back on duty."

Zella, the Cerveau member, marched over. Her eyes trained on her ex-girlfriend. "Marianne, you're going to North Castle?"

"I am." Marianne said.

"I don't like it." Zella glared.

Marianne glared back. "We all have our roles, even the children. Isn't that right?"

Zella stood speechless. Her ashen cheeks flushed, and her eyes moistened, the only hint that she was more sorry than angry.

"Let's go," Marianne said to Tarian and Marcus.

Marianne appeared the frailest of the three royal Sanna sisters with her reedy limbs, but her deportment was strong. She colored her lips in bold red and unlike most Wastelanders her raven black hair didn't possess a single gray strand.

Tarian nodded farewell to Jun and followed the princess north, toward the enormous castle that was once her home. Marianne reminded him of Eleanor not in looks but in spirit—a presence fiercer than her slight frame like an elegant but relentless flame. He'd noticed it earlier when he'd met with the queen and when she'd escorted them to Brianna's lab, but she'd always seemed the messenger not the message. Now she stood in the forefront, and he sensed her power.

Tarian glanced back at Zella. Tarian sympathized with her. Her passion for Marianne burned across her face. Her eyes never left Marianne's gait. Tarian understood that hopeless feeling. As Marianne walked away from Zella, Tarian walked away from Audrey. All they could do was pray for safe returns.

Marianne was an illusionist—a necessary talent for breaking into the castle of a Grand Sorcerer. By the time they'd reached the North Castle, she'd glamoured five times, mostly bland, common folk disguises that didn't require death to consume their identity. In order to enter the castle, they'd need to dominate someone's entire self.

One, two, three malditos fell as if out of thin air when an invisible Marcus grabbed them. Tarian slit their throats and Marianne borrowed their identities. They made an ideal team of assassins. They sank the bodies in one of the many rivers using heavy stones no mere mortal could lift, assured the bodies wouldn't float away.

They walked into the castle as welcomed comrades. Marianne quickly guided them through her old home, down to the dungeons, assuming that's where Lautaro would hold his prisoner. The assumption proved correct, but their uniforms were wrong. They quickly rectified the situation taking the lives of three prison guards and stealing their faces.

Tarian's confidence lifted as Marianne proved extremely useful in skill and knowledge. With a little luck, they'd have Lycott and be gone in a heartbeat.

The path grew damp and dark. They passed a couple more guards without arousing suspicion. Dim lights glowed up ahead. The scrape of chains on stone heightened with each step. A cold chill ran down Tarian's spine. Lycott wasn't the only prisoner. They walked past five cells that held two women and three men. Some huddled in the corner and wouldn't look at them. Others spat and snarled, thinking them Lautaro's guards. But all shared the same horrified fear in their eyes.

Marcus stopped at the sixth cell to gaze at a woman. She stood taller. She winced in pain as her back straightened and her shoulders broadened, but quickly hid the ache behind eyes of steel.

"Sasha?" Marcus asked.

She drew back. Her eyes narrowed in confusion as they fell upon the man that looked like her enemy. A person who'd obviously harmed her, but whose voice sounded different. Familiar. Friendly.

"It's us Sasha. Princess Marianne has the ability to glamour and borrow faces." Tarian motioned to Marianne who stood behind them glamoured as a man in an enemy uniform.

Sasha's shoulders fell. She no longer looked like a fierce immortal, or the inept Awakened hunter that Tarian knew her to be.

"They killed Josh," she said. "They've got me and David. And some mortals from the city."

Marcus paced. "We'll get you out of here."

"What are they doing with you?" Marianne asked.

"Pitting us against malditos."

"Fighting?" Tarian asked as he felt and studied the bars, searching for a weak point. There wasn't one.

"Yes, in an arena. But the malditos are deformed. I don't know what they've done to them, but they're more hideous than before."

"Can you kill them?" Marianne asked.

"Yes, but not easily. Gregory kills them easily and he," she paused and squirmed, "he eats them."

"What?" Marcus' borrowed eyes bulged. He turned to Tarian. "He's gone beyond. He's full Waker."

Tarian's heart twisted as it pounded wildly remembering the warning—*No matter what, they have to stay together until the end.*

"We're going to get you out of here." Tarian looked frantically around for a way to open the cell. "Is there a key, a button, or a release?"

"They slide. It's an iron key but it's very small." Sasha

swiped at the tears cutting a path through her dirt covered face.

Tarian patted down his uniform. Marcus and Marianne did the same.

"I've got one." Marcus pulled the key from the shirt breast pocket. He grinned, but before he could unlock it a dozen guards marched down the hallway.

The leader's face lit as he surveyed Marcus. "Gendry! I wasn't expecting to see you down here." The leader glanced from Marcus to Tarian to Marianne. "You three were scheduled for break twenty minutes ago. Is something wrong?"

Marcus hesitated to speak. His voice would not be Gendry's. He shook his head.

Tarian chanced it and mumbled, "Got held up."

The leader nodded. He banged the cell bars. "This one's a handful." His savage eyes roamed over Sasha.

Marcus shifted.

Tarian readied to defend Marcus if he lost control.

The leader removed a device from his pocket. Tarian was sure of its use—to bring pain to the prisoners. As the man slapped the tool against his palm, he ordered, "Well go on. Be back after your break."

Tarian's mind whirled. His eyes darted at the dozen guards. One could easily slip away and report them. He made the painstaking choice to walk away versus a fight that would surely blow their cover. He needed to see Gregory Lycott, find out the truth. He couldn't go back to South Castle empty handed and with such little information. No. He'd wait it out. Get back to the cells as soon as possible and rescue Sasha. He pivoted and started to leave.

Marcus didn't move. His jaw clenched as he glanced at Sasha.

"Gendry!" The leader studied the outer man that Marcus hid inside. "What's the matter with you?"

Again, Tarian risked a mumble. "Nothin'. Come on Gendry."

Sasha stood tall, her shoulders broadening with strength, appearing less of a prisoner and more like the Guardian immortal Awakened hunter that she was. She gave a slight tilt of her head encouraging Marcus to go.

He grunted but moved on, his stride a heavy shuffle.

Tarian withheld the sigh of relief that filled his lungs as they walked away with their true identities still intact. But no relief comforted the stabbing pain in his heart. He hung his head and promised they'd return. They'd save her and the others, soon.

Once back on the main level of the castle, Marianne took charge. "Follow me." She scaled flights of stairs and whipped around corners with a cat's grace.

Tarian followed her through a door. The room filled with light. A giant pane of glass spanned across the opposing end of the room. This was a viewing room. Shivers of trepidation wove through him.

Marcus hadn't spoken a word. Only loud huffs of air

escaped his nostrils.

Marianne pointed to the expansive pane of glass. "If there's going to be a duel, we'll be able to see it from here. There's an arena below. The window is one way. No one can see in. My father used it to watch his men train. He wanted to see how hard they worked when they didn't think he was around."

Tarian inched forward and peered down. The realm was empty. He released a sigh of relief. "We'll wait up here—"

"For how long?" Marcus asked.

"Long enough to be convincing. We're supposed to be guards on their break."

Marcus glared at him.

Tarian shook his head. "We'll head back down soon."

"We have to get Sasha out."

"I know and find Lycott. According to my sister, they're supposed to remain together."

"We definitely need more information before we head back," Marianne said.

The three of them sat in the room and tried to relax. No one spoke. All of them consumed with their own thoughts and worries.

Eventually, Marianne stood and went over to the window.

"See anything?" Tarian asked.

She gasped in answer.

Tarian and Marcus rushed over. Sasha stood in the arena prepped for a fight. Marcus raised a fist to beat the glass. Tarian grabbed his hand. In a flash, Marianne snatched his other arm. Marcus fought against them.

"That's enough." Marianne said. "We've all lost, and we'll lose even more if we get caught."

Marcus reluctantly conceded. Tarian saw the pain flash across his face and settle in his eyes. The same agony gripped Tarian as well.

There were no words of comfort to ease any of them. So Tarian just stared into the arena and prayed for Sasha's life. She'd beaten them before. She could do it again.

A female maldito slunk into the realm. Tarian understood what Sasha had meant about the maldito's altered appearance. This one was larger and uglier. It moved without grace, stumbling.

Tarian relaxed a little.

Sasha was a Guardian immortal, a skilled warrior, a ruthless hunter. She'd have no issues taking down a wobbly-footed creature. Then the creature lunged and caught Sasha with a force strong enough to throw her off guard.

Now it was Tarian's fist that punched the window. The glass was solid as steel. He welcomed the sharp sting that raced up his arm from the impact. The pain felt far better than the aching anxiety in the pit of his stomach.

The deceptive beast sliced Sasha's arm. Sasha kicked the blade sending it skidding across the dirt.

The fight went to the ground. They rolled pinning each other—roll after roll after roll—until Sasha landed hard on her back. The creature drew a dagger and stabbed her neck.

Tarian cringed. His chest tightening with fear as he studied the gruesome scene below.

As if the sight of blood was too strong for the maldito to resist, it bit where the blood streamed. Its savage mouth ripped jagged, bloody strips of flesh.

Sweat slicked Tarian's palms as the anxious terror built but the immortal healing would begin soon. *Soon*, he told himself. The neck had the swiftest regenerative powers. Tarian peered harder. The process should've started by now. He stepped to the right to get a better angle. Surely, it was the creature's blood. But Sasha's neck wounds gaped open.

Why hadn't regeneration begun? Tarian's heart thundered against his chest. He glanced at Marcus who stood entranced, crushing torment creasing his face.

Sasha wasn't mending. Blood pooled. Red gushed and it never stopped. Sasha bled out, right in front of them. Tarian shook his head refusing to belief it, but her limp and lifeless body was proof.

An agonizing guttural moan escaped Marcus.

Marianne's hand flew to her mouth stifling another gasp.

Tears filled Tarian's eyes. He wanted to run out of the room, destroy everything and everyone but he couldn't. He had to continue to watch, to learn, to find a weakness.

Like an obedient hound, the creature stood above Sasha, its victim, but its wild eyes continued to return hungrily to the blood. Lautaro strutted into the theater for inspection. Once satisfied with the kill, he waved permission for the creature to feast.

Marcus screamed as his fists pounded the glass.

Tarian stumbled as if his legs had just been knocked out from under him. His mind spun. It wasn't real. It's a trick. But he knew what he saw, and he knew he couldn't fall apart.

"Marcus." Tarian grabbed his friend's arm that still pounded the glass. Tarian tugged but Marcus didn't budge. He tried again. "Marcus! Get a hold of yourself. Think of Brianna and Germ and everyone that's counting on us."

Marcus stopped then bolted to the door, but Marianne stood in his way. "Step aside."

"No." She glared. "I know it hurts," her voice cracked. "I know."

Finally, Marcus stepped back. His labored breathing teetered on the verge of hyperventilation.

For a few minutes, Tarian said nothing. Remaining calm as every sinew inside his body twitched to seek revenge, as his rageful blood roared in his ears. It took extreme will, but he stayed collected. He needed his voice to sound strong to not break when he finally spoke, "Those things are worse than a Waker."

Marcus' head dropped and his chest continued to heave wildly.

Tarian remained at the window. He felt he owed it to Sasha. He'd failed her. He'd made the wrong decision in the dungeon. When the scene became too terrible, he bowed his head, and glanced away. Shame crept into all his cells weighing him down.

Marcus turned to Tarian. "Do you think the Pall did that to those creatures?"

Tarian only shook his head as he fought the urge to punch the wall, break something, or race to find Lautaro and murder him. Then movement below caught his attention.

Gregory Lycott stepped out of the shadows. He looked defeated, tired, and sad until the maldito attacked. Lycott's Waker strength flung the maldito across the arena. It landed hard. It slowly got to its feet. Lycott waited patiently for it to try again. The beast rushed back and again Lycott overpowered it.

"Lycott is showing a patience and cunning I didn't see in the Wakers that I hunted back home," Tarian said.

Marcus nodded. "Something in the change. What changes inside us when injected with the Death Serum and then the Awakened Serum?"

"Maybe it's not what changes in the body of a Guardian but what's in the two serums. The common ingredient—ichor," Tarian said.

"That god's blood," Marianne said.

Tarian nodded even though he was skeptical. Ichor came from the skies when the meteor hit but did it come from the heavens? He wasn't so sure.

Marianne turned back to watch then gasped again.

Tarian saw what had troubled her. Lycott shredded the

maldito in seconds then began to feast before Lautaro had given permission. Lautaro laughed and applauded, but the set of his eyes revealed his unease at the lack of obedience in such a dangerous mutant.

Tarian turned to Marcus. "If the infested malditos don't affect Lycott, then I'd bet the Pall doesn't affect him either. Lycott may be able to harness it."

"Maybe but first if Lautaro has ichor, we need to find it," Marcus said.

Tarian nodded. "Find it then get Lycott."

Marcus sneered. "Then kill Lautaro. End this now!"

"Agreed," Tarian said.

Sounds of a commotion came from outside the room. Tarian opened the door. Dozens of Lautaro's men swarmed the hall. He shut the door and leaned against it. "I think they found the dead guards. We need to change our disguise."

"I can glamour us to look like chambermaids, and I can do it without death. I'm sure he doesn't know the faces of his servants. He wouldn't suspect a thing." Marianne's red lips curled. "And I bet I know which bedchamber he sleeps in."

"Alright. Let's do this." Tarian's entire body hummed, thrilled to hunt and kill the Grand Sorcerer.

TWENTY-SEVEN

SOUTH CASTLE — THE WASTELANDS

GUARDIAN AUDREY

As soon as Audrey showed up in the doorway with Prince Theo, Nichola darted past them in a flash.

Piper dashed into the hall. "Nichola!" But the girl turned a corner and was gone.

Audrey grunted. "Where would she go?"

Piper shrugged. "Maybe the garden." She turned to the prince and curtseyed clumsily. "We haven't been properly introduced." She glared at Audrey.

"Oh, sorry," said Audrey, "Prince Theo this is Piper."

"Nice to meet you." Theo smiled.

"Same." Piper's eyes danced up and down the prince's handsome body.

Audrey cleared her throat. "He's come to bind Nichola so you can finally have some peace, and we can be safe should her emotions call the elements upon us." And now the little, unpredictable monster was gone. A scream caught in Audrey's throat and the threat of tears painfully pressured her sinuses. She'd explode soon. Too much chaos and change and uncertainty in one little girl.

"Well, let's get her." Theo sprinted down the hall.

The thrill of competition ate into Audrey. She bit it back. This wasn't a game of chase. She envied the young and their hopeful enthusiasm and raced after them.

They'd roamed the garden, scaled the towers, searched hundreds of rooms, and found no child. Chocolatey goodness bloomed in the air and triggered Audrey's memory. Any child that smelled that would definitely seek it out.

"Let's check the kitchen." Audrey didn't wait for a response. She bolted. And there stood Nichola with a knife in her hand and a terrified Christian at her feet. "Put that down now!" Audrey ordered, then realized Nichola's hands were by her side. Her will controlled the knife.

"Not until he gives me a cookie," Nichola yelled, a fierce storm of determination brewing in her glower.

"I told her there's only one left. Germaine ate them all. This one's mine," the boy stuttered.

Where was Germaine? She wasn't in the kitchen. Audrey hadn't seen her all day.

"Tell her to put that knife away and I'll make more," Christian said.

"Yes." Piper clapped. "Yes. He'll make you dozens."

Christian's mouth gaped.

Audrey was sure he had a limited chocolate supply. "Please, make two dozen if you can, and I'll make sure to get you chocolate enough for ten dozen." She'd force Piper to vade her across the ocean to the Appleton's bakery if she had to.

"Okay." Christian agreed but wouldn't move until the knife dropped.

"The knife." Audrey gestured irritatingly to Piper who had added excited bouncing to her clapping. As if she'd been starved of chocolate too. Audrey clenched her jaw holding back a scream of frustration.

As Piper slowly reached for the knife, Audrey forced her arm still, fighting the urge to snatch the weapon quickly and reprimand Nichola. The child's eyes remained determined but at least she glared at Piper instead of Christian. Then Nichola's stiff shoulders melted, and she released her magic hold over the knife.

"Thank you," Piper said as she carefully caught the falling blade.

The pent-up scream behind Audrey's teeth released as a sigh. "Here's the deal. You can eat the cookies after Christian makes them."

Nichola smiled and her eyes finally softened.

Audrey held up a finger. "If you go back to your room and let Prince Theo have a look at you." Audrey's voice cracked due to the fragility of her patience.

"What does *look at me* mean?" Nichola stepped back into Piper's arms, all demon gone, only little child remaining.

Audrey nodded, pleased to have an understanding. "Well … he's going to give you—"

"Shots!" Nichola wailed and scrambled up Piper who nearly toppled over.

"*No* shots," Theo said. "I promise absolutely no needles."

After a moment, Nichola believed him.

The four of them traipsed back to Piper's room and the exam began.

The ease didn't last. Soon Nichola kicked and thrashed and called them all liars. She wiggled out of Piper's grip like a ferret. Her arms might as well have been slippery tentacles waving about, for they reached far and with great force. Audrey hoped Theo had manacles inside his bag.

"For Pall's sake, girl!" Theo held a foot down with one hand and rubbed his kicked nose with the other.

"Don't call me girl!" Nichola attempted to kick him again.

"Alright, alright. Please cooperate. We want to help you." Theo's words shook on exhausted breaths.

Audrey slipped a needle under Nichola's skin.

Piper scowled. "We promised no needles."

Audrey shrugged. "Remember you'll get chocolate cookies soon."

Nichola's eyes drifted shut, and a faint smile begrudgingly appeared.

Theo's brow beaded with sweat, his cheeks flushed, the veins in his arms popped as he held Nichola's leg until it stilled. He glanced up in awe and grinned at the needle in Audrey's hand.

"I wasn't sure it'd work on her."

"Thank Pall it did," Theo said.

"Did I screw you up?" Audrey asked.

Theo furrowed his brow in question, the expression foreign to him.

Audrey rephrased it. "Can you bind her while she's tranquilized?"

"Yes and no. It's not easy finding the threads of a drugged girl, but it would've been near impossible with her throwing a temper tantrum. And I'm as exhausted as Pall." He let go of Nichola's ankle and fell to the floor. "I'm never having children."

Audrey and Piper snorted.

After a couple of long breaths, Audrey gathered her wits. "Okay, now what?"

"Now you two stand away and be quiet. Or leave. Up to you, I just need to concentrate. I need peace." Theo set his bag on the table and removed a small blade with an elegant mother of pearl handle.

Audrey's shoulders collapsed with fatigue. She'd never appreciated a tranquilizer more than at that moment. At the gleam of the point of that blade, Nichola would've called to all the elements and produced an earthquake or tornado or worse.

Piper squeaked as she watched Theo place the knife against Nichola's skin. "Ouch."

"Shhh," Audrey said.

The prince glared at them.

Piper's fingers tapped, and her knee bobbed.

Audrey laid a hand on her friend's knee and whispered, "She's fine."

Theo drew Nichola's blood from a fine cut, the blade a gentle friend. The amount of blood was so small it bothered Audrey. Surely, he'd need more to bind this clever little witch-demon with the strength of a grown Guardian. But he put the knife down.

Theo sat quietly meditating with the plate of blood next to him. She'd heard blood weavers speak about their work. Some had called it pulling threads from the hemoglobin, plucking them right from the atoms. Others told a more poetic tale of misty columns snaking out of the red syrup, or floating twists of multi-colored energies. Either way, the weaver found the appropriate links to manipulate any given spell.

"This could take hours," Theo said. "She has no rhythm and thousands of threads. It's chaotic."

"Take your time," Audrey lied. She desperately needed him to work fast.

Even though he sat still, meditating his sorcery, his eyes twitched behind closed lids, and his lips jerked, parted, then shut tight. Hours passed, but Audrey and Piper never moved.

Finally, he shook his head and drank water. He yawned then moaned. "She's already bound."

The drowse in Audrey's head from the waiting vanished.

Completely awake, she asked, "What?"

"Her life cord is a deep purple and it's full of knots. Which means her life is intertwined with another's. I found the life cord that wasn't hers. It shares an attachment to her vitals. When I finally found it and unsnarled it, the cord led to Lautaro. I think."

"You think?" Audrey growled.

Theo nodded. "Unless I have a sample of his blood, I can't be certain."

Piper jumped up and tiptoed back and forth nervously. "That's bad … right?"

"Yes."

"How certain are you?" Audrey's patience struggled with conjecture.

"Ninety-five percent." Theo raised perturbed eyebrows.

"And what exactly does this mean?" Even with an exact number, Audrey's brain refused to comprehend a conclusion based on knots and threads. She'd known and trusted magic. Her long life was proof of a strange magical world, and she'd seen many inexplicable things, but she'd also been spoiled with brilliant scientific minds and precise equipment inside Guardian Headquarters. She felt as if she'd stepped back in time, all of science's advancements meaningless.

"It means, if Lautaro dies, so does Nichola," Theo said.

TWENTY-EIGHT

SOUTH CASTLE TRAINING FIELDS — BALEFIRE CITY

GUARDIAN AUDREY

Audrey trailed Christopher as he marched up and down the training lines of young recruits. She recited the awful truth Prince Theo had discovered linking Nichola to Lautaro.

"They must be warned," Audrey said.

"Send the Germ," Christopher said as he corrected a teenage boy's sword grip.

Audrey couldn't even look at the boy's innocent eyes and unblemished skin. He was tough, no doubt, but just a baby. Audrey shook her head as Christopher's words set in. "What? No. I can't send her."

"Why don't *you* go?"

"I need to stay here and wait for Eleanor. And I'm not gifted with invisibility. Neither is Germ. It should be you."

"The girl is good." The voice came from the next row.

Audrey straightened and stood on her toes to look over the children's heads. It was frustrating being shorter than most of the teenage recruits.

Ralph slipped through two duelers.

"Oh, hello Ralph."

"How are you Audrey?" Ralph smiled.

"Not well but thank you for asking." Audrey sighed and shook her head. Germaine was too young and there was no way she'd send her and not Christopher.

"Christopher is needed here. Trust me. Germaine will get the job done," Ralph said.

"I'm sure she's an excellent *human* spy, but this isn't some Blue drug-house in the Wastelands. It's a heavily guarded fortress of creatures. Home to a mad sorcerer."

"Exactly the point." Ralph cocked a brow.

"He's right. She's small and sneaky, and no one knows her," Christopher said.

"She could be killed." Audrey's voiced rose. Didn't anyone understand that children were not supposed to be fighting or spying? Her chest heaved, more screams threatening to burst from her lungs.

"She knows that. Any one of us could be killed." Ralph turned and gestured to the mass of recruits. "After sword training, we take them to shoot targets. These kids are resilient and strong. They've never been coddled like Entente children."

Audrey collapsed in on herself, but it didn't show on the outside. She knew what he meant. She'd grown up during hard times and done stupid, dangerous things at a young age. She absorbed the teenage faces in this training arena—smart, determined, ruthless. Audrey turned to encounter Germaine's invincible stare. She and Lucianna had snuck up on her.

"So this is where you've been spending your time?" Audrey asked.

"Every minute." Germaine stood impregnable, blade in hand, and flushed with sweat.

Princess Lucianna laid a hand on Germaine's shoulder, vouching for the girl's ability.

"Do you have those spectacles?" Audrey asked.

"Of course."

"Did you overhear our plan that someone needs to go to North Castle and warn Tarian?"

Germaine nodded.

"Very well then." Audrey succumbed, but she wouldn't relax until Germaine and Tarian were back at the castle, safe and whole. "Fine. Use the glasses. Try not to get anywhere near Lautaro or his Maldito Apostólos. Just find Tarian. Tell him we need Lautaro alive. Did you get that?"

Germaine continued to stare directly into Audrey's icy eyes. "Yes, Guardian Audrey." Her formal address wasn't a mocked response.

Audrey appreciated her respect. "And take this."

Germaine caught the egg-shaped device.

"Tell Tarian to click it. I've given its double to Franny and trained her how to use it. She's waiting to hear from him. If you can't find him or you get caught—"

"I won't—"

"Don't be foolish. Listen. See this tiny button on the Egg?" Audrey pointed to an almost invisible dot.

"Yeah."

"Click it, and only it, if your life's in danger." Audrey didn't want Germaine messing around and pressing any other spots on the Egg. She needed the Egg for one task, and one task only. It was best if its other features remained locked down. Who knew what Lautaro was capable of tracking? "Franny will come get you. We'll find another way to retrieve Tarian."

Audrey's gut twisted at the thought of saving Lautaro's life should Tarian have the opportunity to kill him, but it twisted worse at the idea of Nichola dying. She was a child after all, and not just *any* child. However, the fact remained that everyone else in this world would be better off with Lautaro dead. She could rationalize the sacrifice of one child, couldn't she?

"I'm not gonna fail." Germaine sheathed her blade and pocketed the Egg.

"Good."

Before Germaine left, she glanced at Christopher. He winked. Then she turned to Lucianna. "Thank you for training me."

"You did fantastic." Lucianna patted Germaine's back.

Germaine turned to Ralph.

Ralph wrapped her in his arms. "I have faith in you."

"Tell Mom and Dad for me." Germaine's parents had left South Castle that morning to bring supplies to the line at the Pall and remain there until further notice.

"Will do," Ralph said.

Germaine slipped out of his grip and disappeared in a flash—the energy and spirit of youth.

TWENTY-NINE

ESURIENT DHAUMRA'S LAIR

GUARDIAN CHANCELLOR ELEANOR

Eleanor collected stones along the mind path in Dhaumra's garden. An amethyst crystal caught her eye. She picked it up and rubbed it between her fingertips. "You'll make a fine amulet." All crystals were useful but the ones along this trail were the most powerful she'd ever held.

She continued strolling, awaiting Dhaumra's return from the daily moon council meeting which could last hours. The list of attendees was confidential. The Guardians of Dare High Council may be the only guests, or they may be one of many. She suspected leaders from South America also sought council having had dealt with the Grand Sorcerer's deceptive take-over for years.

Eleanor hadn't attended the LMCI (Life-Magical, Cursed, Immortal) conference in two turns. They met every ten years or when needed, as in this case. For her the affairs of the Entente of Nations always took precedence, too many scheduling conflicts or so she told herself. Truth was she'd found them boring, a bunch of elitist creatures bragging or complaining.

"You look lovely in the moonlight." Dhaumra's voice a whispered breath on her shoulder. He slipped his arms around her waist. Her back melted into the curve of his chest.

She leaned her head back and felt the life—the solace— she could have if she'd just say the word. They bathed in the light he called moonlight, but it wasn't. It was barely afternoon, or at least, she didn't think she'd slept that long.

His lips kissed her neck. His hand caressed the plain of her stomach then trailed up to cup her breast.

She spun out of his arms. "You will not seduce me until after I have my information."

A Cheshire grin pinched his golden, feline eyes. "With a promise like that I'll tell you everything."

She strolled back inside and sat down on the silk embroidered sofa. Her racing heart and her fearful, rolling stomach made standing a challenge.

He took a seat beside her. "I alone cannot defeat the smokey Pall with its powerful origin enchantments. I have tried. This is my territory, and it shames me." His head dropped.

Eleanor lifted his chin with a gentle touch. "Don't be foolish."

He laughed. "You're right. I'm a foolish old creature."

She smiled. "What do you know of it?"

"The last war stirred the dark magic. This is magic older than I am. It has conquered my powers as well as others. Lautaro believes it is the end of the Esurients' reign. Someone has filled his ear with a prophecy, has told him it is a natural evolution. His time to rule this world has come. Maybe he is correct, for the old smoke is drawn to him, but I will not lose without a fight. I walk the planes of possibilities and have seen many outcomes, some victorious some not. There is still hope.

"I'm powerless inside it, but it does not hurt me. It also doesn't reveal its secrets to me, but it has secrets. I've watched your mortal men go in and die. I've seen your ghosts go in and nearly die. Lautaro will die too if he lingers in the mist without protection. But the girl," he paused, his stare drifted to another dimension, searching for something she couldn't see. "The possibilities have shown her to harness its power."

"She is the key." Eleanor loosed a long breath.

"As long as she harnesses it for good. The smoke has no allegiance yet. It waits for her. And she is too young to act out of reason. She will act for love. I've seen this. She will act for love, and once her father—the one she calls father—dies, she will act out of pain, which will have devastatingly harmful effects. I see her turning against Lautaro, but I also see her turning to him as a father figure. I fear," he paused, but this time his gaze stayed present. It dove deep into Eleanor's eyes. "If she was older, more skilled, less emotional … but …" He shook his head.

"She needs her actual father." Everything inside Eleanor grew taught with worry, twisted, and gnarled like an old tree weaving its roots into her chest.

"We need many variables to align perfectly or else the Pall will absorb us all, slowly and viciously."

"And what of the other information I gave over?" Eleanor tensed. She may have doomed her Entente people to a lethal outcome.

Dhaumra's face paled, and Eleanor's heart plummeted.

"Tell me," she begged.

"They will of course thoroughly fact check, but it looks as if your intelligence is accurate. The portal Lautaro opened to retrieve the ichor has allowed the Pall to spread across the continents."

"What precautions are being discussed?" Eleanor held her breath as she awaited the answer.

"My dear, you know we cannot allow the ichor to exist. The High Council's claims of its destructive capabilities hold much weight. The cavern must be destroyed, and the portal sealed to contain the Pall in the Eastern Wastelands."

The gravity of Eleanor's helplessness crashed down. She hung her head. "When will it happen?"

"Soon." Dhaumra pulled her into him. She didn't resist his caress.

"Maybe I can persuade a most humane demolition." He kissed her hair.

His words were kind, but she knew how these things worked. Sacrificing the few to save the many. She remained locked in his embrace for hours, letting time lapse, procrastinating the inevitable, losing her senses in his roaming hands.

THIRTY

THE STREETS — BALEFIRE CITY

NERVE SPY GERMAINE

Germaine moved like a breeze through the streets of Balefire. Unlike the Guardians and Elite soldiers that practically glowed with their healthy untainted skin, Germaine's ashen tone blended. Skin layers deep with toxins from the air, water, and soil.

She slunk around corners like Pall shadows. Her senses heightened to acute awareness in this unfamiliar city. Its differences from home struck her. Litter didn't engulf the streets of Balefire. Crumbled stone buildings had been rebuilt. Roofs remained intact and protective. The kids too young to fight played, gathered, and read. Back home they thieved, scammed, and shot up Blue. Those kids were tough, tougher than the teenagers training with Christopher, but they weren't heroes. Germaine wanted to be a hero, to protect and build like the people of Balefire.

In her mind's eye, she saw it—her future as one of those heroes. But not all of these city kids with heroic potential would live. They were too weak. Only the tough would survive. Princess

Lucianna was tough and beautiful with shimmer on her eyes and cheeks. Germaine hoped to live in a future world where she could put shimmer on her face and be beautiful while fighting fiercely.

As she roamed nearer to North Castle, the streets quieted. Fewer motorized bikes, less people walking, no more children. She was eerily alone until she heard the buzz of a scooter and felt the weight of someone's stare. Shivers of warning showered her skin leaving goose bumps.

A flash of red whizzed past. She followed it around the corner and spied Sam on the red motorized scooter. The scooter halted. A cloaked figure appeared, stepped from the building's shadow.

Before Germaine could hide, Sam spotted her. Sam donned nice clothes, leather gloves, and new shoes. Germaine hadn't thought about Sam since that night. She remembered the gold chain. By the looks of it, Sam had scored well.

A smile formed on Germaine's face. She was truly happy for Sam and curious. The necklace was a valuable metal, but it was thin. She was surprised it fetched so much.

Would Sam suspect she was there on Nerve business? Maybe Sam was still interested in joining the rebels. But stopping to chat about it wasn't ideal at this time. Germaine's brain conjured up escape routes, excuses why she was there and what she was doing.

Sam nodded to the person under the hood then glanced back at Germaine.

Germaine stared into Sam's eyes for answers. They transformed from grim gray to radiant steel, sharp as the edge of Lucianna's sword. *Why?*

By the time Germaine's sixth sense ignited, it was too late. She should have known Sam was up to no good. Germaine realized she'd just stepped smack in the middle of one of Sam's dirty deals. She turned to run when someone grabbed her. She yanked her arm, but her captor yanked harder, securing her against an expansive stomach.

She glanced over at Sam and her mystery date. Germaine knew that they saw her struggling. They knew what was happening but neither moved to help. Germaine focused hard, but the face under the hood remained a black hole. No clue if it was human, creature, male or female, but she sensed an evil within its presence.

The cloaked figure said something to Sam, but Germaine was too far away to hear the words. Sam's eyes met Germaine's then returned to the face under the hood. Sam grinned as if concluding their negotiation. Then the mysterious person strolled in the opposite direction past several alleys and vanished.

Shit, she cursed her situation. *Sam just bargained me off.* Her heart plunged and fear poured out of her in sweat. *What debt was owed to that cloaked figure? How'd she know I was here?* Her mind flooded with unanswered questions.

The scooter revved as Sam turned the throttle. She sped away then slowed to look back, and for a brief second, Germaine thought maybe she'd return, then the motor screamed. Sam shot out of sight.

The girl whose hand covered Germaine's mouth spoke, "You really pissed off your friend. She paid us to keep you overnight. So let's have some fun."

That's no friend, Germaine thought. And neither was this girl. She tried to bite her hand, ignoring its nasty smell. She had a plan. She'd draw blood, spit out its filth and run, but the girl pressed harder. The fleshy insides of Germaine's lips dug into her teeth. She tasted blood. Hers. Forced to inhale the smell of the sweaty fingers, vomit hit the back of her throat. She convulsed.

The girl released her hand and Germaine got an instant of fresh air until a boy shoved a mouthful of cloth down her throat and bound it around her head. *Where'd he come from?* The cloth smelled better, but she thought she'd suffocate as the vomit threatened to rise. She attempted a swallow. It helped, for now.

Her eyes searched for more kidnappers but found none. They were alone. There was no one around to help her. Anxiety crept up her spine. She recognized the one that stuffed her mouth. The cruel boy with evil eyes, the one with Jinx that night she'd caught the Guardians at Nichola's house, the boy that looked as if he enjoyed drowning kittens. The tall, big one that held her from behind must be his girlfriend. She was strong and lifted Germaine off the ground, took her down an alley and into a dark room. She thrashed and kicked but the girl was like iron.

Kitten-drowner had stringy gray-black hair and a wiry frame. He bound Germaine's wrists behind her back so tightly it felt like a ring of fire.

When she realized she was free from the girl's belly and her legs unbound, she bolted. She was fast, but kitten-drowner was faster. He caught her, shoved her to the ground, and kicked her stomach. She doubled in pain and couldn't wrap her arms around herself which made it worse.

"Not so tough now, are you? I knew I'd get you sooner or later. Show you I'm the boss." He grabbed her hair and yanked her head back then landed a solid punch to her cheek. Her tongue puckered at the tang of blood and her teeth ached.

He hoisted her up by her hair and forced her to bend backwards over a table. Her knuckles crunched as her wrists flattened between her spine and the wood. The awareness as to why her legs weren't bound slithered through her. The large girl pinned her shoulders flat. As much as she squirmed, she couldn't get free. Her knee, however, thrust upward and landed hard between the wiry boy's legs.

He stumbled back. "Pall! You bitch." He coughed then snarled.

She thrashed and wiggled during his absence. It did nothing. The large girl was too strong and with one hand still holding Germaine down, she hit her in the head with the other. Germaine's brain throbbed, her vision blurred, and her body went limp.

Fog. Confusion. Piercing pain electrified her. Warm fluid slid down her side. Blood. Once her mind cleared, she realized wiry boy had bit her. Half of her clothes had been ripped off her body. She felt as cold and exposed as a piece of raw meat.

How had this happened? Wasn't she just envisioning herself as a future hero? She expected this from the scum running through the streets under the tower around the Wastelands, the Blue addicts or the homeless teens, but not here, in the city that promised hope. But these two were the worst kind of Wasteland scum and somehow, they knew she'd be here. Somehow Sam had double-crossed her.

"You think you're better than us. I saw it in your eyes that night. But you're not." Kitten-drowner's hot breath hit her face like steaming garbage. "You're nothing."

She turned her head refusing to allow his lips too close to hers. She wouldn't inhale his breath. Never! She tried to knee him again, but he'd figured that trick out. He had a firm hold on her legs. His skinny arms were deceivingly powerful. She struggled but he held the position of advantage.

"Do it!" the large girl growled.

What is he going to do to me?

"Shut up. Keep her still."

I'm tough. Don't cry. She repeated over and over in her head. She wouldn't cry no matter what awful abuse he would enact. Only a single tear defied her orders and rolled out the corner of her eye. She ignored it, focused on the wall. Failure welled inside her.

The large girl growled again, and kitten-drowner grunted as Germaine continued to make it difficult for them. Wiry boy punched her ribs, momentarily paralyzing her with the ache.

Agony throbbed her side then the torture extended down to her toes. Her mind raced through the pain, her father's and mother's faces clear behind her closed eyes. More tears spilled. Then Ralph's face came to her. He'd had such confidence in her abilities to succeed in the mission, and now she feared she'd die here, a failure, a disappointment, a weakling. It had all gone so wrong.

Then the room fell silent. The scumbags no longer bickered. The heavy breath from the wiry boy disappeared along with the guttural growls from the big girl. The silence spoke louder than the scream that died in the back of her gagged throat. She told her body to fight, but it didn't obey. Her limbs were tired. Her core ached. Exhaustion overcame her entirely. Her back collapsed into the knuckles of her hands bound behind her. If not for the fear, she'd be in unbearable pain.

Silence. Numbness. Then a whisper. She must be going crazy from the beatings. She'd gone nuts. There it was again— whispers in the dark. Her eyes went wide. Then the wiry boy's head landed between her breasts. Warmth bloomed on her stomach and spilled over her side. More blood. Not hers. His.

She screamed, but she was still gagged. She looked up at the awful girl's face. Surprise in her eyes, just before the bullet split her face and she toppled over.

Blinking through the tears, she searched the dimly lit room.

Maria!

A blue haired, bronze skinned woman stepped from the shadows. She rushed to Germaine, ripped the gag from her mouth. Germaine gasped. Life and energy filled her lungs.

Maria sat her up then unbound her hands. "You're safe now. Are you okay?"

Germaine nodded. She felt the sobs but forced them quiet.

"Did he …" Maria let the silence ask her question.

Germaine shook her head.

Maria pulled clothes out of her backpack and covered Germaine's bare breasts. "Can you stand?"

Germaine nodded and stood. The gravity brought all her anger and sadness down. The sobs erupted then she collapsed into Maria's arms.

Maria held her and kept her standing strong. "It's okay. Let it out. You're safe. You're safe."

"Thank … you … I … thought," Germaine tried to speak between sobs. "He almost … If you hadn't—"

"Shhh. Almost doesn't count." Maria stroked her hair as they hugged, patiently waiting for her to gain strength.

With one giant gulp, Germaine straightened. She wiped her eyes. She snorted back snotty tears. She checked to make sure she was completely clothed, no longer exposed to the harsh eyes and greedy fingers of cruel rats.

Germaine's eyes fell on Maria's gun. "It whispered to me."

Maria smiled. "It's called a silencer. Pretty awesome, huh?"

Germaine grinned. She kicked kitten-drowner's ribs until she felt them crack. She searched out her spectacles. They'd been flung across the room along with her blade. She tucked them both into her pockets. The Egg had managed to stay inside her discarded clothes. She collected it without looking at the ripped threads and bloodstains.

Germaine swallowed down the rage, disgust, and humiliation. She gave another hard kick to each body. "I have to get inside North Castle." And when Maria didn't complain, didn't warn her, didn't feel sorry for her, assertion filled her like a swarm of dragons. She could fulfill her mission and tell no one of what was almost taken from her. She trusted Maria would never breathe a word and she wondered why. She didn't ask.

Maria put an arm around her. Together they stalked the winding alleys leading north. Glares of murder fell upon all that glanced their way. Germaine fought the urge to stab random people that crossed her path. She saw the ghost of Sam's face in everyone. Sam would pay.

The city spread far, and it took hours to cross it on foot. Once within yards of North Castle, she put on her spectacles. Slowly her eyes roamed through each window. She saw one that glowed. The spelled spectacles highlighted a Guardian's aura in neon orange. She slid the spectacles off her face and hit the ground hard. Her slight frame allowed her to slip through the rails of the fence. She skipped from bush to bush until she managed to find a shadowy crook and waited for Maria to catch up.

Her eyes lifted then darted around the white stone. Dirt stuck in the cracks and crevices like jam between bread. A spectrum of browns built up over time, each layer, each smear, a mark of time. Who'd walked its halls, slept in its beds? Who'd died at the hands of murderers, suffered at the hands of rapists? Who'd lived a gloriously happy life and birthed many children? Could she scale it, or would she fall to her death?

Maria caught her shoulder. "I think I should stay down here. Hide over there in those bushes. Wait for your exit. I can go for help if you're too long."

"Okay. That's probably a good idea." Germaine shivered, but her unwavering voice and practical words hid her fear. She wasn't ready to be alone.

"Tarian, Marcus, and Marianne are already in there. So, I really think having an ally on the outside is smart. Is that okay with you?"

It wasn't but she said, "Yeah. It's okay."

Germaine's fingers reached for a notch, then another. Her toes found tiny holes to slip into. She never looked down. She reached a guarded balcony. As soon as the guard roamed in the other direction, her slender legs swooped up and over. She hunched like a cat and prowled around a corner.

The guard repeated his steps coming toward her, but she hid just out of his sight. Again, he stopped at a certain point then turned and retraced. With his back facing her, she stepped out and through a door. She constantly looked over her shoulder. She could still smell that filthy girl's frying-pan hands and feel kitten-drowner's eager breath. Terror sent shivers down her spine, but her tenacity grew and pushed her forward. She no longer wanted to be a hero. She would be a hunter.

I'm the hunter, not the hunted! But as much as she repeated those words, the fear lingered.

THIRTY-ONE

SOUTH CASTLE — BALEFIRE CITY

GUARDIAN AUDREY

Audrey zoomed through the castle halls. She'd just spoken with Eleanor. The news was bad. Eleanor hadn't confided everything. Audrey had heard the hesitation in the Chancellor's voice. However, what Eleanor had offered made Audrey sorry she'd entrusted a teenager to return Tarian to her.

Disastrous!

She got to Piper's room and almost barged in but thought better of it. She knocked then focused on the detailed pattern of the rug at her feet so as to not burst from anxiety.

Piper opened the door, looked her over, then asked, "Don't you have the cookies?" Her whispered words had a sharp edge.

Cookies! She felt it in her bones that Tarian was about to kill Lautaro, dooming them all, and Piper wanted cookies.

"You promised cookies!" Nichola howled.

Audrey had forgotten.

Nichola's eyes were rimmed red from sobs, her hair a tangled mess, lunch and dinner sat uneaten on the table.

"We're having a bad day," Piper said through gritted teeth.

"I can see that." Audrey almost slumped and gave up, but she found the ember of determined strength deep inside her and stroked it to full flame. "I'll be right back."

Audrey hurried to the kitchen. As Christian had promised, two dozen chocolate chip cookies awaited her on the counter. She would've hugged the boy if he'd been there. She grabbed them and raced back to Nichola; all the while stunned by the ridiculousness of it all.

Audrey calmly waited until she'd eaten three cookies and the red in her cheeks had faded.

The child looked content, so she risked, "Nichola, I need you to unbind yourself from Lautaro."

"No!" The word blasted a scream that lasted so long Audrey almost doubted it came out of her.

"I know you know what you are." Audrey inched toward her.

Nichola opened her mouth in protest but didn't scream, instead, a long sigh escaped.

"You're special. You can help us all. Don't you want to save Piper?" Audrey hoped she sounded sincere and not furious.

"Of course." Nichola sunk onto her bed. "But you want Daddy dead. You'll leave him with that evil sorcerer." Sobs choked any more words she tried to say.

"I can guarantee we want him back."

Nichola shook her tear-drenched face.

"I'm being honest. He has the ability to kill immortals. We don't want that in the hands of a mad sorcerer. Tarian is there right now trying to get him back—"

"Tarian hates Daddy!"

Those were the wrong words. Nichola drew on the element of air. The contents of the room swirled violently. A chocolate cookie slammed into Audrey's face.

Piper stole time and the tornado of objects froze. Nichola glared at Piper.

"Get out, Audrey. I'll deal with her," Piper said.

Audrey didn't move.

Piper's face turned red with strain. "I can't hold this for long."

Dejected, Audrey shuffled out of the room. She jumped when the door slammed shut. The lives of everyone she cared about hinged on two kids. She wanted to scream, wanted to pound the walls, jump out the window.

THIRTY-TWO

Germaine entered a dark, musty, and cluttered room. She made her way through the cobwebs to another door. It squeaked as she opened it. Thankfully, no one was on the other side. She proceeded from door to door listening and hunting, careful not to topple the marble busts and vases that perched atop pedestals marking the halls. Then she hurried up a stairwell that ended abruptly and she nearly fell to her death.

She drew back, heart racing. *That was close.* She gasped for breath. Once her breathing steadied and her nerves calmed, she peered down at the long drop she would have taken if she hadn't been paying attention. Her heart pounded again. She had no fear of heights, but she did have a reasonable fear of falling.

Shaking off the terror, she rushed down the steps then through another hall with more doors. The maze of halls and doors soon dizzied all sense of direction. Some were pristine while others were almost too dilapidated to walk through. She'd become discombobulated. It should have been easier. But she would succeed. She would not lose. Not after what she'd been through. Now more than ever she needed to prove she was the best. She wasn't a failure.

Tarian could be anywhere. She smothered the howl clawing up her throat. He had to be in this part of the castle because she'd seen the glow through the spectacles.

She sighed and risked opening several more doors. Then she heard voices mutedly drifting from next door, or upstairs, she wasn't sure. Her feet climbed another set of stairs, and the voices grew louder. Words melted as if coated with honey.

A hand gripped her mouth. Panic looped her neck like a noose. Her heart hammered as the morning's torturous episode revisited her.

"Shhh. Germ. It's Marcus," he whispered.

She slammed her teeth into the flesh of his hand and bit down.

"Ouch." Marcus released her. "Why'd ya do that? I told ya it was me."

She gulped in oxygen. Tremors and anxious butterflies stormed inside her.

"Hey." Marcus put a hand on her shoulders. "You alright?"

She backed away nodding vigorously in between shortened breaths. She swallowed. *Get it together!*

"It's okay." Marcus reached for her, but again she backed

away. His eyes melted, and his round cheeks puffed full of concern. "Are ya sure you're okay?"

She nodded, breathing steadily. "You just caught me off guard. I'm good now." She hoped her lie convinced him.

"This way." Marcus frowned then he led her into the next room.

An extra-large bed with a bulky frame and several silk pillows occupied the center of the room. Chest of drawers and other furniture sat against the wall. Tarian stood next to Marianne. He held a square case with something gold inside. A boy Germaine recognized from the Wasteland streets stood with them.

"Germ!" Tarian's voice whispered and his eyes darted looking for others, but it was only her. "What are you doing here?"

"Why is he here?" She pointed to the boy.

"This is Luke. He's one of the orphans that got captured during the takeover. He led us to Lautaro's bedchambers to retrieve this ichor." Tarian extended the container so she could have a better look. The glob of golden lava was somehow suspended inside the box.

At the mention of Lautaro's name, she remembered her orders. "You can't kill the Grand Sorcerer."

"How did you know we were going to?" Tarian's brows knit, and rage spread red across his cheeks.

"Audrey feared you would if you got the chance."

Tarian huffed a small laugh. "It was his idea." He pointed to Marcus.

"Nichola's bound her life to Lautaro's. We need to get out of here and back to South Castle." She unzipped her jacket and tossed the Egg to Tarian.

Recognition lit Tarian's eyes. "That's Elite gear. Where'd you get that jacket?"

Germaine sighed. "Maria is waiting on the ground. It's hers."

Tarian nodded then looked at the Egg. "We're not supposed to use these."

"All I know is Audrey told me to tell you to click it there." She pointed to the nearly invisible button.

Tarian shook his head. "I might as well hold a neon target to my head."

"You have to trust Audrey," Marcus said.

"I agree." Marianne's sharp nails nervously clicked together.

Before they had the opportunity to click the button, Lautaro's muffled voice came from outside the door.

Luke shoved them all into a closet. He wasn't much older than she. He was a clever thief and good at Wack. He'd slept on the tower once or twice. She wondered how he'd made his way here.

Lautaro barged through the door. "Luke?"

"Good evening Grand Sorcerer. I was just turning down your bed."

"Tonight is magnificent. Isn't it, son?" Lautaro asked.

"It is. Only a sliver moon though."

"Yes. But the skies know I'm coming to claim them. I can kill the unkillable." The Sorcerer's laugh rolled through the room like an avalanche.

Luke mimicked his laugh but to Germaine's ears it sounded hollow. She hoped his eyes concreted the lie, but they mustn't have.

"What is it boy?"

"Nothing, Grand Sorcerer … I'm not one for violence."

"Hmm. Well, I guess some of us are meant to serve in other ways."

A long pause followed. Too long. Germaine's eyes widened. Tarian shook his head, but it didn't ease the worry brewing inside her gut. No sound. No movement. Nothing.

He knows. Germaine rocked from toes to heels in panic and whispered, "He knows."

Tarian hit the button on the Egg. Nothing happened.

Suddenly, Marcus disappeared and just when she wished she had that ability, a tingling raced up her limbs. Marianne had grabbed her. The strange sensation was coming from her touch.

"What's happening?" Germaine whispered.

Marianne placed a finger to her lips and Germain froze. Together they took a small step backward hitting their backs against clothing. Marianne was using her illusions. Germaine noticed a sheerness to their bodies as if they were blending with the fine silk shirts and velvet jackets that hung inside the closet.

Tarian hit the button again. Nothing. He still held the container with that gold stuff and just when he tossed it to Marianne, the door swung open.

Lautaro stared at Tarian standing seemingly alone in the closet and the box of ichor soaring through the air then falling to the floor.

Marianne couldn't catch it. If it disappeared, became glamoured, in front of Lautaro's eyes, she'd risk getting caught. The precious case of golden liquid lay on the floor inches away from their feet.

THIRTY-THREE

NORTH CASTLE — BALEFIRE CITY

GUARDIAN TARIAN

Tarian's mind worked fast as Lautaro stood inches away, dazed at the sight of a Guardian in his closet.

Even though Tarian could see Marcus, he knew Lautaro couldn't. Tarian threw a stern glance at his friend in warning. He hoped Marcus understood that he needed him to protect Germaine.

Marcus snarled but remained hidden.

Tarian stepped forward palms splayed in surrender. The teenager's life was all that mattered.

"Call my men," Lautaro ordered his boy servant.

Luke's gray eyes hardened to iron.

Tarian's heart twisted. He reached for his blade, but he knew it was too late. Luke was going to do something stupidly brave. Tarian couldn't save the boy, but he could prevent more bloodshed.

Lautaro whirled on Luke. "Informer!" In one graceful movement, the sword was unsheathed and sliced the young man's neck.

Germaine gasped.

Tarian shut the closet door and prayed Luke's yelp echoed so loudly in Lautaro's ear that he'd missed Germ's slight intake of air. Tarian lunged blade out. His effort weak, meant only to draw attention away from the closet. It worked.

Lautaro raised his sword to defend the blade near his ribs. "I don't wish to kill you Tarian."

"There are far worse things than death." Tarian leaped over the dead boy's body, burst past the bedchamber doors, and out into the hall. He raced down the corridor's maze.

Lautaro closed the distance behind him.

Two guards rushed toward him with murder in their eyes. Tarian thrust his blade in the gut of one and ducked out of the path of the other's two-edged claymore, but not before it nicked his side. Pain struck hard and keen. Tarian held a breath and swallowed it away clearing his mind of the sting, his skin already mending. He moved on, scaled the banister to fall several stories. He landed hard and rolled, bounding back to his feet. He flinched as his bones ached from the shock. As quick as they'd broken, they welded back together. But it didn't matter, for he'd only taken two steps before being forced to yield. The needle thin sword pierced his throat. He felt the acid burn and went down gagging. A thin, tall maldito kept him pinned to the floor like a skewered mouse.

Lautaro's footsteps thundered down the stairwell and up the hall then stopped at Tarian's head. His boot lifted, and Tarian braced for a kick to the face, but it never came. A shuffling of a dozen men encircled them.

"Take him to a cell," Lautaro ordered. He turned to a decorated guard. "Search the entire interior and grounds. He wasn't alone."

THIRTY-FOUR

NORTH CASTLE — BALEFIRE CITY

NERVE SPY GERMAINE

Germaine swallowed the next gasp that crept up her throat. It took great effort to withhold it. Her horror manifested in a squeeze of Marianne's hand. Germaine held it tightly as her body trembled. She feared if she let go, she'd scream or collapse. To Marianne's credit she didn't flinch.

They were trapped. Germaine suspected and hoped Marcus was there too. She couldn't see him; however, she could see Marianne. Her eyes bounced to a window and Germaine nodded.

Lautaro would come back soon and Germaine sure as Pall wouldn't be there when he did. She leaped to the window's edge, but the glass stuck, until an invisible hand wrenched it free.

"Thank you, Marcus," she whispered.

Marianne picked up the box of ichor, but she couldn't hold on to it and climb to the window. She scrambled around the closet, shuffling through clothes and shoes.

Germaine's stomach knotted. Marianne was wasting precious time.

Finally, Marianne found a bag and shoved the box inside then looped the strap around her shoulder.

"Come on," Germaine whispered.

"Go! Both of you," invisible Marcus added.

Marianne didn't hesitate, didn't ask Marcus' plan, didn't wish him well. They all knew Marcus was far too large to jam through the small window.

The decline was nearly impossible, a straight drop. Twenty stories high or more. Germaine's slender, strong fingers cautiously grasped miniscule ledges of protruding stone. Her narrow feet wedged into crevices too small for a sparrow's nest. She hoped Marianne wouldn't stumble and bump into her. They'd fall to their deaths for certain.

The agonizing trek to the bottom lasted too long. The place would be surrounded by the time they reached the ground. Nevertheless, a rush of relief flooded through Germaine as her foot finally touched down but before she could flee, Marianne grabbed her. She forced Germaine to flatten against the wall. Lautaro's men scattered everywhere. And she couldn't tell a *maldito* soldier from a human one.

Marianne said, "They can't see through my glamour."

Germaine prayed it was true. Apparently, it was as the men marched past without a glance. They must have looked like blocks of yellow limestone.

Marianne exhaled then said, "Run."

It was the longest two-hundred-and-fifty yards Germaine had ever run. They reached the woods, found Maria, then cautiously plodded through the night dodging malditos and sketchy street people. None had the resolve to discuss their failures, and the uncertainty of Marcus' and Tarian's fate crushed what was left of Germaine's spirit.

THIRTY-FIVE

SOUTH CASTLE — BALEFIRE CITY

GUARDIAN AUDREY

The news of Sasha's death and Tarian's capture hit hard. Audrey's heart broke knowing her love would be in that horrific arena fighting for his life. The worst part—she had to stay in South Castle doing nothing but the grim task of reporting the news to Eleanor, who remained with Dhaumra.

"Your people need you Chancellor." Audrey wielded Eleanor's title like a keen blade, her anger seething just below her skin's surface.

"Agreed," Eleanor said.

"Good," was all Audrey replied, biting back the sharp remarks on her tongue regarding the strange eternal Eleanor chose to spend her time with while Tarian suffered at the hands of that wretched wizard. Her only comfort was knowing that he had Marcus protecting him.

The next day stretched painfully into night awaiting orders. With Tarian and Marcus gone, and Sasha and Josh dead, the gravitas infected every room, hall, closet in South Castle. So they drank wine and tried to carry on a sense of hope.

Christopher's glass landed hard on the table next to the box of ichor. The square of gold like a lurid centerpiece. "Lycott's alive and Sasha's dead. What kind of world are we living in?" Joe opened his mouth, but Christopher cut him off, "Don't give me any of your God's plan bullshit."

Audrey jabbed him under the table. He'd drunk too much wine. And she really needed to find a safe place to store that box of ichor.

"Okay. I'll simply say the Lord works in mysterious ways." Joe's positive words couldn't mask the terror eclipsing his face. He hadn't bothered with lenses, so his black eyes sunk hauntingly into their sockets.

Audrey rubbed Christopher's back. She felt just as miserable. The fact that Marcus hadn't been discovered when Marianne escaped was the only thing keeping her hopes up. Maybe he'd remained undetected. They were Guardians, the strongest ones at that. They'd survive. They would. They had to. She forced her chin up.

Christopher's face reddened then he raised his goblet. "Touché."

Everyone toasted.

"And to Maria." Christopher's voice rose, as did his wine glass.

"To Maria." Everyone toasted.

Maria rolled her eyes. "Thanks. It's great to be here instead of out there."

"What a blessing you ran into Germ," Lucianna said. "She mentioned you saved her from a street fight."

Maria nodded.

Audrey wondered why Sparkplug was being unusually quiet. "Have you heard from Gabe?"

"Yes, not too long ago. He wishes he was here," Maria said.

"Huh," Audrey huffed, now truly confused at Maria's dry demeanor. She studied her a little longer until Maria caught her and gave her the stink-eye.

Audrey looked to Jun for help, but the Xia Preta crossed her arms and scowled. Audrey's heart darkened despite the ray of hope she tried to force through it.

"We need him, all of them here. President Lloyd is an ass." Jun frowned then took a swig of the blood mixture in her wineglass. Jun had stormed into South Castle demanding answers the minute she'd heard of Tarian's capture. They'd bonded last autumn after being flushed through Rain's Gate, out of the Entente of Nations, and into banishment. Now, like the rest of them, she sat dwelling in drink, furious and helpless.

"The election is in four days. He promised troops at that time, win or lose," Audrey said. Four days was an eternity. How many would die in four days? Could Tarian survive four days? She couldn't wait that long. She'd figure out something. She doubted she'd stay in South Castle through the night, but she couldn't be rash. She couldn't help Tarian if she got caught or killed. And she truly did have faith in Marcus.

"What we need is for my sister to solve this puzzle, and now she's distraught over Marcus. When I left, she was babbling nonsense." Princess Lucianna ran a hand through her smoky locks.

Prince Theo laughed, "You left her with Marianne. No wonder."

Joe stood. "I'll relieve her. She needs rest."

"The exhausted leading the exhausted. Wonderful." Prince Theo snorted.

"Theo," Princess Lucianna scolded. She stood out of respect and smiled. "Thank you."

Joe nodded at the princess then gently patted Audrey's back before he left.

Everyone looked bone-weary.

"I think wine time is over," Audrey said. "We need our strength."

Audrey and Maria were the last to leave.

Audrey sighed loudly and shuffled to the door.

"What is it, Sergeant Gualtiero?" Maria asked. "You've been eyeballing me all night."

"You seem upset." Audrey would normally confront Maria head on, but with Tarian captured she just didn't have it in her.

"I'm fine," Maria said in a very *not fine* tone.

"Okay." Audrey strolled toward the exit. She knew she'd

lit the fire, and now she'd let the flames burn.

Maria threw up her hands. "I'm fine."

Audrey's hands splayed palms up in surrender. "I didn't say anything."

They strolled on in heavy silence.

"If anything, I should be asking you if you're fine," Maria said.

Audrey blinked back tears. "No, I'm not fine, but I've been doing this for hundreds of years, so I guess I'm accustomed. And Tarian is the strongest Guardian. With Marcus there too, I feel okay about their safety. It just sucks to be here not knowing what's going on over there."

"I get it. I'm sure that's how Gabe feels back home."

Audrey nodded and they ambled on in silence.

Maria turned the corner to her quarters then stopped. "How long will Germaine's parents be gone?"

Audrey twitched at the surprise change of topic. "I'm not sure."

"I think she needs them. She's just a teenager."

"Sure. I'll get them here immediately." Come to think of it, Audrey hadn't seen the little spy all day. Something must've happened in the city, something that would warrant Maria leaving her post. She'd gotten marks for abandoning but blew it off. Maria was a complicated hardass, but Audrey knew she respected the vow she took—honor, duty, Entente.

"Thanks." Maria bowed her head and plodded down the

hall.

Audrey stood dumbfounded. She walked to a window and peered out. The city forever trapped in a hazy gloom. The towers of North Castle peaked above the low fog. Some of the towers rose proud and magnificent while others were weak and frayed from the attack but still standing with honor as if to say, *You'll never beat me.*

"Or me," Audrey whispered, defying her fragmented spirit.

THIRTY-SIX

ENERGY DISTRICT — THE ENTENTE

EMA CADET GABE ORTEGA

Music roared from speakers. The thump of drums and rattle of maracas encouraged the toe tapping of the two families gathered in celebration. Songs sang from joyous lips. Gabe hadn't seen his family this happy in a long time.

Maria's brothers clapped as the women danced around them. Little Ava moved energetically not knowing the exact choreography, but she would. Every kid in the town knew the dances that had been passed down since the meteor hit. Their families had made this town. It wasn't much, but it birthed their heritage and customs.

Tonight's festivities sprung from Gabe's visit and proposition. He'd told Mike Lazaro of his intentions to marry Maria and asked for his blessing. Mike had given it and quickly gathered the families together in his home to celebrate. Then began the ritual meant to bestow good fortune upon the young couple.

The impromptu ceremony of food and dance lasted late

into the evening. Normally these celebrations were planned months in advance with the bride in attendance. Normally the girl to be wed wasn't beyond the border in a wasteland, and normally young peoples' futures seemed more solid. But lately, an urgency had settled in Gabe's bones. When the girl he loved had set off across the ocean, all certainties in their future thinned to a delicate layer of ice. If it was destined to shatter, then he needed to fulfill all of his desires now.

Gabe sat outside. The warm summer breeze carried the smoke that spiraled from his cigar.

Maria's eldest brother said, "I appreciate you following the old customs."

"Sure." Gabe puffed.

"No, I mean it. You've both gotten out of this place. You're Entente Elites. You didn't have to come here and get our blessings, but you did. That says a lot."

"I know it's what Maria would've wanted."

Carlos slapped a hand on his knee. "I'd love to see her face when you propose." He smiled, lost in childhood memories of his sister. "I'm so proud of her … and of you."

"Thanks man."

Carlos nodded. "It's true. I'm glad. I'm not sure what's gonna happen to this mine. Weird shit is goin' down."

"Like what?"

"Like horror movie stuff. Shadows that steal your mind. And Dad's really upset. Worried for his men. This wedding announcement is just what this family needs." Carlos puffed and his eyes glazed over.

Gabe had heard similar stories about something called the Pall over there in the Wastelands where his Maria was. He prayed every night for her safe return. The tone in Carlos' voice scared him. Just what had he seen? "Shadows, huh? Have you seen—"

"Boys! Get in here," Nadia ordered.

Carlos jumped to his feet at his mother's request. The opportunity to question him further lost. More wine poured from carafes, more music sounded from speakers. The family rejoiced in love, and no one dared mention the shadows under the ground.

Sonia Ortega beamed at her son. "I wish you could stay the night."

"Me too."

"You look well. So strong." A tear escaped into one of her wrinkled valleys.

Gabe swallowed his guilt. He hugged her. She trembled in his arms.

"Oh, mi príncipe." She sniffled and squeezed him. "We're so proud of you. So proud. You've given me something to look forward to. The wedding will be a delight."

When he pulled away, he saw her wide smile. She'd returned to his energetic, joyous Mom from his boyhood. The woman with big smiles and musical laughs. The mining town had sucked a lot of pleasure out of her, but he'd given it back. He held her hand for as long as he could, but it was late. He had to return to the EMA.

Gabe said his goodbyes then slid into the EMA issued vehicle and voice commanded, "Destination: Military District, Entente Military Academy."

The car drove away from the music and laughter into the darkness of the desert night. Shortly into the trip, the floor of the vehicle vibrated as if the ground beneath shook. Gabe glanced in the rearview mirror. A fiery eruption devoured the horizon behind him in bright orange flames against a midnight backdrop.

"Turn around," he voice commanded. The car turned and drove back toward the town he and Maria grew up in, toward the wall of fire.

Facing the force of the devastation, Gabe's heart stilled. The heat from the distant inferno warmed his closed windows. Oxygen eluded him, and for seconds he feared some strange, rare hazard with his car, a gas leak or something. He couldn't breathe. His eyes stung. His mouth parched. But it had nothing to do with his vehicle. Shock held him in its wicked clutches.

His brain refused to comprehend the placement of the blaze. It must be beyond the caves, maybe in the mountains. It couldn't be the cavern system mines or the small town that surrounded them. He'd just left there. Left his family. They were celebrating.

It couldn't be.

They were all alive and full of life. He'd sat at the dinner table with all four of her brothers. The food. The wine. The laughter. He'd kissed little Ava's soft youthful cheek. He'd hugged his mother.

Sorrow ballooned inside his chest until he burst out in sobs. He frantically wiped his face and forced sense into his mind.

It couldn't be.

"Drive faster!" he ordered the car.

It couldn't be.

But it was.

THIRTY-SEVEN

GUARDIAN VILLAGE

HEALER TERESA

At the Inn, Teresa shivered violently. She tucked herself tightly under her sheets but remained terrified. She'd slept alone and wished she'd stay the night with Patrick. Shudders detonated inside her. Her blood throbbed from the beat of her thundering heart. Her doe eyes stretched wider than usual and filled with tears.

The bedroom door cautiously opened. "Teresa?" her mom asked.

As Carolyn's shadow drew near, Teresa saw the worry crease her mother's forehead. She must've screamed but couldn't remember.

"What's wrong dear?" Carolyn flipped the switch that turned her bedside lamp on. A wave of shock rolled over her face. "My goodness honey, you've turned ghostly white. Is it Tarian?"

Teresa shook her head. "The cavern system's gone." Her voice sounded distant and cold, detached from the chaos coursing through her.

"Oh sweetheart." Carolyn gathered Teresa into her arms, squeezing tightly to stop the tremors.

"I failed. I saw it. If I'd only been a better seer. I missed the signs that I can see so clearly now." Tears rolled down her cheeks. Her mother's rocking embrace began to soothe. She stopped shaking. Her head cleared.

"Hope! Call the Appleton's. I'm sure she saw it too. She'll be terrified." Teresa jumped out of her bed then stumbled from lightheadedness.

THIRTY-EIGHT

SOUTH CASTLE — BALEFIRE CITY

IMMORTAL LAVENDER WITCH PIPER

Piper jolted out of bed, sweat pearling along her forehead. Instinctively, she checked the small bed next to hers. Nichola sat upright, big amethyst eyes staring ahead at nothing, one tear rolling down her face. Then she strolled to the window. Piper followed. They both gazed upon the ordinariness of the city and the extraordinariness of the Pall.

Nichola whispered, "Was it is real?"

"I think so." Piper inhaled deeply.

Nichola reached Piper's chest in height. She'd grown inches in only days. Was Nichola a child that could weave a growth spell? Piper feared so. Shivers of despair for the girl's discarded youth crept over her flesh like the soft touch of spider feet, while the horrifying dream vision haunted her blood. This was going to be a very bad day.

Piper let out a long sigh. "Well, let's get dressed. Eleanor will be arriving and once everyone learns of the explosion ..." she paused thinking inwardly, choking on sorrow. "Maria. She needs to know before the others. She must know first."

Nichola's face scrunched in confusion.

"If the cavern system exploded, Maria's family may be dead," Piper explained.

Nichola swiped the tear that had escaped and focused on it.

Eleanor looked more ragged than ever and yet remained poised as she walked into the castle.

Piper greeted her without pleasantries, waited a beat then cried out, "Why?"

Eleanor studied Piper's pleading eyes and Nichola's aggressive shimmer. She shook her head. "How do *you* know? *I* have not gotten confirmation yet."

Piper gasped and stumbled. "But you knew."

Eleanor reached out to steady her. "I knew there was a chance they'd do it."

"We dreamed it or felt it." Piper gestured to Nichola who nodded.

"Dhaumra told me they would vote on it. I left before I knew the verdict. Esurients Ryu and Yoshin must have plane walked the instant the yes votes were counted."

"Is it all destroyed?" Piper asked.

"Possibly."

"I don't understand." Piper rocked on her toes, sadness bursting inside her.

"It was a portal."

"What?"

Eleanor nodded. "Margaret confirmed it. I suspected when Audrey told me of the malditos disappearing for a long length of time then emerging with a container full of something."

"No," Piper said.

"I'm afraid so. I feared once the High Council informed the Esurients on the use of ichor in the Death and Waker serums that the action would be swift and strong."

"But why didn't they warn people? Thousands could be dead." Piper barely got the words out. Sobs clawed up her throat threatening to spew, but she swallowed her sorrow. Nichola held her hand and watched her closely. She couldn't fall apart.

"I cannot fully understand or explain the actions of the Esurients. I know it had to look like a natural disaster," Eleanor said without a hint of an apology. Too many years of explaining the actions of the Esurients hardened on her face.

Piper sighed and rocked more on her toes. The only thing keeping her steady was Nichola's grip. "Now it's gone. All of it." Piper shook her head. "What if we need it again? This is irresponsible. Rash."

"But in the wrong hands, in Lautaro's hands, it is our

downfall." Eleanor's attention turned to the girl. "Gregory Lycott is unaffected by the infested malditos. He's able to kill them. He's a powerful weapon. Do you understand?"

"Yes." Nichola's wide eyes looked up at the elegant Chancellor with an undeterred expression of stubbornness.

"Will you unbind yourself so we can kill the Grand Sorcerer?" Eleanor asked.

Nichola shook her head, her jaw clenched.

Eleanor swallowed, straightened, and dismissed the girl. "Very well then."

The exchange unnerved Piper. "I don't get it. The Esurients haven't intervened in mortal affairs for centuries. Why now?"

"This isn't a mortal problem. The Pall will either shade this planet or enlighten it. The shade will bring all evil creatures to power. The world will turn dark. And it will be a millennium before light can shine." Eleanor turned to Nichola. "You are the piece that will tip the scale. But you alone do not determine the direction in which it will slide."

Nichola nodded, but her expression remained indifferent.

"Please excuse me. I'm scheduled to meet with the queen. We need to get our Guardians back and tame this Pall." Eleanor didn't get far.

Maria darted in like a rabid fox. Face flush from tears, mouth foaming with rage, eyes fixed on the Chancellor. "Stop it! Rewind time or plane walk backward, whatever the fuck you do.

Do it!"

Piper rushed to intervene. Insulting the Chancellor was a crime that warranted an arrest.

Eleanor gently waved Piper at ease. "I understand. I've lost centuries of loved ones, but unfortunately, I cannot do what you ask. It was not my order. Whether you like it or not, Esurients have had a hand in mortal lives since the beginning of time. This may sound cruel, but your family died to save millions." Eleanor shut her eyes obviously remorseful. When she opened them, cold black coals bled through her green lenses and leveled solidly on Maria. "I'm sorry for your loss. I truly am." Eleanor pivoted and walked toward the queen's tower.

Maria staggered. Her shoulder slammed the wall. She slid down, pulled her knees into her chest, and screamed. The scream broke quickly. Tears welled in her eyes and choked her breaths.

Nichola grabbed Piper's hand and tugged. The child's eyes full of compassion.

Relief that Nichola wasn't a heartless monster after all surged in Piper's heart. The girl had been so malicious and uncooperative lately. Piper could barely sleep without nightmares and anxiety for Nichola's soul.

Nichola tugged harder.

Piper shook her head and pulled the girl away from Maria. "She doesn't want our sympathy. Not yet."

Confusion stole over Nichola's face.

"I know it's confusing. But it's too soon. Maria will need

us, and we'll be here for her. Right now, she needs to be angry at all of us."

Piper walked Nichola to the window. The sun rose beyond the clouds, although it didn't shine through, its warmth did. Piper encouraged Nichola to push her cheek against the glass and feel the light. "If you hurt for Maria then you know what you must do. Use the light. Feel the power of good."

Nichola turned away, all compassion gone, replaced with rancor.

"A heart that beats for one's own desires will easily go dark." Piper gently tucked the girl's golden hair behind her ear.

Their lavender eyes met. Mother to Daughter. Piper had been placating the young witch, but that ended now. She'd call to the Lavender Witch blood that coursed through her and strengthen their bond. She'd felt the fire, seen the explosion, envisioned a world without the warmth of the light, and it terrified her. She never wanted that dream to come true.

THIRTY-NINE

The guard's foot struck Tarian's stomach again. "And stay down!"

Tarian curled up on the cold, stone floor and watched the boots that had pummeled him step out of the cell. The door slid and locked in place.

"I'm preparing the cell next to you for your lovely Audrey. You can watch what I'm gonna do to her." The guard's laugh rumbled up from his bowels. "You'll wish you *could* die." The laugh echoed as the guard strolled away.

Tarian swallowed his rage and hugged his knees. He could've shot up to his feet, but he refused to be goaded into stupidity again by mere words. They'd send him into the arena soon, and he needed to conserve his energy.

A Marcus only Tarian could see whispered wisdom in his ear. "Don't be a fool. Let them talk. Who cares? You're on the ground like a slaughtered pig for what?"

Tarian grunted. He'd heard it over and over after each beating.

"For stupid pride. You gotta think kid. Here." Marcus shoved a plate full of red berries and hard-boiled eggs through the slot. Marcus had been delivering words of encouragement and sneaking in food that wasn't drugged over the last twenty-four hours.

Tarian slowly sat up and took in a deep breath ignoring the pain shooting up his back and through his ribs. Every muscle ached and throbbed. His regenerating cells worked overtime. It took a few seconds but finally he managed to stumble to the food and eat it. The meal brought clarity—reason began to overshadow his despair. Audrey was safe. She wasn't in this horrible dungeon, and he had to stop defending her honor just so they could weaken him for the true battle yet to come. He'd be in the arena soon and face a monster far more superior than that guard.

The anger built again. "When I'm free, that guard will pay. I'll make him regret every vile word. Every blow."

Marcus sighed. "Eat and rest."

Tarian launched the empty plate across the cell. It shattered. The noise loudly bounced off the stone walls. He waited for punishment, but no one came. Marcus still stood there shaking his head. He kicked the ground stirring the dirt.

Finally, a whisper cut through the dust clouds. "I'm gonna leave. Scout around for more answers."

Tarian nodded then hung his head in defeat. Marcus had

become his sounding board and too often, his punching bag. They'd already argued. Tarian wanted Marcus to go back to South Castle, be safe, work out a plan of attack with the others, protect Audrey, but Marcus refused. He'd do more for the cause remaining invisible and snooping around North Castle for answers. Maybe he was right but rotting away helpless inside a cell banished all sanity.

"Chin up."

Tarian straightened.

"And go lie down." Marcus' gruff voice traveled past the bars and shoved Tarian.

"I am." Tarian threw up his arms and shuffled to the pile of hay. He lay face up, hands behind his head and forced his eyelids shut.

Hours later, he awoke to the sound of boots shuffling.

"Marcus?"

The cell door scraped open, and the guard's voice hollered, "Let's go!"

They walked down a long, slopping corridor then a guard slapped his back.

Tarian tripped into the blinding light. His eyes eventually adjusted to the brightness. He blinked and backpedaled finding the wall and flattening against it. He glanced around the empty circular space.

He had no weapon, but the dirt floor was riddled with rocks. He focused, noting each stone that might prove a worthy weapon. Most were tiny, good only for a brief toss of distraction.

Some held enough weight that if thrown precisely could possibly blind an eye.

Tarian had been steeling his mind for a fight against Lycott, but he figured Lautaro would first send out a maldito, weaken him up. And that's exactly what he did do.

The maldito that stepped into the arena looked like the monster of a gruesome fairy tale. Long, straggly hair slicked back with grease that ran down its face in shiny tears. Eyes as dark as bull's shit and an extra-large bull-head to match. Scars and tattoos covered its naked arms and torso. It wore rugged boots and thick pants.

Tarian remained in his Guardian uniform, which was tough as well, but filthy. If the monstrosity could smell, maybe Tarian could knock it out with that. It wasn't just him that smelled. The stale stench of sweat, ripe order of vomit, and the copper tang of blood had been ground into the dirt and stone of this place. It was worse than any athletic locker room Tarian had ever been in.

The maldito charged first. Tarian stepped out of the way and let the beast crash into the stone behind him. The beast staggered just enough for Tarian to land a solid kick. The maldito stumbled but didn't fall. Once it regained its footing, it came at Tarian again. Tarian blocked a jab but missed the hook that landed square on his temple. White stars bloomed in his vision before he felt the all-too-familiar, gut-wrenching pain of a kick to the ribs. Blood and bile saturated his tongue. He choked.

Tarian didn't have time to regret his mistakes as two blades fell to the arena floor. The beast ran and snatched both blades. It sent one whistling through the air. Its point drove into Tarian's arm. The other one didn't follow.

Tarian ripped the blade from his tissue, warm blood slid down his bicep. "You should've kept this." He twirled the blade between his fingers mockingly.

A grin spread crookedly across the maldito's bullish head. Its lips remained tight, but Tarian assumed the teeth hidden behind them were sharp as knives.

"Man, you're ugly," Tarian said.

The beast came again with both speed and power. Slashing the blade in brutal, broad strokes. Razor sharp steel clashed. The beast had the strength of fifty. They sparred back and forth. Tarian got punched again, but this time he was prepared. He feigned weakness. Crouched. Then met its thrust with his own. His blade slipped deep between the monster's ribs, but the beast cocked a brow and seemed unfazed.

Another lunge from the maldito threw Tarian off balance. He lost his footing on the grains of sand and landed on his back. The maldito flew like a demonic night creature and landed on top of Tarian. Its gray dry lips curled back revealing what Tarian had already thought, extremely sharp, rotten teeth. The maldito bit into Tarian's shoulder, tore the flesh. Blood spilled and pooled from the deep gash.

The maldito raised his head and came down again, but Tarian rolled and jumped to his feet. His heart pounded. The air hit his exposed musculus fibers like tiny needles.

Tiny needles? His flesh stitched slowly back together. His mind raced back to Sasha's fight. Her bite hadn't healed.

He had no time to contemplate. He dodged the beast's blade and blows with elegance as if he'd skipped right past them. He turned and sliced the beast's back. Blood splattered on the stone and dirt. The maldito turned to find Tarian's strikes rain down continuously. Tarian sliced through its thick beastly flesh and shoved it back against the wall with a foot thrust to its torso. Tarian's blade stabbed through an eye socket. The beast howled in pain. Finally, he'd found the sweet spot. Tarian smashed its head against the stone until the beast fell limp at his feet. He shoved the blade through its heart and felt the pulse of its last beat.

Tarian backed away. It would be a bad idea to turn his back. He had seen what it had done to Sasha. But in the few areas where the beast had sunk its teeth, Tarian already felt the tingle of healing. He breathed heavily and swallowed thick saliva. His tongue dry and lips crusty. He needed water.

He stared up at the black windows. He couldn't see through the glass even with his immortal sight, but he knew they saw him. He grinned and stood tall. He marched to the dead maldito, went to grab him but a sharp pang shot up his arm stopping his reach. The initial blade wound refused to heal. He adjusted and utilized the unharmed arm. Tarian clasped the cursed creature's greasy hair and drug him in ritualistic, primitive circles.

"You cannot beat me!" Tarian's animalistic howl echoed around the arena.

FORTY

GUARDIAN VILLAGE — THE ENTENTE

HEALER TERESA

The headache persisted. Teresa knew Tarian was in trouble. The pain of the explosion still lingered in her veins and amplified her thoughts producing nightmares during the day. She couldn't close her eyes without seeing the agony slashed across her brother's face. She'd become almost useless which no doubt made her pain worse. She'd already prepped the infirmary and inspected it three times over.

"Where is he?" Her outburst caused others to glance her way. "Has anyone heard from Patrick? He should've been here by now."

No one answered. They just shook their heads and went about their business.

Teresa plopped into a chair. She rubbed her temples attempting to soothe the ache pounding inside her skull.

A hand touched her shoulder. She knew it and tilted into it. The back of Patrick's hand caressed her soft cheek. She looked up. The sight of him relieved some of her suffering.

Patrick stood with an older woman, younger man, and small child.

Teresa jumped to her feet. "Hello."

The survivors nodded. They wore a weary sadness on their faces. Ash dusted their hair and smudged their clothes.

"Teresa, this is Nadia Lazaro, her son Carlos, and her granddaughter Ava. Maria's family." Patrick turned his gaze from Teresa to Maria's only surviving family members and continued, "This is our best healer, Teresa Prescott."

Carlos held out his hand. Teresa took it. He gripped with determined strength. He was their rock. He'd be Teresa's go-to. She looked him square in the eyes and said, "I'll make sure Maria knows you're alive."

Nadia's breath hitched.

A small smile curled on Carlos' somber face. "Thank you."

"You'll stay at my mother's apartment," Teresa said.

Nadia shook her head.

"We don't want to impose," Carlos spoke for his mother.

"Nonsense." Teresa seized Nadia's hand. It took a moment, but the woman's eyes finally lifted to Teresa's. A jolt of torment pierced Teresa's mind, a flash headache, then it was gone. "I have a little sister. I think this will be best for your granddaughter."

Nadia swallowed then barely whispered, "Yes. Maybe she'd enjoy that."

Teresa had her purpose now, her mission.

Teresa had kept busy all day long and yet the headache remained.

"Are you still in pain?" Patrick asked.

"Is it obvious? I don't want the patients to think I'm ill."

"I'm not sure anyone else noticed, but I know you."

She smiled at the beautiful immortal she loved more than anything.

"I don't know too much about seers, but I think you're battling something that wants to come through."

Teresa sucked in a breath of air. "Of course! That makes sense. I'm fighting the vision when I should just embrace it." She paused as a wave of confusion washed through her like nausea. "But how? What do I do?"

"You rest. Relax your mind."

Teresa's shoulders fell.

"What is it sweetheart?"

She hated the torture apparent on his face. His deep concern drew wrinkles out of his smooth forehead. She ran her fingers across the lines. They disappeared.

"Maybe if I'd done that instead of running around thinking the world was coming to an end, then I could've predicted when and where the explosion was going to happen. We could've stopped the gas leak or whatever caused it."

"I don't think it exploded due to natural causes."

Teresa's doomsday fear spread again. Her first instinct was to kiss Patrick, to hug him so tightly and never let go, but she resisted. This time she exhaled, released the panic, and listened.

"I think this was the work of the Esurients and the High Council. There's nothing you could have done to stop them."

"Why?" Teresa's voice broke as she choked back tears.

"I can assure you they had good reason and the safety of the world in mind, but … well … no sense dwelling on things we can't change. Let's concentrate on what we can. You rest and let that marvelous brain of yours find truths, and I'll continue to work on the solution to our troop's illness. Deal?" He smiled wide.

"Deal," she said then kissed him.

Patrick brought her to an infirmary bed and tucked her in. "Rest here. I'll come back in an hour."

She opened her mouth, but Patrick placed a finger on her lips. "Shhh. The Lazaros are fine. I'll call your mom to check in, and the rest of the survivors are being tended to."

Just as he'd promised, one hour later he pulled back the magical barrier.

She'd just awoken. "You were right, relaxing my mind and accepting the visions worked."

"What did you see?"

"My brother rotting away in a dungeon and fighting a monster in an arena. There was a traitor, a cloaked figure, in there too. The treacherous person wore a cloak with the hood drawn up. All I could see were long, skinny fingers gripping two girls, one good and one bad." She shook her head. "I don't know these girls. I just felt their intentions. The traitor's hands squeezed as the girls tried desperately to get away."

"Was the traitor female or male?" Patrick asked.

"I don't know." She'd seen it all so clearly. Every part except the most important—the traitor's face. At least, she had more confidence. "I'll try again tonight."

Patrick pulled her into him. "You'll learn your craft. Just give it time."

She sunk into his embrace, fearing Tarian didn't have the luxury of time.

FORTY-ONE

SOUTH CASTLE TRAINING FIELDS — BALEFIRE CITY

GUARDIAN AUDREY

Sweat slicked Audrey's forehead. She breathed hard from the physical exertion. Maria's breaths came quick and shallow as well. A smile whispered across her face, barely a hint, but a smile, nonetheless. She had good reason not to smile. Audrey had glimpsed that same cautiously bitter smile when she told Maria the good news—her mother, her niece, and one of her brothers had survived the explosion. Maria didn't jump for joy, didn't ask to make contact with them. She'd just thanked Audrey and wanted to fight.

"That felt good," Audrey said between pants. They'd sparred for nearly two hours. "You've really improved, cadet." A mocking grin cocked her cheek.

"Thanks Sergeant Gualtiero. So, when do we get to go over there and kick ass?" Maria turned toward the north.

Audrey's heart sank. She didn't want to look north, think of her love trapped and tortured. Think of what Teresa had mentioned, a cloaked traitor. If not for the illness, she'd bring Tarian's sister over the seas to Balefire. Put her in closer proximity. Maybe it would open her mind's eye.

"Soon. Just waiting on weapons," Audrey said.

The hawk flew out of Brianna's tower window.

Maria's eyes shot skyward. "Is that …?"

Audrey nodded. "Joe's making an aerial assessment."

"Why doesn't he just fly into North Castle? Give us an update."

"How many birds have you seen around here?"

Maria's face dropped.

"He'd be spotted and captured before he got the chance to do anything. Besides Lautaro knows Joe can shift to a hawk's form. The element of surprise is gone. He could have snipers on watch."

"I need water." Maria waved her empty canteen then strolled to the water refill station that was set up mid field for all the trainees.

Audrey followed. As they walked in silence, Audrey's attention drifted to the many rows of sparring trainees, most too young and thin to wield a blade properly. Christopher and Lucianna stalked the rows assisting and advising them, their gladiator bodies enhancing the contrast of the youths' frailty. A little farther Ralph, Axon, and Jen led the Nerve Rebels in an exercise. They drilled with proper technique and strong form. A twinge of hope flickered in Audrey's heart, but she didn't dare encourage it.

She swallowed her misgivings. *It'll be enough. It has to be.* Her eyes floated back up to Brianna's lab then fell back to Maria whose stare trained on Germaine.

"It's too much. She's shaking. Her muscles are way past fatigue." Maria shook her head.

"Germ's been acting different since she returned. I tried to get her to play with Nichola, give Piper a break, but she refused without reason."

Maria's brow furrowed. Her eyes scrambled for something to look at besides Audrey or Germaine.

"What happened?"

Maria's eyes landed hard on Audrey's icy blues. "Cruel kids happened."

Audrey waited for more elaboration. None came. Her mind shuffled through reasons. "Regular city kids or one of Lautaro's?"

"All I know is if I hadn't happened to be stationed there, tasked to look for operational cells, she'd have been raped, maybe murdered. So no, these aren't regular city kids. At least, I hope not because if so, why in the hell are we bothering to save this place?"

Audrey's eyes returned to Germaine. Her sparring partner got the better of her and she fell, landing hard on her butt. She stayed down, bowed her head, and hyperventilated. The teenage boy reached out to help her up to continue their practice, but she smacked his hand away. He stepped back, allowing her the space to wobble back to her feet.

"Do you want to stop?" the boy asked.

"Yes," Maria answered for her. "Drink this." Maria put her canteen to Germaine's lips. Germaine gulped, but half of the water spilled. Germaine would need a dozen glasses to regain the energy she'd lost fighting in this humidity.

"You're tough. I enjoyed training with you. Maybe, I'll see you tomorrow." The boy smiled, nodded, and walked away.

This place wasn't unworthy. Plenty of decent people lived in the Wastelands, but there were a lot of vile nasty people too. Even so, Audrey's gut knotted with stubborn prognostication. Children as spies. Children as warriors. Children as criminals. These children were pawns. Who had placed cruel children in Germ's path? Who knew of her mission to get a message to Tarian? Who had Teresa seen in her vision?

She glanced around at the newer faces—the Nerve Rebels, the Royals. Could she truly trust them? She hadn't wanted to send Germ, but they'd insisted. Ralph and Princess Lucianna had eagerly offered her up. Audrey closed her eyes in an attempt to blackout the nag of betrayal.

Christopher waltzed around the troops, smiling and full of confidence. She recalled he'd also deemed Germ capable. She shook her head again, but the suspicion that coincidences were as rare as Maria's smiles determinedly clung to her thoughts.

Audrey insisted Maria tell her everything. With much coaxing, she finally relayed what Germaine had told her.

Audrey listened, her eyes glancing skyward then back

down to Maria. "Come on. I've got an idea."

Maria and Audrey awaited the hawk's return then sent him on another errand. After he returned with coordinates, the two soldiers left South Castle.

Audrey had a hunch that Germaine hadn't stumbled into one of her friend's tricks by accident. She'd been led there. Teresa's description of a cloaked figure holding two girls, one good and one bad, fit this narrative. It had to be related. Audrey just needed to find out how. The last thing she wanted was to interrogate Germaine and make her relive the horrific experience. Instead, she'd settle for the foggy vision of a seer and the secondhand information Maria had lent her, along with a little luck and a lot of fight. She could always count on Maria to seek revenge, especially now, when a good vendetta with a lot of bloodshed would be the perfect outlet for Maria's mournful rage.

FORTY-TWO

WEST TOWER — SOUTH CASTLE

NERVE SPY GERMAINE

Germaine scaled the west tower, directly opposite the east tower where she spent most of her time. The east belfry housed her bedchamber and Brianna's lab, but she wanted to gaze west toward home, toward the Wastelands.

She squinted as hard as she could, feeling the strain on her brow and cheeks, but she couldn't see her old streets or the tower she missed so much. She longed for her parents, and her eyes drifted around the landscape wondering where they'd been sent. Would she tell them she'd been kidnapped? Would she trouble her mom with the frightening details? Shudders traveled through her. She wrapped her arms around herself and imagined her mother's embrace.

From this height, she saw the labyrinth of Balefire and guessed at the spot where she'd been caught. With determined eyes, she searched for the hooded figure, the one who bargained for her torture. Revisiting that day made her head pound. She blamed Sam, and if she ever saw her again, she'd beat the shit out of her, but the stranger put Sam up to it. Of that, she was sure. Sam was too much of a coward to concoct any plan on her own. Her eyes closed allowing her mind to remember the face hidden under the hood's shadow. She hadn't seen it that day, and she couldn't conjure it now.

Frustrated she leaned against the cool stone letting her feet dangle. She'd climbed high but not as high as when she scaled the tower, but she sat above the trees. She missed her tower. She didn't know why. It was full of Blue addicts and homeless kids looking for a score. Here she had everything she could ever want—good food, cozy bed, Princess Lucianna befriended her, chocolate, and a library.

A library! Her head glanced back again so she could peer into the window. She thought she'd hallucinated, but the room was there past the glass. Books stacked high on shelves. Tons and tons of them. She hadn't realized west tower housed a library.

Three people gathered around a table reading and laughing. Her heart ached. A girl with spectacles she'd never seen before sat next to the boy from the kitchen.

"Christian." His name popped into her head then her mouth began to water at the thought of chocolate chip cookies. She searched the table for a plate but saw only books, paper, and colored pencils.

A boy with his back to Germaine sat at the table too.

Every once in a while, the girl looked up from her book at him. He made her laugh. Something tugged at Germaine's heart again. Then the boy turned around and stared straight at her. It was the boy from field training, the one that out skilled her. His face widened in shock at the sight of her—a girl perched ten stories above the ground. Fear and guilt fell like a stone to the pit of her stomach. She hadn't meant to spy.

He marched over and opened the window.

"I ... I ... I'm sorry."

He shook his head. His eyebrows knitted together. His hands wrapped around her wrists, and he pulled her inside.

Germaine opened her mouth to apologize again but seeing all the faces staring at her she fell silent. Her stomach groaned with disgrace.

"Are you okay? What happened?" the boy from training asked.

Her breath hitched in surprise. "You're not mad?"

"Mad?" He shrugged. "Germaine, how in the world did you get up here? I thought I was going crazy. I thought one of the giant ravens I've been reading about suddenly came to life." He laughed.

"Elijah, who is this?" the girl with the brown shaded gray skin asked. Her complexion wasn't the magnificent bronze of Maria's skin, but enough to add life to the typical Wasteland skin, and Germaine envied her for it.

Elijah turned to face his friends. "This is Germaine."

"Germ." Her head fell then jerked back up. She didn't know what had come over her. Why did these kids make her feel as if she was on display, a specimen to be judged? "Everyone calls me Germ."

"Well that's horrible." The girl pushed her spectacles back up the bridge of her nose.

"What's your name?" Germaine asked curtly.

"Teodora, and no one calls me Teo or Dora."

Germaine huffed. "Well, I have a purpose."

"Oh yeah. What's that?" Teodora's steel gray eyes cut into her.

Germaine swallowed her answer. She'd always been proud to be a spy for the rebels, but she feared they'd judge her harshly.

"She's a spy for the rebels," Elijah said with a huge smile. He turned eyes all a glow at her.

"Are you?" Teodora asked as if she didn't believe her friend, but she seemed almost as impressed as Elijah.

"Yes." Germaine answered in a tone without bias and studied their reactions. They all smiled and leaned in. Her heart filled with joy and relief. She nodded. "I'm good at climbing. I love to be up high. It's peaceful."

"I imagine it is. That's why we come in here." Teodora leaned back in her chair as if to encompass the entirety of the library in one slight movement.

"I love books. I had no idea there was a library," Germaine said.

"You can help us." Elijah took her hand and lead her over to the table.

"Quinrella arrived with the children, thank the Pall, but all the children's books are in North Castle," Teodora said.

Christian shook his head. "It was destroyed."

Teodora sighed. "That's right. I forgot."

"Who's Quinrella?" Germaine asked.

"She looks after the orphans, and she's our teacher," Christian said.

"A teacher." Hope bloomed in Germaine's heart.

Christian nodded. "Yes, she schools us on math and science. Well, she used to. I assume she'll resume now that she's back."

Math and science were precisely what Germaine wanted to learn about. Shivers of delight ran over her skin. She wondered if they had the proper materials.

Christian grunted. "If we're not sent to war."

Gloom settled over the table. Teodora adjusted her glasses again. Elijah shifted his weight. No one spoke for a minute or two.

"Anyway, we're searching for anything a young child might find interesting. So far we've come up short so we're making books," Teodora explained.

"Really? That sounds fun." Germaine's stomach fluttered as if her mother's fingers tickled her. Loads of colored pencils scattered the table or stood bundled in a cup ready to be plucked and used.

Teodora smiled. "Terrific, Germaine. Think of a story and start drawing it up."

Christian passed her a stack of papers.

Elijah pulled out the chair next to his and motioned for her to sit down. She did and he scooted close to her. The gentle nudge tugged at her heart yet again, but it didn't frighten her. She knew she'd found her place and this time it wasn't among thieves.

FORTY-THREE

BRIANNA'S LAB — SOUTH CASTLE

IMMORTAL LAVENDER WITCH PIPER

The door to Piper's and Nichola's room flung open. Piper leaped
for Nichola and gathered her into her arms' protection. Every
sinew in Piper's body clenched until she realized it was Eleanor.

"Goodness, Chancellor. You terrified me."

Characteristically Eleanor, she didn't offer an apology. She
delved into a tirade. "Henry refuses to send troops. I practically
groveled, and all he'd commit was weaponry." She shook her head.
Disgust creased her forehead.

Piper dizzied following Eleanor's pacing steps with her
eyes.

"I warned Dhaumra. I knew this would become a
problem." Eleanor continued pacing. Her eyes darted as if in her
mind the conversation went on. Anger close to madness wrinkled
her normally placid demeanor.

Piper squeezed Nichola tighter. Eleanor's erratic behavior
was out of character. Piper feared her next move.

"Tragedies only unite the mortals and prejudice them. Henry can't risk the election. Not now. When every man, woman, and child is rallying around the cavern system. They need all the help they can get. If he sent soldiers over to the Wastelands, the nation would revolt. It'd be political suicide. I understand. His hands are tied. Not to mention the mysterious infection the homecoming soldiers are contracting and bringing back with them."

Eleanor stopped pacing, which frightened Piper even more.

"Weapons are good. I appreciate them. I would have liked more aircrafts but we have one. The advanced firepower should successfully take out North Castle and retrieve Tarian and Marcus. Then what?" She threw up her hands. "We still have the Pall." At that point, she pivoted, stepped toward them and stabbed a syringe into Nichola's shoulder. "You understand." Eleanor's eyes had returned to calm emerald orbs and looked deeply into Piper's.

Piper shook her head. She didn't understand. For a brief second, her heart stopped beating, fearing the worst then she realized it was the same sedative Audrey had used days ago. Before Piper could ask questions, Eleanor scooped the girl up and waltzed her up the tower stairs to Brianna's lab.

Piper scurried behind them. "What are you going to do with her?"

"Find her power." Eleanor scaled the stairs at vampire speed. She laid Nichola on the couch where she swabbed the inside of her cheek, cut some of her hair, and pricked her finger. She took the samples over to Brianna.

Piper remained left behind and furious, and that fury almost manifested into witch wind, but she stifled the rage. Carefully, she inhaled and exhaled controlled breaths that cooled her temper. She convinced herself Eleanor's intentions were good, although her methods questionable. Everyone was burdened with heavy stress. Piper sat down, rested Nichola's head in her lap and tried not to fall apart.

Piper sat as still as her tranquilized daughter, watching the two women work. The older, more experienced immortal was a classic beauty, but her brown hair was untidier than Piper had ever seen it. Her Chancellor's eyes were as fierce and determined as ever. Drops of blood dotted her lips as she bit them in frenzied concentration.

The youthful princess witch was neither a fierce bombshell like Lucianna or a traditional refined beauty like Marianne. In fact, as Piper inspected her, she was really quite average, and yet, she seemed the prettiest of the three Sanna sisters. Piper's eye traced a blue-black streak that wove through Brianna's ashen gray hair noticing it had dulled. Stress had stolen its shine.

Eleanor was flustered, but Brianna was downright manic. Piper had to look away. Watching them suffer failure after failure would only thrust Piper into the same state of delirium.

I must stay calm and strong for Nichola. Heck! For all of us.

Piper's stare locked on the shelves. Her eyes roamed the

titles, savoring the intricate foiling and sturdy bindings of the antique books. She admired the shelves entirety—the books, the glassware, a couple outdated microscopes, and loads of different textured ingredients in a spectrum of colors. All neatly arranged and ordered just like Piper's stacks in the village library. But out of all the fascinating things, the voluminous grimoire with its tobacco brown, stag hide leather called to her.

Piper shook off the sensation and returned her attention back to the two women.

Eleanor and Brianna peered into microscopes and circled the long tables studying their array of flasks and beakers. Some boiled, others misted. Vapors coiled like wicked serpents through the air. A hood covered one of the experiments, and there'd already been two explosions, luckily properly contained.

Piper twitched at the memory. She sighed, content to sit far away and observe.

Eleanor left the table of glassware and trudged to the stand that held the grimoire. She removed her gloves and gently turned its pages, her eyes skimming the words. Her fingers stroked the hinge then abruptly stilled.

"That's what I was telling you about. Marcus is sure they've been taken for a reason, and he believes it's the missing key to this solution." Princess Brianna shook her head. "I just can't imagine it. Those pages have always been gone."

"How close were you to your grandmum?"

"Close." The single word struck like a dart to a bullseye.

"Then she wouldn't have handed over her most prized possession to the witch she believed could yield its secrets and not have explained the missing pages."

Brianna took off her gloves and drew her arms around herself.

Curiosity got the better of Piper. She could no longer ignore the pull of that book. She reluctantly left Nichola and crossed the threshold that divided the sitting room from the lab. "Do you mind if I have a look?" Piper hovered over the grimoire.

"Please do," Brianna said.

The velvet soft pages hummed under Piper's fingers.

"You feel it, don't you?" Brianna's eyes opened wide.

Eleanor's forehead creased with puzzlement.

Piper nodded.

Brianna huddled next to Piper, obviously excited to share the experience. "There's a lot about a horse, an amethyst, and a schorl throughout the volume, and just before the missing pages it mentions a shield, and I've heard schorl referred to before as a psychic shield. Here read this page and tell me what comes to you."

Piper held the page that came before the missing grouping. There were only four sentences written in large scrolling script. "In fog and mist there is a gift guarded by a fire dragon. You'll need the talisman and the shield. Violet et Noir. One cannot fare less the other."

"Schorl is black tourmaline. The stone has electrical and magnetic properties. It has also been thought to deflect negative energies," Eleanor said.

"Or ground them." Brianna's eyebrows lifted.

"A psychic shield to ground the negative entities." Piper bounced as conviction effervesced through her veins, blood cells pin-balling throughout her. "A shield. That's it. If Nichola is the key to the Pall, she needs a shield."

"I'm hungry," Nichola's groggy voice crossed the room.

Piper's stomach growled in answer. She bid Eleanor and Brianna goodbye. With Nichola in hand she descended the many tower stairs then ventured into the kitchen. They found Germaine in the kitchen as well, talking and laughing with three other teenagers.

"Germaine!" Nichola charged straight into Germaine's arms.

Warmth eclipsed Piper as she watched Germaine take Nichola by the hand and lead her over to the others. Chocolate chip morsels spilled from the ripped opening of a bag. One of the boys tossed a chip at Germaine. His eyes sparked when she caught it in her mouth and grinned.

"Your turn," Germaine said to Nichola.

"Okay." Nichola shimmered with joy. If the other kids noticed they didn't let on. Nichola missed the first toss but caught the next. "I did it!" She beamed.

Piper's heart crowded with hope, but her mind brimmed with questions. *What or who was the shield?*

"Guess where we've been?" Germaine asked Nichola.

The little witch shook her head.

"In a library."

"A library!" Piper snapped. She'd been half listening and half lost in her own thoughts. "Where is it?"

"In the west tower," Germaine said.

"That's fantastic." Piper smiled. Maybe she'd get a chance to look around, hunt for answers. If nothing else, she just wanted to inhale the wonderful musky smell of paper and old leather.

FORTY-FOUR

NORTH CASTLE — BALEFIRE CITY

GUARDIAN MARCUS

As maldito guards trampled the ancient rugs and wooden floors Marcus floated through Eminence Castle a ghost. In transparent form, he still had mass so if someone should get too close, they'd feel the point of a sword. He'd poke them just enough to prompt a shift as if an annoying insect had just stung then he would slide past unnoticed. He made no sound, but on some surfaces, his hefty footprints resulted in indentations. Trampling through mud or snow never worked out well. Luckily, on worn thin rugs and wooden floors he left no trace.

He'd been gone too long. He'd promised to return in time for Lycott's fight. Although, he wasn't sure it mattered, as he hadn't been able to slip through the gate and into the arena to assist Tarian in the first battle. The gates were too fast and narrow.

Unlike Tarian, he was free and needed to search for information—plans, escape routes, Pall data, anything to stop Lautaro. At the moment, worry and guilt had no place in his mind.

He clenched his jaw and narrowed his eyes, forcing clarity and resolve to take over and guide him onward.

After finding nothing of any significance, he snuck into the makeshift infirmary. Lautaro employed a well-equipped and manned sickbay. Marcus hovered around a grotesque old witch rubbing a foul-smelling ointment on a guard's stab wound. She capped the ointment container and set it on the counter. Marcus swiped it and tiptoed out of the room.

The trick would be getting the container back to Tarian. His weapon and the special guardian uniform he wore were designed to detect the change in his cells and vanish with him, but a glass jar didn't have the same nanotechnology. Mostly he held the container high above his head, and it worked since he was significantly taller than the many that walked past. On occasion, he'd had to pause, set it on a table, ledge, or windowsill and pray no one realized its misplacement and grabbed it.

Carefully, he managed his way back to Tarian. "Here mate." A square container jetted into Tarian's unit.

Tarian snatched it before a guard noticed the floating box. "What's this?" He unscrewed the lid and gagged. "That's awful."

"Rub it on the blade wound. It's still not healing, right?"

"No. And I don't get it."

"Yeah, that's strange."

Tarian rubbed the ointment over his open wound. "Wow. It's tingling. I assume that's a good thing. It feels better anyway."

"Good."

"Listen don't stay here wasting time with me. Go find out something useful or go get help."

"No need to go get help. They know where we are. They'll send for us as soon as they can. Right now, I need to keep you alive."

Tarian scoffed. "I'm fine. I heard them say something about Lycott not being fit to fight. So I think I have some time. Have you found him yet?"

"No, I haven't found him. It's a big castle."

"Half of it is destroyed."

"Well, it's an enormous half." Marcus grunted. "I'm goin' now."

"Okay. Don't worry about me." Tarian blew out a mouthful of frustrated air.

Marcus made no comment. He was worried, extremely worried. He liked Tarian, and more so, he loved Audrey like a sister. It'd break her heart to lose Tarian. And Joe. His stomach dropped and flipped about ten times. He had to find Lycott.

Lycott could be imprisoned behind any of the several locked doors Marcus had pulled on. But he stumbled into a dark room full of books and leather chairs—a study that hadn't been used recently. Marcus had already scoured the bedchamber, but as he'd suspected, Lautaro wiped it clean after finding Tarian in his closet. But this room was a new treasure. Had Lautaro moved all his prized possessions here?

Marcus took note of the layout in case someone decided to

join him. Only one door leading in and out made for a less than ideal escape. He sighed and went about opening drawers and shuffling through pages, until he came across a page that seemed familiar. He'd felt that velvety texture before. He tugged gently. The pages were old and fragile. One edge frayed. The first page numbered four hundred and ninety. He flipped—four hundred ninety-one, ninety-two, ninety-three, ninety-four, and ninety-five.

He stared at the discovery. Thrilling shivers rolled over his thick skin. Whether these pages held the answers to unlocking the Pall or not, Brianna would be ecstatic to have them back. But for as much as he wanted to return the pages, he couldn't sneak away and leave Tarian.

People gathered and spoke just outside the door. He tucked the pages under his uniform snug against his chest and waited. The voices moved on, and so did he. He found the tower he'd ascended with Brianna the night he rescued her. He opened the door Brianna had opened and stepped into the stairwell he'd carried her up, but there was no up. The entire tower had been demolished. Crumbled stone piled high to an open sky. The bedroom he'd only glimpsed that evening—gone. A sudden emptiness overtook him. He would've loved to see her room, roamed around, read her books, felt the softness of her pillows. What color had she painted the walls? A childhood blown away by a mad man. He looked to the open sky and thought of Piper. *She could vade here, couldn't she? Lautaro couldn't spell this, could he?*

It was irrelevant and he had to get his head back in the

game. He patted his chest reassuring his senses the pages were still there. Safe and sound. He had to get back and check on Tarian.

He strolled along the empty corridor less worried than before now that he'd found something useful. He passed a leg of the castle that had aroused suspicion earlier when he hadn't had time to investigate. It was dark and vacant. He slipped into the shadows as the hallway rolled downward in a steep descent. No stairs just a sharp decline. Wicked paintings of old royals lined the hall. He recognized a few and flinched. They'd scared him in life centuries ago and still now with those evil eyes trailing his movement as if he wasn't invisible.

A woman's voice cut in whispered ribbons through the darkness. Marcus halted. He snapped back to the pictures on the wall. Ghosts? Were they speaking to him?

He shook his head. *No! Nonsense.*

And it was nonsense. The voice belonged to a real person. Another voice spoke. It was deeper. A masculine tone. Marcus stalked closer until he reached the sources.

Jen stood in front of one of Lautaro's Maldito Apostólos holding a bayonet with an engraved brass hilt. She held it with caution. At first, Marcus assumed Jen's wariness was due to its delicate beauty, but on further notice he concluded she feared touching the steel. *Why?* Her eyes opened wide and wild, fear burning in them. The strange transaction drew Marcus' scrutiny.

The Apostólo wore gloves and sheathed the bayonet attentively.

Marcus listened harder.

"This one is more potent?" the Apostólo asked.

"Yes. Tell Lautaro this is the strongest," she said.

The Apostólo grunted, secured the sheathed sword to his belt, and walked away.

Marcus flushed hot. So hot he worried a red aura encircled his invisible body. But the Maldito Apostólo left, and Jen's shoulders relaxed, undoubtedly relieved to be rid of that hideous creature and none the wiser of Marcus' presence.

Jen slinked off and Marcus followed. She turned west at the spot where he would've turned east to return to Tarian. His mind split. Follow Jen or go warn Tarian of the poisoned blade.

He followed her. She led him straight to Franny. They vaded before he had the chance to confront them.

Marcus reached Tarian's cell too late. He was passed out on the abhorrent hay pile.

"Psst." Nothing. "Psst." Still nothing. "Tarian!" Marcus whispered louder to no avail. Drool leaked from his friend's lips and his chest heaved. A loud exhausted sigh escaped Marcus, "They drugged him."

Marcus paced in front of the prison bars. Up and down. Down and up. He'd raked his blonde curls a million times. He'd bitten his lips and tasted blood. Ultimately, he had to rely on Tarian's savvy ability to fight and live. He was the strongest Guardian of Dare. He'd survive. He must. Marcus wouldn't let his mind think otherwise.

Marcus had to leave. He had to get this intel to Eleanor as soon as possible. He made a last attempt to rouse Tarian, but all he got in return were snores.

"Good luck friend." Marcus bounded out of dungeons up to the main level and rushed out into the night. He ran on rage and revenge. Lavender Witches were a horrible, racist bunch. The only trustworthy one was Piper. And Jen. The burn of hatred for this traitor made his blood boil. As soon as he got the chance, he'd rip her head from her body.

FORTY-FIVE

SOUTH CASTLE — BALEFIRE CITY

GUARDIAN AUDREY

Audrey and Maria skirted around town on scooters. The city was littered with them, but they were slow. Nothing like the hoverbikes back home. Audrey wished she had the sleek titanium death rocket, but instead, she'd settled for a scooter that had been tinkered with to achieve the great speed of forty-five miles-per-hour. At least that was ten-miles-an-hour faster than anyone else's.

I might as well be riding a turtle.

Maria matched her thought. "This piece of shit is slow."

Audrey grinned.

They whipped around their target building, which luckily stood south of the line. Earlier a skinny girl with short hair had parked her scooter and entered the facility. This information was gathered by the hawk.

"There." Maria pointed at the cherry red motorbike. It stuck out like a firefly against a midnight sky.

The place was some sort of hotel or hostel or rehab center.

Audrey and Maria waded through a room full of young adults hanging around. Some spent their time with purpose either reading or playing games, others stared blankly as if lost. Audrey guessed they were homeless—the abandoned children of the Wastelands. A stout woman called out a name. A girl, maybe fifteen, walked up to her then sat. The woman took notes, then measured and weighed her. This was some sort of recruitment center to place the homeless children either in a job or on the battlefield.

Audrey's head whipped around. Standing room only. How many orphaned children lived in the city? But no one matched the description of the girl they searched for.

Maria ventured down a hallway and Audrey followed. The girl they were looking for lay in a crumpled heap at the end of the hall. All of the fury Audrey had prepared to heave upon this treacherous teenager faded suddenly. The pitiful sight of her frail body broke Audrey's resolve. Sam was dead. By the looks of it, she'd overdosed on Blue.

Audrey kicked the wall. This traitor was clever and ruthless, and Audrey had almost had them. She knew she was right. Sam and Germaine had to be the two girls in Teresa's vision. They had to be. She couldn't remain a step behind.

Maria sniffled then rubbed her nose. Crippling pain hollowed her eye sockets. She looked as exhausted as Audrey felt. They'd set out on a victory journey of revenge and blame and come up short.

"She was a pawn." Audrey shook her head. "I'm sure the

cloaked figure Germ told you about sold her the Blue. It was either poisoned or she'd been given so much and the temptation to feel nothing was too great. Either way, Sam can't tell us who the person is now."

Maria stared at Sam's body for seconds before speaking. "I'd read about drugs like this. We were taught in school about how awful drug addiction had been years ago, but this, those books didn't do the horror justice. Her veins." Maria lifted Sam's wrist. Sapphire lines snaked and webbed up and around the whole of her arm like a tattoo. A blue liquid dripped from the corner of her mouth. Her eyes stared at nothing. Blue bled from her gray irises like watery ink.

Audrey remembered the Bar District. The enchanted little vials that floated down from the starry sky of Hu's and Jun's nightclub. A drug that filled partygoers with glee, delighted them with confidence, and allowed them to be seduced by vampires. Drugs hadn't entirely left the Entente, but they'd become rare after the war and reconstruction.

"Let's go. We'll tell the lady at the front. I'm sure Sam's not the first kid to OD in this place," Audrey said.

Maria wiped another tear from her cheek, and Audrey regretted the flatness of her voice. Maria was a human with armor as thick as rhinoceros' skin that kept her emotions in check, but with the recent loss of most of her family, those plates of armor began to flake away leaving her humanity exposed. Audrey almost wished for the sting of tears, but it'd been a long time since she'd shed actual tears for a stranger. Her heart hardened with each year that she lived as an immortal among humans. She used to think of herself as a human. She wondered when she'd stopped. Watching empathic sadness morph Maria's face, wet her brown eyes, steel the pink from her lips, made it crystal clear she'd crossed a plain somewhere in her long life. One she wished she hadn't.

On their return to South Castle, they met up with Marcus. He rushed from the woods. Alone. Audrey's heart stopped beating for a second. She both hated and welcomed the despair, happy to feel human again, but not at the bargain of Tarian's life. Once she read the look of sorrow in Marcus' eyes, she wanted her numbness back.

"What? Where's Tarian." Audrey braced her mind for bad news, but she didn't have enough inner steel to protect her heart.

"He's still there. In a cell. But he's alive." Marcus pulled the papers out from under his suit. "I found these."

"The missing grimoire pages?" Audrey asked.

"Yes, and I saw Jen …" Marcus continued recapping all he'd witnessed.

Hot, rageful blood flooded Audrey's chambers with each word Marcus spoke. Her heart's rapid pumps brewed a relentless tornado inside her.

With the cloaked traitor no longer a mystery, Audrey gave orders, "Maria, find Germ and stay with her at all times. Marcus, bring the pages to Brianna. Get Eleanor to look at them as well. And one of you get a message to Teresa. Tell her what you've discovered. It'll set her mind at ease."

Maria and Marcus nodded in unison as Audrey stormed away to retrieve Christopher and Lucianna. She had to get to the bottom of this betrayal before the weapons arrived and the fighting began.

Audrey pinned Axon and Ralph against the wall. She'd suspected they were lovers and found them when they were most vulnerable. Each of her slender hands wrapped around their necks, squeezing with the fervor of ten immortals. Her short stature didn't curtail her high reach and both men rose on their toes to prevent choking.

Christopher and Lucianna scoured the room leaving no drawer unopened or pocket unchecked. They found nothing linking them to Jen's or Franny's treacherous behavior.

"They're clean," Christopher said.

"Where's Jen and Franny?" Audrey growled, her stare as hard and cold as a diamond of ice.

"Here! In their rooms?" Axon was clearly confused.

Audrey released them. They dropped, knees buckling.

"What is this? Just barge in here and accuse us of … of … what? What have Jen and Franny done?" Ralph rubbed his swollen throat as fire glared from his gray-wolf eyes.

"Yes, this is uncalled for. We are working *with* you!" Axon placed an arm around the younger man. "Are you okay?"

Ralph nodded.

The pit in Audrey's stomach grew—solid and suffocating. She'd acted out of spite. The two men that stared back at her were honorable and she'd disrespected them. Shudders of shame trampled over her.

"I'm sorry. You're right." Her fingers dug into her scalp as she paced. "Marcus has returned. Tarian's still imprisoned over there. The fights in the arena—"

"How'd you come to work with a Lavender Witch?" Christopher asked.

"Franny came with your Senator," Axon said.

Ralph turned to Lucianna. "She knows your family well."

"Yes, long ago," Lucianna said.

"And Jen came after?" Audrey asked.

"Yes, after the Senator got half our rebels killed. We realized our mistake. He tried to make us a militia. We're not."

"Franny actually warned us not to trust him. I can't imagine her a traitor." Ralph looked to Audrey as he wove his fingers through Axon's.

"Why not? She betrayed the man that brought her to you. She's been working with Lautaro this entire time." Audrey shook her head disgusted at her own stupidity. How could she have been so naïve? Lautaro's tentacles reached and wound further than she'd thought.

"What's your proof?" Axon asked.

"Right now, two things. My gut, and Marcus saw her inside North Castle with Jen poisoning blades to kill Tarian."

Axon gritted his teeth.

"Why?" Ralph's eyes narrowed.

"Lautaro and the Lavender Witches have been working together for many, many years. My guess is she was just spying. He needed to keep an eye on the Nerve. Make sure you all didn't pose a threat. She was probably spying on Zachary too. Keeping Lautaro abreast of that fiasco. Lautaro's no fool."

"She befriended grandmum decades ago. We trusted her," Lucianna said.

"This has been a long, thought-out plan." Audrey said. "I'm not sure which came first, her friendship with your grandmother or her partnership with Lautaro."

"And Jen? What's her gain?" Axon asked.

"Money. I'd guess. Maybe he's promised her a place in his new regime," Audrey snarled. "Or maybe some kind of revenge. She despised Tarian from the first."

"We have a limited number of fighters. We need to know who we can trust." Lucianna fidgeted, apparently done with the small talk.

"You have my word. You can trust us. We have nothing to do with Jen's or Franny's betrayal." Axon raised their joined hands in a gesture on conformity.

"I'm glad to hear that. Unfortunately, I can't trust people's word. Those that will be assigned an Entente weapon will first undergo questioning under truth serum. I hope you understand." Audrey never looked away, she never wavered, her fiancé's life depended on her strength.

"I completely understand," Axon said.

Ralph glared. His face still, lips pressed together.

Christopher stared deeply at them. "Get dressed and ready. Gather your rebels. Meet in the training field in an hour. We're expecting the weapons today. Once they arrive, those that pass the truth test will need to be trained to operate them. Then we charge the line, bring Tarian home, and destroy Lautaro."

"Truth serums aren't fool proof," Ralph said.

"I know, but I can tell a lot about a person when I interrogate them," Audrey paused, "I believe you'd do the same for your loved one."

Ralph nodded.

Axon sighed. "We're here to save our homeland. There should be no doubt when we go raid the North Castle."

Audrey studied the two men. She liked them. She'd liked them from the first day she'd met them. She desperately wanted to trust them. In her bones, she did and hated herself for the invasion of privacy she'd thrust upon them, but Tarian's life hung in the middle. She had to be certain. She couldn't arm traitors with lethal weapons.

FORTY-SIX

BRIANNA'S LAB — SOUTH CASTLE

IMMORTAL LAVENDER WITCH PIPER

The pages practically glowed as Piper read them aloud. "Prophecy 713—The Shadow veil falls on mortal kind. Unbound particles flow. Untamed dark magic reborn. Fire and spark. A deathly void. Thrice the world will have collapsed. From ashes cometh city. The sphere will grow. She will grow as well. Babe to young lady. Unnatural transition. He fades, death comes slow. The great horse is not to be trusted. The horse longs to seize her, use him, and master the sphere of smoke. Darkness will spread. Esurient rule will end. Listen to the children. Listen to the never dying. Or be governed by the Terrible Horse for centuries."

Piper looked up from the page, understanding racing through her like hot lava.

Brianna's head tilted. "You know what it means?"

"I think so."

"Please explain your thoughts." Eleanor's face appeared pensive with her own ideas.

"Well, we know the shadow veil … particles … deathly void, that's all the Pall."

Brianna and Eleanor nodded.

"The horse is Lautaro." Piper stared at Eleanor for confirmation. "He shapeshifts into a giant, fire-casting horse."

"What?" Brianna shook her head. "All this time, I've been searching for a hint to his grand wizarding powers. A horse?"

"And the babe to young lady is obviously Nichola. The *he* referred to may be Lycott but that's questionable. And listen to the children. Well, that's Hope, maybe Teresa too. I'm sure of it."

"Who's Hope?" Brianna asked.

"A young girl back home that now has visions after being attacked by a Waker."

Brianna's eyebrows lifted. "Marcus told me about those."

"Hope told me about Nichola and Lycott before I'd even met them. And she said they had to stay together till the very end. If we're to follow the grimoire's instructions, then Nichola needs to be with Lycott. Somehow, they need to go into the Pall together. He's the shield remember?"

Eleanor pointed to the words in the prophecy—*He fades, death comes slow.* She flipped to the next page and pointed—*Death takes one.* Eleanor's eyes drifted to Nichola.

Piper understood.

Nichola looked up to see them all staring at her. "What?"

"Oh, just good news. We should have this all solved soon," Piper said.

Nichola smiled then fell back onto the sofa. "I'm bored. You said Dad would be back soon."

"He will." The lie stung like hornets on Piper's tongue.

"Should we mix the ingredients?" Brianna asked.

"Yes," Eleanor said.

Brianna dashed to her cabinet.

Piper read off the list of items as Brianna took them from the shelf. "… And an amethyst crystal."

"I have one." Eleanor pulled a brilliant amethyst amulet from her under her shirt collar. She unhooked the necklace and handed it to Piper. "It's been cleansed just as the book requires."

Piper returned to the pages and read. "Amethyst amulet for magical protection. Frequently cleanse." She looked up and smiled at Eleanor. "When battling the shadows wear the amulet. She takes the energy. She forms to either light or dark. Balancing crystals. Sacred Buddhism crystal. Stronger when adorned by the pure of heart. All is balance. Positive requires negative. Light requires dark. Shadow requires fire. Amethyst requires schorl shield." Piper stopped reading and exhaled.

"And look. My grandmum wrote—*the woman with amethyst eyes, the awakened, and the one they call First Born. Triangle. The parents in nature and nurture.*" Brianna pointed to the scratchy ink. "That's her hand. I know it. Before she died, she could barely write. Her hand jerked too much. And that means the pages were stolen when grandmum was very old, maybe just before she died."

"If Franny is a traitor, she could've used her vading ability.

She could've popped in and out of the castle completely unnoticed." Piper's eyes widened with curiosity. She rocked back and forth from her toes to her heels.

"Yes." Eleanor's one word spoke volumes.

The three women read the last sentences in silence not risking Nichola's ears.

She is young and pure. He is old and obscene. Death takes one. Violet et Noir. Next to it written in the grandmum's shaky script— *The awakened is a never dying monster. Evil, untrustworthy, but a needed shield. A sacrifice.*

The foreboding meaning hung in the air like haunted spirits.

"Okay. We must blend the ingredients." Eleanor said.

Brianna opened each container. Cinnamon. Galangal Root. Dried peppermint leaves. Dried rue. Dried vervain. Dried vetiver. She poured them in one-by-one while Eleanor stirred. Lastly, Brianna poured in the oils—sunflower and olive. She ground black tourmaline stones to a fine powder then folded the coarse powder into the mixture. It blended to a sticky brown paste.

Again all three women turned to the girl.

"Do we mark her now?" Brianna asked.

"Not yet." Eleanor glanced at the clock on the wall. "We have time, maybe hours. Watch for the flare then smear the girl before vading to the Pall." Eleanor walked to the door.

"Where are you going?" Piper asked.

"To the hollow mountain." Eleanor pulled the nickel

dragon from her pocket.

As soon as Eleanor held the talisman, she slid out of sight.

"Where'd she go?" Brianna asked in surprise almost spilling the potion. She quickly screwed the lid on the container.

"To get help from her Esurient friend." Piper turned to her mysterious daughter. Nichola knew her task, her fate, probably more than Piper did, but at the moment, Nichola sulked like an average child stuck in a room full of adults. Piper walked over and placed the amethyst amulet around Nichola's neck.

Nichola twirled the amulet around in her fingers. "It's so pretty." She giggled musically.

Piper mentally documented this particular smile that spread wide across her face and these trills that gleefully flew from her tongue. No matter what happened, at least she'd have these memories forever etched in her mind.

FORTY-SEVEN

THE LINE — BALEFIRE CITY

GUARDIAN AUDREY

The weapons had finally arrived, and the truth tests had been administered. No other traitors existed. Battle initiation began.

The blasts hit the enemy line that divided the city. Chaos broke out. Metals clanged. Explosions burst. Cries of death pierced the battlefield and smoke thickened the already heavy air. Flames sprang forth in all directions. Audrey's eyes and nostrils stung.

Enemies rushed her left and right. She had no time to protect herself from the smells and particulates. She shoved some aside and buried her sword in others. Blood and sweat stuck to every inch of her. The ground soddened with gore. She leaped over corpses like gruesome stepping-stones to squeeze her way through. She had a blessed gun but wielded her diamond blade instead. She had a long way to go before reaching North Castle. That would be the true fight, and she'd need every blessed bullet.

Tired and growing impatient, her mind jumped with thoughts of Tarian—rescuing him, finding him alive. Or not.

Marcus and Christopher, Lucianna and Briggen, shared her goal. They fought alongside her creating holes for her to slip through. She needed to get to the other side, run toward North Castle. It seemed near impossible as her blade found more and more hearts to pierce and bellies to gut. These malditos didn't go down with just one stab. It took four or five. She wasn't sure how the bones or blessing worked. Were some bones more powerful? Did blades blessed by a higher ranked clergy kill faster? She hoped not. She liked to think the purer the faith, the more powerful the blade, regardless of rank. Maybe evil was just a tough bitch to kill. She'd certainly lived long enough to witness its almighty power.

Audrey made the mistake of looking out across the line. Youthful faces wincing in agonizing terror. Big liquid silver eyes opened wide and darting around for survival. Marianne did well to glamour as many as possible giving them some advantage, all while she slashed and kicked the enemies down. Audrey was truly impressed. Then a young boy fell.

"No!" Audrey's heart split open. She veered off course to help the young ones, but Marcus yanked her back.

Audrey's panic-stricken face whipped around and landed on Christopher. "Fire! Use the blasters. Now!"

Christopher and Briggen loaded up and took out several enemies.

The cool chill of relief eclipsed her bones, but it was brief.

"I don't want child casualties. You hear me!" She screamed at Christopher.

He nodded and edged toward the youngest recruits.

The ally leaders scattered the long line. She hadn't even seen Axon or Maria or other fellow Guardians, Rebels, and Elites. Too many battles fought at once—a sea of red with an escape hole. Her hole. She dove through it followed by Marcus. They raced into the city's darkness, away from the crimson line, and toward North Castle.

FORTY-EIGHT

ARENA — NORTH CASTLE

GUARDIAN TARIAN

Tarian woke suddenly. Head pounding. Heart racing. His eyes darted madly around the cell. For an instant he'd forgotten his location. That's when he knew they'd drugged him. How long had he slept? What day was it?

"Marcus… Marcus?" Tarian whispered.

No response.

Time dragged on without a visit from anyone. He paced wondering what had happened to take his only connection to the outside world away.

What'd you find Marcus?

He gripped the bars, looked as far down the corridor as possible, then leaned his forehead against the iron. His mind envisioned Audrey. Her honey burnt hair like silk through his fingers. The sharp line of her jaw that he loved to kiss, trace its edge with his lips. The crystal eyes that only he could soften. He longed to bury his head in her neck and inhale her red clover fragrance. To caress her and feel her heart beat against his chest. He had to survive. He needed at least one more night with her.

The guards swarmed his cell, gathered Tarian, and marched him toward the open gate of the arena. Once again, a guard thrust him brutally out of the darkness and into the blinding light. Exploding white spots obstructed his vision. When they cleared, he swept the stone and dirt room with his eyes. He was alone. A gleaming double-edged, two-handed broadsword and an iron dagger hung on the opposite wall. They dangled like rabbit meat tempting a hungry dog.

It's a set up, but I need weapons.

He remained alert as he strutted across the arena feeling like a walking bullseye. He'd give anything to hold his Elite assault weapon and shatter every window so Lautaro could no longer hide behind them. Instead, he wrapped his fingers around the leather-bound hilt and lifted it from the wall.

He waited. Nothing happened. The arena stilled. Eyes he could not see, watched him. Their stares prickled his skin. His gaze traveled around the room briefly pausing to glare at each window until one opened. A guard held someone in a Guardians of Dare uniform. It was a woman about Audrey's height and weight with a bag draped over her head. The woman struggled and muffled sounds came from under the hood.

"Audrey!" Tarian rushed to the wall under the window. He tried to scale it but there were no holes to slip his feet into, no divots to grab hold of. For all his superior abilities, scaling smooth vertical surfaces wasn't one of them. His fists pounded the stone until bloody. He paced as agonizing terror stifled his lungs. He gasped and choked. His mind couldn't focus. He looked up again and scrutinized the woman. Was it her? He knew her so well and yet she was covered completely under clothes and cloth, he couldn't be certain. The uncertainty tortured his soul. But she was alive whoever she was. He inhaled. Letting faith grow with that fact and give him strength to fight.

He steadied his feet, gathered his weapons, tightened his grip, and waited for the monsters.

A maldito stumbled into the arena, apparently experiencing the same blindness that Tarian had. He took advantage of the maldito's momentary confusion and flung the dagger directly into its heart. It collapsed then sat up and pulled the dagger from its chest, a grave mistake. The loss of blood was far too great. The maldito couldn't stand. It fell back. Its head thwacked the dirt.

Tarian ran to retrieve the dagger. He got within inches when another's fingers wrapped around it. The dead maldito's blood dripped from the blessed blade. The new monster stood taller and wider, his features more deformed and his teeth filed to deadly points.

The bound woman muffled a whimper, but Tarian didn't dare risk a glance at her as he circled the beast cautiously. Tarian's arm stiff from his previous wound, the skin healing but at a mortal's rate. The stench of the salve Marcus had stolen lingered, a reminder to avoid the blades at all costs. They were obviously blessed in order to kill malditos, and if they could mortally wound him, they'd been poisoned as well.

His mind went to Sasha's murder. He'd viewed it over and over while trapped in his cell and still he couldn't remember if she'd bled out from the bite or the stab wound. All that flashed in his mind's eye was the blood and her wilting face as the life slipped from it. Centuries of life snuffed out. The emptiness of his frustrated heart because he couldn't save her tortured him in that lonely cell, but in this arena under the bright lights, wading in the stench of death, the thought gave him stubborn courage. That would not be his fate or the fate of the trapped girl above. Not if breath still passed into his lungs.

The beast lunged. Tarian leaned out of reach, his stare never veering from the blade. The monster lunged again. Tarian side stepped and brought his sword down hard on the beast's back, but its thick leather binding barely split. Tarian backed away. He gave himself a good distance to run and leap. His speed was too fast for the maldito monster to retreat. Tarian's foot landed hard on its jaw. The crack of the break echoed throughout the arena. The beast howled.

Tarian glanced up to check on the woman. Her predicament was unchanged, but Franny stood next to her. A deep violet bruise circled both of her teary eyes, her nose was bloodied, and her hands were bound behind her back. Her pitiful appearance distracted Tarian just long enough for the dagger to spike his side.

The monster forced the blade in then ripped it out.

A starburst of red crossed Tarian's vision as the wound throbbed in pain. He bent and cupped the gash just under his ribs. Perforated muscle tore as he tried to stand. Again his immortal healing ability didn't manifest. Tarian swallowed the agony and ran his sword through the maldito's center. Just as quick as he'd run it through, he pulled it out and swung it ferociously across its neck, nearly decapitating the beast.

His gaze again rose to the two hostages. Franny's pleading eyes drove deep into Tarian's wounds like jagged, twisting knives.

"Let them go!" Tarian yelled. "You're a coward, Lautaro!"

Two challengers entered the ring—one large and strong, the other crumpled like dirty laundry.

"Lycott," Tarian muttered to himself.

Lycott didn't look well but he did look wicked. His sunken black eyes hungered for flesh. His ridged yellowed fingernails were sharpened and crusted with dried blood from his last kill. He stood on a skinny frame.

Tarian knew better than to underestimate a Waker, even a boney one. He planted his feet and forgot his pain. His eyes darted from beast to beast. They both charged at once, and Tarian didn't know which to slice first. Thinking of Nichola, his hand shifted the sword's mark to the belly of the maldito.

Simultaneously, Lycott pounced the beast and tore its flesh with sharp teeth. To Tarian's disgust, he swallowed it. Bile burned as it hit the back of Tarian's throat, but he forced it back. Lycott had just made a conscience choice to save Tarian. That was unusual behavior for a Waker. Somewhere deep inside that monstrous exterior, humanity prevailed. Tarian now had three lives to save. The hooded woman that was or wasn't Audrey, Franny, and Lycott, not to mention his own.

His immortal synapsis ricocheted and burst. Confidence and energy rushed through him. The stabbed and bitten maldito attempted another strike. Tarian's fist landed on its jaw like a bullet. The maldito's head flung back as it fell knocked out.

Lycott watched the beast land. He waited for it to rise again, but it didn't. Then he turned to face Tarian. He growled, but a tear escaped his black soulless eyes. A voice guttural and barely audible escaped his lips. "I won't fight you Tarian. I won't."

Tarian nodded.

Lycott winced as the torment of his inner conflict devoured him inside. With each betrayal of his nature, his body weakened.

Tarian grabbed the dagger and the blade then flung them into the booth with the hostages. Each hit its target. The woman's hood fell. Jen stood stunned. Relief and disappointment flooded Tarian. He longed to see Audrey's face, but not in this horrible place.

"Run," he yelled to the women then turned to gather Lycott. Determined to find a way out he scanned the arena for any escape. None. They were trapped like cockroaches in a glass jar.

FORTY-NINE

Tarian squinted. Did his eyes play tricks, or had he actually seen Audrey behind the gate? Maybe the blades had poisoned him, making him delusional. He shook his head and blinked. The gate slid open.

"What are you waiting for? Get out of there!" Audrey yelled.

Holding Lycott in his arms he ran toward her. As he slipped through the gate, gunfire erupted. The sound made his heart rejoice. Those were Entente weapons, and Lautaro's army had nothing worthy to oppose them.

Tarian wanted to hold her and kiss her, but he had to settle for a smile.

She tossed him a firearm.

They rushed up the ramp away from the dank cells. They were empty. There'd been innocents trapped. He'd heard their cries for help, their whimpers of fear. Had they been freed? Tarian's spirit lightened a little with hope.

Marcus stood at the top of the ramp with a wide grin. "Hey man! Sorry I left you bro."

"I understand." Tarian's smile faded as his breath quickened. "They have Jen and Franny. We need to get them out of here."

Audrey frowned and Marcus grunted. They both shook their heads simultaneously.

"What is it?" Tarian asked.

"They're traitors." Vengeance spilled from Audrey's lips.

Confusion clouded Tarian's mind. He recalled what he'd seen. "But they were bound and held at knife point."

"An act. I saw Jen poison the blades and then meet up with Franny," Marcus said.

"But I—"

"Where are they?" Audrey's eyes glared wild with determination.

"In one of the viewing rooms. Fourth floor I believe." Rage grew in Tarian. He'd tried to help them. He'd almost risked Lycott to save them.

Audrey spoke into the Egg. "Jen and Franny are here. Find them. She can vade. She's probably Lautaro's escape plan." Audrey looked up at Marcus. "Go up ahead and make sure it's clear."

Marcus vanished.

"We have to get to the Pall as quick as possible," Audrey

told Tarian.

"Do you know how to stop it?"

"I hope so." Audrey's eyes shifted to Lycott. "Is he okay?"

Lycott grunted.

"He's a fighter." It blew his mind that he actually felt admiration for Lycott.

"Well, we need him. Don't die, Gregory," she scolded.

"I'll try not to," Lycott's gruff voice garbled.

"Marcus left you because he found the missing grimoire pages. Eleanor said they've translated them." Audrey shook her head and picked up her pace. "I don't know. It didn't make sense to me, but Piper will be there with Nichola, and she knows what to do. All I know is you and Lycott are both intricate parts of the plan." Audrey stopped abruptly. "Are you okay?"

Tarian's legs wobbled. His side and leg wound burned. Blood slicked his flesh. His palms became too sweaty to grip Lycott. He collapsed.

"Marcus!" Audrey screamed.

Lycott stumbled around trying to keep out of Audrey's way as she fell to her knees next to Tarian.

Marcus appeared.

"What's wrong with him?" Audrey asked.

"The poisoned blades. There's a salve in the infirmary."

"Get it now!"

Marcus vanished again.

Tarian's head lay in Audrey's lap. She gently stroked his

sweat soaked hair. "Stay with me," she whispered.

He nodded. His eyes struggled to focus on her wonderful angles. He loved her. "Love," he barely whispered.

"Save your strength honey."

Love, the word and the emotion, whirled through his body. Fire devoured his flesh and yet his soul was at peace. He drifted in and out of consciousness until he smelled the nasty odor of the ointment. Oily stickiness slapped onto his side and leg. It tingled. The fog in his brain slowly cleared. Audrey's ice blue eyes came into focus as they stared down into his.

"Can you stand?" Marcus asked.

Tarian cautiously got to his feet. The world tilted on the wrong axis throwing him off balance. Audrey caught him. Eventually the ground leveled under his feet and the vertigo stopped.

"Don't mean to rush you bro, but Lautaro's set this place on fire," Marcus said.

Audrey flashed Marcus an anxious glare.

Tarian took one step, then another. "How?"

"Barrels of oil and fire breath," Marcus said.

The lines surrounding Audrey's eyes deepened.

Tarian took another step. "I'm good. Let's go."

Marcus scooped up Lycott who looked paler by the second and they ran. As soon as they reached the first floor above ground the heat hit them. They covered their faces. Black smoke snaked through the halls and irritated their eyes.

"This way." Audrey ran in the opposite direction of the smoky tendrils straight into a pack of guards. She shot two but the third came at her from the side knocking her weapon to the ground. He landed a hard blow to her back. She lunged forward, landed on her knees, back arched in pain.

Tarian's fist found the guard's throat. He'd aimed for the jaw and missed. His coordination still off from the poisoning. It didn't matter. The deadly chop crushed the guard's windpipe. He was a human and dropped to the ground asphyxiated.

Marcus kicked two more sending them wobbling to the floor.

Tarian unsheathed his sword and sliced through their bellies. Their cries of pain ignored as he rushed to Audrey who shakily returned to her feet. She held his hand for support, and they continued forward.

Marcus took the lead. They ducked into a room to avoid more approaching guards. More fighting meant time and energy lost. Although, when they slipped back out into the hall, they had no choice but to pop two more. Luckily there were only two, and Audrey didn't miss.

Jen turned the corner. "Oh thank God. I thought they'd kill me. Franny betrayed us."

Audrey pointed the gun at Jen. "Put your hands up."

"What are you doing?" Jen asked.

"Do it!" Audrey demanded.

Jen's hands slowly rose. "I'm on your side."

"Search her."

Tarian took one step in Jen's direction, and she reacted. Her hand shot to the weapon tucked under her belt, but she never got the chance to withdraw it. The bullet pierced between her eyes, taking her life within seconds.

Tarian closed his eyes. Relief and disgust churned his gut. Instant death didn't seem a worthy punishment for a woman so viciously selfish, but she'd never betray them again and that felt genuinely satisfying.

Finally, they reached the cycles.

Marcus exhaled, "Good. They're still here."

A whole fleet of shiny cycles awaited them.

"Do you know the code?" Audrey asked.

Marcus flashed a sly grin. "I've only roamed this entire castle at least twenty times. Of course, I do. You ready with the flare?"

Audrey nodded.

Marcus ignited three sonic bikes. He drove off with Lycott strapped to him looking as ghastly as ever.

Audrey lit the flare then sped off. Tarian followed longing to get as far away from this place as possible.

After traveling miles and regaining his steady balance, Tarian glanced back. North Castle lit up the horizon, a fire torch fit for a giant. People jumped from the windows to escape the flames. Tarian's chest hollowed with regret, so much history lost, and he was certain Franny had vaded Lautaro to safety. The sour sting of bile filled his empty chest. He returned his gaze to his destination and propelled the cycle to top speed ignoring the constant ache of his wounds and throb in his head.

FIFTY

NORTH CASTLE — PALL'S EDGE

IMMORTAL LAVENDER WITCH PIPER

The wait seemed endless. Nichola had drifted off to sleep hours ago.

In the distance, Piper saw the flames through the foggy air. North Castle had been hit. It wouldn't be long now, but it felt like forever. She startled at each burst of fire. Her twitchy concentration gave her a headache. It became difficult to distinguish a flame from a flare until finally a red line shot high above everything else.

"That's it!" Piper yelled.

Brianna met Piper at Nichola's side. The little girl tossed and turned, groaned and cried in her sleep. Brianna unscrewed the cap, scooped up a dollop of potion, and anointed the smooth forehead of the young Lavender Immortal Witch.

Nichola's eyes popped open. "Is it time?"

Piper nodded and held out her hand. They vaded as Brianna said, "Goddess bless you."

Piper and Nichola appeared in front of the Pall. The enormous tiger leapt, its striped face and sharp fangs inches from the soft skin of their faces.

"Hello Hu." Piper patted the top of the tiger's head.

Hu purred then growled. With long powerful strides the tiger encircled them as they waited for Audrey and Tarian.

Nichola's hand stiffened in Piper's. Nichola stood so still she could've been petrified. Her amethyst eyes jumped and looped as if listening to someone or something.

"Nichola?" Piper shook her.

Nichola's possession continued as if the Pall signaled to her, sending her instructions.

Piper wrapped her arms around Nichola holding firmly, protecting her daughter from whatever demon hunted her. Nichola remained entranced and Piper squeezed. Nothing happened but the air thickened with anticipation. The noise of the war raging in the distance silenced. The cat stilled to listen.

A loud crack like the slap of a whip sounded then Lautaro and Franny appeared. They grabbed Nichola out of Piper's clutches, and vaded.

"No!" Piper screamed.

The tiger bounded, but his fangs bit only air, and his claws swiped at nothing.

"It's no use." Piper crumbled to the ground unable to think or move, completely exhausted from the hours upon hours of little sleep and loads of worry.

The tiger paced a circle around her, snarling sharp teeth, and glaring amber eyes.

Piper drew her knees to her chin. "I know Hu. I'm not going into the Pall without Tarian and Gregory Lycott. Don't worry."

The tiger snorted and paced. Every few minutes Hu bobbed his cat's head from the Pall to Piper. Growls of frustration slipped between his teeth.

Piper understood his agony at being stuck on guard but desiring the chase, itching to save the girl and eat the sorcerer. Her heart pounded and skipped making her dizzy. She hugged her legs and rocked trying to calm her crackling nerves.

FIFTY-ONE

THE PALL'S EDGE

GUARDIAN AUDREY

The cycles zoomed to within an inch of where the tiger prowled. Tarian, Marcus, and Audrey hopped off. Lycott nearly fell off.

"Where's Nichola?" Audrey asked.

Piper shook her head. "Lautaro and Franny vaded her away."

"They're in the Pall," Audrey said. "Let's go."

Tarian's arm crossed Audrey's chest blocking her.

Audrey stomped her foot. "Dammit Tarian. I'm going." She looked to Marcus, who looked to Piper

"You can't help us in there." Piper gestured to the fog a few yards away.

"Why not?" Audrey's gut twisted and ached. She was a Guardian of Dare, Tarian's protector, his fiancée. How could she let him walk into that trap without her?

"According to the grimoire, the three of us have to enter together—a triangle of sorts. It's the only way to stay alive in there." Piper's finger swabbed the potion she'd made earlier with Brianna and Eleanor. She smeared Tarian's forehead and her own. Lycott readied for his anointment, but she recapped the container. "I'm sorry, Gregory."

His eyes closed calmly. "I understand."

"You are her shield." Piper reached for Lycott's hand. He took it. With her other hand, she reached for Tarian's, and he took it.

The threesome walked hand-in-hand into the gray mist.

Tarian glanced back and smiled. Audrey's stubborn tears finally streamed down her face, but he didn't stop moving away with the others. The three bodies became shadows that gradually darkened before blending into the Pall. Soon she saw nothing. The immense strain on her heart nearly broke it in half.

Minutes passed bitterly slow. The tiger paced, Marcus grunted, and Audrey's fragile heart sank deeper, her fighting spirit drowned by impotence. The tears had dried on her face and itched, but she didn't possess the energy to scratch them away. She appreciated the annoying reminder.

A scream echoed.

"Tarian!" Audrey called, intensity returning to her limp body and energy jumpstarting the beat of her heart.

Marcus readied for action but stopped short.

The helplessness scraped and clawed her insides as she gazed at Marcus' blues and saw the same torment. What could they do? Nothing. They were stuck in horrible limbo. She lunged toward the fog, but Marcus grabbed her arm and pulled her back.

Her desperate eyes looked at Hu. His tiger's eyes bore into her like two intense suns burning fiercely.

"Go," she whispered.

He sprinted into the shadows.

She didn't think her heart could sink or break any further, but it could, and it did—dust where a heart should be.

FIFTY-TWO

INSIDE THE PALL

GUARDIAN TARIAN

Tarian pulled the others along. The mass of shadow mist thickened the farther they strode. Incredibly, Lycott's strength grew, and soon he sprinted faster than Tarian. They couldn't release each other's hands, but they managed the cumbersome journey.

A breeze swooshed past. Tiger stripes a blur in the fog running alongside them.

Tarian moved on feel and intuition as his eyes struggled for any light or color. He followed Hu's lead trusting a tiger's senses above his own.

Hu apparently had never had cause to venture this far because his path zigzagged until finally slowing to a prowl.

Tarian strained for noises or voices in the muffled cloudy air. He heard nothing but the scrapes of their feet. They trudged on—a lopsided triangle and a big cat breaking through the continuous wall of fog, like pulling open curtain after curtain after curtain of gray mist.

Finally, red shone through the shadows. Hu raced ahead. Tarian followed dragging the others. They stepped from the smoke into a clearing. Light poured in but not from the sky. It was a dome. The shadow smoke lifted high above them, but it still existed blocking all sunlight. The light came from fire, but the area didn't fill with smoke.

Flames fluttered and floated upon a pool of water. It marked the middle of the dome. Their bodies were points on a circumference. Nichola stood on the other side of the pool a direct diagonal line. Lautaro and Franny held hands about forty degrees south of her. A witch with long red hair kneeled next to Nichola smiling and coaxing. Tarian remembered a redheaded Lavender Witch that hunted Vixy, the young Lavender Witch insurgent that had helped Tarian find and fight Lautaro just a few months earlier.

Nichola's mouth opened wide. Tarian studied the shadows flowing from her or into her. He couldn't make out which direction they flew, but either way the sight disturbed him. By the strained cords of her throat, Tarian assumed she devoured them. Ribbons and ribbons of smoke filing into her little body without lengthening or widening. Where did it all go? She did age though. Her eyes narrowed and her lavender irises darkened to a bruised purple. Her soft cheeks hollowed, and her jawline thinned to a razor-sharp edge.

Lycott let go and rushed toward the water, but the heat shoved him back. He switched and raced around the pool. The redhead hissed. Nichola held out a hand. She willed an invisible barrier that he couldn't pass. He stretched his arms toward her, but the witch whispered something and Nichola turned away from him.

"What is she telling you?" Lycott screamed above the crackle of fire and wind of shadows.

Nichola's eyes closed, and her shoulders dropped but she didn't stop. Life drained from her with each inhalation of gray mist.

"She's lying to you! Don't believe her. She's wicked and evil."

The redhead Lavender Witch flung a shadow ball and struck Lycott. His body hurled across the dome. He landed with a thwack.

Nichola shut her mouth. She whirled on the witch. The girl's powers had gained the strength of the Pall, and she thrust them on the redhead. The witch flew farther and with more force than Lycott. But unlike Lycott who remained curled on the ground in pain, the witch flew back to Nichola's side as if nothing had happened.

Lautaro smiled encouragingly to Nichola as he gripped Franny. She was his lifeline, as Piper was Tarian's.

Franny used her free hand to stroke and shape the flames into a barrier that slithered from the water and divided Lycott and Nichola.

Nichola didn't like this. She whipped her hand in the direction of the fire and shoved it back on Franny. Hateful rage filled the girl as the purple in her eyes continued to darkened, and the muscles under her skin corded. Her skin stretched taught around bones.

Lycott got to his feet and turned to Tarian and Piper. "It's killing her."

Tarian turned to Piper. "Is it? Do you know what she's doing?"

Tears welled in Piper's eyes, and it took a minute for her to find her voice. "Her mark is gone. I believe, by swallowing the negative energy, she's becoming negative energy. She will be a dark force, possibly the darkest force."

"Can you do what you do?" Tarian's voice cracked as his blood pumped frantically through him.

Piper's face scrunched in confusion.

Tarian lost all words, his mouth parched, his tongue swollen. Finally, he forced out the question, "Can you stop time?"

"No. I tried." She sighed and looked back across the water. Her fingers fastened around Tarian's.

FIFTY-THREE

THE PALL'S EDGE

GUARDIAN AUDREY

The Pall shimmied.

Audrey stopped pacing. "Has it always done that?"

"I've never seen it sway before." Marcus stood closest to the shadows. He swept his arm through the fog. "Feels the same."

Audrey returned to the path she'd been pacing. Her utter helplessness sucked the fluid from her marrow leaving her hollowed to the core. If she stopped pacing, she'd collapse into a heap of brittle bones. And she was set on doing just that, if Tarian didn't come out alive.

She couldn't lose him. All the wedding foolishness she'd hated so much, she now longed for more than anything. So when she started to feel the shifts, the pressure, the tiny nuances of change in the Pall, she feared she'd be left at the alter—this gray, dismal alter—alone to continue year after year without him.

"Did you feel that?" Audrey's panicked voice called out just as Marcus, Brianna, Theo, Jun, Maria, Germaine, and

Germaine's friend Elijah walked up.

Maria led the group. "Hello Audrey."

"What are you doing here? Take the kids back to the castle at once!" Audrey ordered.

"Fine," Germaine said, "We'll go fight on the line."

"They stay," Maria said.

Audrey turned to Maria and glared. "Then they're your responsibility."

"Fine." Maria accepted the challenge.

Audrey focused on this stubborn gang of seven. "Well! Did any of you feel that?"

"I did," Germaine said.

As if she'd been lifted from under a pile of rocks, Audrey's chest lightened. She beamed at the teenager thankful she'd stayed. But her seconds of glee whisked away as the smoke stopped swaying back and forth and picked one direction. It twirled, first a slow breeze, then gradually building.

Everyone backed away with fast feet, but never taking an eye off of the whirlwind. A colossal tube of swirling shadow smoke that inhaled energy swelled and darkened spreading a sense of anger and making it hard for anyone to feel hopeful.

Audrey glanced around to see if the others felt the Pall's effects. They did. They hunched, their knees buckled, and soon all fell on their hands and knees. The force pulled them down, and it was an effort to keep from lying down, giving up.

Screams cut through the cacophonous vacuum. People

were being sucked in. Why weren't they? Then she saw the circle drawn in the mud, Brianna's work, and Theo sat with eyes shut and hands at work on invisible threads. Maria's body engulfed Germaine like a turtle's shell. Elijah held tight to them. Marcus crawled to Brianna until they could finally lock hands. Audrey's stare found Jun. Her muscles corded under black leather as she refused to give in to the crushing pressure.

Invisible talons shredded any hope she had that Tarian would survive. She heard her inner mind scream, *No!* She shook her head and forced her thoughts elsewhere. She prayed for the soldiers on the line, begged God to help Marianne protect the children. Prayers were all she had, her body was trapped in an endless loop of misery fighting just to remain upright and not be sucked up into the whirlwind.

Where was Eleanor? She'd said she had a plan, that she'd convince the Esurients to offer their ancient magic.

After what seemed like hours, the pressure and pull lessened giving Audrey the ability to draw her torso up, but she remained on her knees for stability. A shard of light peeked through the gray fog as if a cat had scratched a gash in the curtain.

That's a good sign. Right? It must be. She dared to be positive.

Refusing to let the nausea get the better of her, she stood. Something stirred. She wouldn't get caught on her knees. If this was going to be her end, she'd fight.

FIFTY-FOUR

INSIDE THE PALL

GUARDIAN TARIAN

The cat crept as cats do, and before anyone knew it, the tiger had positioned itself within striking distance.

Tarian's eye caught Hu's tiger ambers. They both stared at each other in desperation. Milliseconds mattered now. No time to question the rationality of decisions. He didn't even know what decision was the right one, so he nodded granting the big cat its choice.

Hu lunged. Massive tiger paws batted gray ribbons, but they still flowed into Nichola, one after the other, never ending. He roared at her. Surprisingly, she roared back, or more the shadows did. The cherub-cheeked girl had morphed into a demon. He leaped onto her.

Piper gasped and stepped forward. Tarian squeezed her hand and held her back.

Nichola flung the cat onto the burning water. The tiger cried out before succumbing to the sizzling flames, but he didn't sink. Instead, he laid atop the liquid a bright tiger-shaped flame.

"Daughter. No!" Piper's scream resonated like a rocket inside the dome. They all covered their ears to relieve the pressure she'd created.

Nichola shut her mouth. The shadows kept coming, but she refused them. They layered and shaped into human form. Shadow ghosts longing to join Nichola, begging her to take them in again but her mouth clamped shut. Light returned to her eyes as if she'd just seen Piper for the first time.

Her head whipped to Lycott. "Daddy?"

"Go to them," Lycott said.

Nichola shook her head.

Tarian and Piper held out their free hands to her.

"Say something to her." Tarian's voice trembled. His knees weakened from exasperation. "She's listening."

"Nichola please. Remember your friends … Germaine, Brianna. Call to the light. Please daughter!"

Tarian wondered if he should speak up. Call to her as a father. He feared he'd sound insincere and make it worse. Piper sounded so impressively bold and loving. He admired her strength and tried to steal some of it through their connected hands. He felt a bond but very little strength. It took great effort just to keep his arm lifted and his hands reaching toward his daughter, but he wouldn't drop his arm or his eyes. He'd never abandon the fight. The shadow ghosts could not win.

Nichola's scared eyes darted to the evil creatures

surrounding her, some made of flesh and bone and others only shadows. A wave of goosebumps rolled over his skin.

"Gregory, you are the shield," Piper yelled.

Lycott frowned. "Forgive me daughter." His two black soulless pools of midnight widened as he relinquished his control to the Waker inside of him. His skin paled from head to toe giving the illusion of weakening, but it was just the opposite. The vivid and wild wickedness overtook him filling him with immense vitality. His lips parted and the shadowy wisps swirled and danced their way into his mouth, his elongated throat smooth unlike Nichola's strained cording. The shadow ghosts reveled their way into Lycott. He seduced them. And like a siren's call the redheaded witch and Franny floated toward him as well.

Franny dropped Lautaro's hand. The sorcerer cried out in agony as he fought to shift into the giant mare. Only a phantasm of a horse appeared for an instant then melted away. Franny had been his breath, his connection to the miniscule amount of nontoxic life that lived inside this circle. But she and the redhead couldn't resist the pull of Lycott. After all, they were sinister creatures.

Tarian glanced at his fingers as they intertwined with Piper's. She kept him alive. Like cursed creatures or immortal ghosts, Lavender Witches could survive inside the Pall. Tarian wasn't cursed nor was he gifted with invisibility, so he squeezed Piper's hand not trusting the smear of potion to sustain his life.

Lycott and the two Lavender Witches formed a triangle of the negative. The toxins and dark magic swelled in Lycott as he inhaled the gray tendrils. His eyes emboldened.

Would it seduce him? Would he choose evil? A heroic impulse to run and kill that wicked triangle tugged at Tarian's heart, but he wisely knew his place. His duty remained with Piper.

Piper and Tarian inched closer to Nichola with fingers stretching, reaching for their daughter.

She drew her hands into herself, her eyes never leaving Lycott. She bit her lips and whimpered. A veil of determination fell across her face and her mouth reopened. She sucked, but the mist wouldn't come to her now.

"Please Nichola, trust me." Piper pressed her hand to her forehead against the potion then held it out to Nichola. The girl slipped her slender fingers into her mother's. A line of light formed indicating a sealed bond.

Tarian copied Piper and pressed his hand against his forehead then he offered it palm open to Nichola. She glanced at it then turned to the man that had raised her. She watched him darken, all goodness crumbling and dying.

The tiger that lay on the water awoke and grew and burned. A cloaked figure of smoke sat atop the enormous fire tiger.

"The fire dragon," Piper whispered as a grin curled on her lips.

Dhaumra's arms stretched long and wide up to the sky. "Vejiye va oji!"

Nichola glanced upward as did Tarian and Piper. A sliver of azure sky broke through the storm of shadows.

The wind strengthened, attempting to pull Piper, Tarian, and Nichola apart. Tarian hadn't secured the girl's grip and he felt her slipping away. He knew the triangle was critical. The wind pushed mightily against him, but he managed a step and a reach.

Nichola wouldn't commit. She withdrew.

His eyes pleaded and moistened with tears. He loved her. He cursed the tardiness of his feelings. How could he convince this little witch of his love? He pushed against the wind and managed another step. His reach now an inch closer, but he could only brush her skin with his fingers. He fought the resistant current, but its strength outmatched his own. He could only keep reaching and hoping.

Piper tugged at Nichola and nodded, but she remained stubbornly still.

The wind continued to whirl deafeningly catching their hair and clothing up into cyclone swirls. Their feet lifted off the ground. If Nichola didn't complete the triangle, they'd all get sucked into the darkness.

Nichola held back her hand, hugged it to herself. Her head bowed and her eyes shut.

Piper's forehead wrinkled. Shimmers of deep purple erupted from her as her arm stiffened and her elbow locked. Her magic valiantly fought the pull. "We need you daughter. The world needs you."

Nichola looked to the tiny opening of light above. Her tender face turned rigid again, and her eyes turned ten shades darker, but her hand jetted out, and Tarian didn't hesitate. A bolt of electricity zoomed around the triangle as soon as their grip locked. Their feet solidified on the ground, and the mark reappeared on Nichola's forehead. It glowed, as did Piper's and Tarian's.

A lump of confusion caught in Tarian's throat. It tasted bloody and sour. Would the mark hold? What was it? His eyes found Piper's and asked the question silently.

Piper smiled. Her eyes softened.

Relief gushed through him, washing down the bitter clot of bewilderment.

Nichola's head tilted to the fragment of light. She parted her lips and blew. The sky above expanded. Light gradually eclipsed the dark. Shadows faded.

Lycott smiled. His true self shined underneath his Waker skin.

The young, powerful girl that breathed light, smiled too. The brilliance of her eyes returned. Her cheeks blushed pink.

As the light battled the dark, Lycott dragged the shadows and the witches closer to the tiger of fire.

Lycott glared at the beast. "Do it now!"

A blaze of flames burst from the tiger's mouth. The ghosts of the dark howled. The witches shrieked. Lycott grinned. As they burned to ash, the dense grayness thinned to fog to smoke to mist to clear air. A tiger made of fire remained with an Esurient Eternal poised on top.

The last of the light to escape Nichola shimmered too

brightly to look at. She swallowed it. Her shoulders collapsed, tears gushed from her eyes, a smile spread across her face. She glanced from Piper to Tarian. They fell into one another. None let go. Tarian hugged them to him. He kissed the top of Nichola's head and mouthed *Thank you* to Piper. She winked.

The last shadow burned into pure light and the tiger of fire melted into the water. The Esurient with the smoke cloak stepped across to another plane.

Tarian, Nichola, and Piper stood alone next to the corpse of Lautaro. They finally let their hands drop free.

FIFTY-FIVE

Germaine had never seen a blue sky. Wonder fluttered inside her as the gray haze that had forever covered her world reduced, then melted away. The brightness that followed assaulted her eyes, and she turned away in fear.

"What's that?" Germaine squinted at Audrey.

Audrey chuckled. "The sun."

Germaine smiled and whispered, "Oh, that's the true sun."

Audrey took Germaine's hand and softly squeezed it as she looked at the space where the Pall had been.

Germaine saw nothing but miles and miles of field, trees, and rocky hills. Not only could she see into the distance now, but it was full of color too.

Elijah slipped an arm around her. She dragged her eyes away from the brilliant new world and glanced up at him. His eyes brimmed in awe just as hers did. He looked away for a moment to gaze down at her and smile. She smiled back. They both turned back at the miracle manifesting before them.

Audrey's tearful eyes stared unblinking. Marcus shifted his weight, an arm securely wrapped around Brianna's waste. Jun paced. Theo sighed. Maria took hold of Audrey's other hand. None of them appeared joyful.

Germaine turned to Elijah. "Doesn't anyone see the miracle?"

"They do. They're just worried," he said.

"Me too, but it's gone, that's good." Germaine's voice grew louder. She dropped Audrey's hand and slunk out from under Elijah's arm. She threw her arms wide and gestured to the sky and the open land they were all staring at with miserable expressions. "It's gone! Whatever they did they found the light." But still, no one smiled. "Stop it!"

"It's wonderful. I'm sorry." Audrey shook her head, a frown on her face where a smile should be.

"Don't be—"

A piercing screech called from the sky.

All heads tilted upward to see the hawk. It circled and cawed.

Audrey bolted. Her speed and power blew a gush of wind that rustled Germaine's dirty gray hair.

"There they are." Brianna tugged Marcus forward.

Everyone rushed to greet the three figures.

Audrey got to them first. She threw her body onto Tarian leaping into his embrace. They kissed with a passion Germaine had never witnessed before. It forced her feet still and her eyes sharp. She absorbed what she saw. He loved her and she him with a force that Germaine could feel. The air hummed. She wanted that.

Her eyes scanned and found the part of the sky she could look at without having the strong rays of the sun blind her, then she focused on its brilliant blueness. Once she'd satisfied her curiosity, she turned her face back to the sun, closed her eyes, and let the sunlight sink into her cheeks. Her skin warmed one layer at a time like a velvet soft touch stroking its way into her blood. The sky embraced her kindly. Maybe now she could dream about silly things like love and boys. Elijah.

Fingers tugged her shirt. They'd pulled for a few seconds before Germaine paid attention. It was Nichola, smiling at her.

"Are you happy?" Nichola asked.

Tears welled. Germaine blinked fast. "Very."

Nichola surprised Germaine with a generous hug.

"I almost couldn't do it," Nichola's voice cracked.

"Almost doesn't count." The wise words formed on Germaine's tongue without effort, and she understood. She'd had a lot of *almosts* in her life that had haunted her, but Nichola had given her a definite light so dazzling it incinerated all her *almost* ghosts away.

"I couldn't save him." Nichola hugged harder and buried her head in Germaine's shoulder.

"I think it was meant to be this way. I'm sorry."

Nichola nodded but didn't let go.

Germaine regarded the group and witnessed many smiles, laughs, and tears. Piper assisted a hobbling Jun. She cried the loudest.

Elijah stepped into Germaine's line of sight. His eyes smiled as he stood alone, selflessly watching her embrace the peculiar girl. She made room and he joined in, a cozy huddle of three.

FIFTY-SIX

SOUTH CASTLE — BALEFIRE CITY

GUARDIAN TARIAN

Maria didn't receive permission to go home. None of the Entente Elite soldiers had. Her tour had been extended indefinitely. Balefire City needed to be rebuilt. The Wastelands had a future, and its citizens needed help. But everyone knew the soldiers' extensions weren't philanthropic. It was quarantine. The Wastelands contaminated people. So, when a stocky guy with military-cut black hair arrived in the toxic town, everyone knew why.

"Love kills all diseases. Don't you know?" Gabe winked.

Maria rolled her eyes and shook her head then snatched his hand and pulled him into her. Their mouths hungrily kissed then tasted each other's cheeks, chins, eyelids, and necks.

Tarian stood awkwardly next to them wondering if they were ever going to stop kissing.

"El burro!" Maria shoved Gabe back and punched his arm.

Tarian howled with laughter.

340

Maria turned on him. "You knew about this!"

Tarian shook his head. His eyes bulged as he searched his mind for a lie, an excuse, a witty comeback. Nothing. "Ah … nah … maybe."

"Tarian," Maria scolded, but he only laughed louder, and Gabe joined in. "This isn't funny. You just sentenced him to death."

"Don't be so dramatic," Gabe said.

Instantly, Maria's face reddened, and steam could've been coming from her ears.

Tarian sobered up fast. "My sister just told me today that they're close to finding a solution."

"A cure, Tarian?" Maria questioned.

"Not sure if it's a cure or a vaccine or what."

"It makes a difference, Tarian."

The way she kept emphasizing his name made him uncomfortable. Maria was hotheaded, and he'd expected she'd be upset, but he worried she was right.

Gabe strolled over and gently took Maria's hand. "I love you. My family is gone."

Maria choked with both sorrow and joy, her eyes smiled but her lips frowned.

"You're all I got."

"Ahem." Tarian smirked.

"Sorry bro, but I ain't sleeping with you."

Maria nudged her boyfriend.

Gabe turned his attention back to her. "You're my world, and if that means we got some wacked-out disease, then so be it." He kissed the tip of her nose.

She giggled.

Gabe glanced around. "It's not so bad. Tarian said the people are nice."

"Some are." She smirked and collapsed into him.

"Come on, Audrey can't wait to see you," Tarian said.

They followed Tarian up the spiraling east tower stairs of South Castle. North Castle wouldn't be livable for a long time, even with a little magic. The Balefire citizens and the Nerve Rebels worked long, hard days with machinery and technology the Entente had supplied to restore all that Lautaro had destroyed. They'd rebuild their new country, but it'd take time and patience.

Audrey, Germaine, Teodora, and Piper sat at a table hunched over photos. They sprung up when they heard Tarian enter.

"It's so good to see you." Audrey barreled over and hugged Gabe.

Piper beamed and kissed his cheeks.

"I'm Germ."

"I'm Teodora."

"Nice to meet you both." Gabe shook each outstretched hand.

"What's going on?" Maria's fists went to her hips as a scowl crossed her face.

"Well—" Audrey began to explain when Piper jumped in, literally jumped.

"One of the weddings is going to be here … in Balefire … so you can attend. We're having two weddings." She clapped her hands together in delight. "Two!"

"We wanted you to be a part of our special day," Audrey said.

Maria's knees buckled. Gabe caught her and carried her to a chair.

Tarian's heart hitched. Strong Maria had nearly collapsed. She'd been his first friend at the EMA. She'd stuck up for him when others hadn't. He could, and would, always count on her. He'd never envisioned a time when she wasn't fiercely independent. But she'd been through so much.

Tarian didn't know what to do, but he had to do something. He pulled a chair up next to her and placed an arm around her. "Audrey and I couldn't imagine a wedding without our best friends."

"Thank you." Maria's eyes welled with tears.

"Maybe it could be a double wedding." Tarian cocked an eyebrow at Gabe.

Gabe chuckled, "Maybe."

"Yes!" Piper squealed. "Three! Oh goddess. Three. A double wedding here and one back at the village." She rushed over to Maria. "Pale yellow? With your skin tone. Yes. You'd dazzle in lemon chiffon."

"Not gonna happen Piper." Maria's eyes rolled until they landed on Gabe then her lips curled into a heartfelt smile. "I want my own special day, and I'm sure Audrey does too."

Tarian felt Maria's shoulders relax under his arm. "I think lemon suits you." He gave her a friendly squeeze. "Your tart personality."

He got a swift elbow to the ribs.

FIFTY-SEVEN

BURNING TIGER POND — BALEFIRE CITY

AUGUST 1, 2122

GUARDIAN AUDREY

Audrey found Jun skipping stones into the pond. She picked up a flat rock, perfect for jumping water, and flung it. Her rock skipped and hopped alongside Jun's until both sunk.

"Mine went farther," Jun said.

Audrey laughed.

"I miss him." Jun rolled another pebble between her fingers then tossed it.

Audrey bent to scour for a smoother stone. "Me too."

"I don't know if I can ever go home."

It'd been a couple of months since Lautaro's death. Audrey had wondered why Jun hadn't gone to visit her mother. Only mortals were quarantined not creatures. The question remained unasked. The silence between them lengthened. Only the plopping of skipping stones interrupted the awkwardness.

Eventually Audrey said, "Yeah, this place has grown on me

too."

Jun rolled her eyes.

"Sorry, I didn't mean to—"

"It's fine. I put the nightclub up for sale."

The words punched Audrey hard in the gut, but Hu was the magic of the bar. She'd probably sell it too if she was Hu's sister and business partner. She couldn't imagine what it'd be like for Jun to go back and run it alone.

A memory flashed through her. On her first night visiting the club, Hu had created the illusion of a forest. It was a maze and he'd prowled it in his tiger form. When he'd transformed back into his human body, he had attempted a kiss, but she'd bitten him then they'd danced. He'd tried to seduce her with his preta lure. She'd been furious with him. However, after several long days of being trapped in a deserted world, not too different than this one, they'd become fast friends. He'd risked his life and saved her and Tarian. And as if that wasn't enough, he and Jun had risked everything to help save the world from the Pall.

"And Qui?" Audrey dared to ask about their mother.

"Not good."

"I hope she's coming to at least one of the weddings?"

"She is. I'll bring her here—to Hu's pond. I think that'll help her heal."

Audrey nodded. She didn't trust that her voice could successfully squeeze past the lump in her throat.

"I think. Or I choose to think, that we weren't cursed all

those years ago, we were saved. His life was saved just so he could rescue the world." Tears streamed down Jun's sharp cheekbones, but her voice remained solid as if determined not to let grief break it.

Audrey swallowed and tried to find a worthy voice. "That's a beautiful idea. And I agree."

"Your vows should be here."

"What?"

Jun nodded wildly. "Yes. You and Tarian should pledge your love here. Right here." She pointed dramatically toward the ground.

Audrey glanced around. The water shimmered silver. The sun cast golden flecks that magnified the glimmering ripples, as if diamonds sailed the swells. Mountains rose majestically in the background no longer strangled by ugly fog. Now that the sun could kiss the ground, green grass blanketed the fields and wild colorful heather grew madly. Audrey couldn't deny it would be a spectacular place for a wedding ceremony. The reception could still be held in the castle as Piper had planned. It was only the first day of August. They had one more week before the wedding. It wouldn't be too difficult to switch the ceremony's site.

"You see it. Don't ya?" Jun stroked her spiked hair as she gazed longingly past the water, over the fields, and to the mountains.

"Yes."

"Listen." Jun's intense stare scrutinized.

Audrey thought she had been listening, but she concentrated harder. She heard a few bird songs. The bird's slow return east had filled the local children with surprise. Audrey loved to watch their expressions when they saw a new bird's nest or heard a new bird song. She thought of their smiles now. But that wasn't what Jun meant.

She listened past the bird's music, past the tinkle of water, and swish of grass. She couldn't place any other sound. Maybe the hum of an insect. What else? What did Jun want her to hear? She closed her eyes.

Audrey gasped and her eyes flew open.

"You heard him?"

"He whispered." Chills ran through Audrey. She'd heard the pond whisper. It wasn't words per se, just a hushed murmuring *I love you.*

"And all this was covered by that fog. That wretched gray muck." Jun turned sincere eyes on Audrey. "Maybe this is what called to those kids. Those stupid kids that just walked in. I thought them a bunch of fools. But maybe I was the fool."

Again, Audrey fell silent fearing speech would bring tears. Instead, she looped her elbow through Jun's spidery arm and drew her close. Neither woman was a hugger, but they wanted and needed to be close to each other in that moment. The sharp blades of grief shredded their stubborn past differences and bonded them.

FIFTY-EIGHT

BURNING TIGER POND — BALEFIRE CITY

AUGUST 7, 2122

GUARDIAN AUDREY

A breeze rippled across Burning Tiger Pond then swept the tendrils of hair from Audrey's cheekbones. She inwardly thanked Jun for suggesting this location. It seemed to gather more beauty with each day that passed.

She stood knees knocking and palms sweating at the edge of the glistening water. Many locals were already touting the pond's healing properties. Eleanor had even sent a sample of it back home to Patrick in the hopes that it might improve the Sanoxine. All Audrey knew was its wonder could not be matched. She'd have spectacular pictures to look back on.

Little white flowers wove wildly through an archway above her and Tarian's head. The sweet honey smell perfumed the air all around them and their guests. She hadn't felt happiness this fierce since the birth of her daughter, Isabella, hundreds of years ago. Her spirit buzzed as if millions of bees sprung from the flowers to pollinate her senses. It made standing still and listening to Joe recite the vows extremely difficult.

She tried to calm the rampant excitement zinging through her by staring deeply into the chocolate eyes of the man she loved more than immortal life itself. He beamed back at her, which only rattled her more. The energy between them became too much for a hardened soldier girl that had long ago built a fortress around her emotions, so she did the only thing she could, dropped her gaze to the floor. The sight of her bare feet centered her. She had jokingly threatened to wear combat boots giving Piper a near heart attack.

Robin egg blue toenails captured her attention and hence calmed her butterflies. Piper had taught Teodora, Nichola, and Germ the art of nail beautification once the shipment of assorted colored nail powders reached Balefire City. Germ was surprisingly skillful and had dipped and prepped Audrey's fingernails and toenails to perfection. They'd had an intimate girl's night slash bridal party putting all the finishing touches on the dresses, hairpieces, bouquets, and such.

The ballet-slipper pink, silk skirt hem swayed in the wind gently brushing its slipperiness against her ankles. It felt as if she waded in the glistening water and the waves lapped at her feet. The silver lamé bodice clung to her chest, defining her modest breasts and narrow waist. She'd felt exquisite when Tarian's breath hitched at the sight of her walking down the aisle.

She gripped the stems of the bundled wild heather bouquet in order to gather the courage to glance up again. The last thing she wanted was for Tarian to fear she had doubts. She had absolutely none. She couldn't have said that a year ago or even a month ago. All doubts that had once paralyzed her vanished. She no longer cared that he was hundreds of years younger. The fact that he was Joe's son no longer plagued her nightmares. Instead, she felt she belonged to the perfect family. And the immature teenager she'd been sent to protect at the EMA had grown into a wonderfully strong man that could protect her.

Her eyes found his once more, and he smiled a heart-melting, belly-flipping, butterfly-awakening, devilish grin. Passion shot through her blood like a tidal wave. Her lungs expanded, but the metallic fibers of the bodice wouldn't give forcing her breaths to shorten. She prayed she wouldn't pass out.

Tarian took her hand, his thumb softly stroking her palm, banishing all angst. He said, "I do."

Shivers trampled under her skin and fluttered her heart. He was absolutely perfect, and she quickly returned, "I do."

It broke her heart to step out from under the precious archway and away from the water's edge, away from Hu's spirit, from his whispered blessings. Yet, at the same time, her heart pounded with anticipation for the next stage—the reception. They were in for a night of glittering elegance. Sharing their wedding with all their new friends brought a delight to her bones that couldn't be described in words. And this wasn't like her. She wasn't a giddy person, but it was impossible not to get caught up in the festivities.

Of course, she missed Tarian's family and the villagers, but they would do this all over again the following month at home in the village. This ceremony was a symphony of natural beauty with a touch of magic pixie dust to harmonize the opposing beats. But the party Piper had planned for the village would be a bazaar to tantalize all senses, an explosion of shiny color and glittering metallics that would stretch beyond imagination, literally. A circus of light and dance. A rowdy celebration to reminisce the centuries past and embrace the hope of the modern time. Pints would spill and raucous laughter would ring out until the morning.

Which would she prefer? She didn't know. She'd always imagined all her friends and family celebrating at once, not split an ocean apart. It made her stomach sour. Somehow the Great Entente War still had its claws embedded in her and her loved ones.

"Are you okay?" Tarian asked.

"Of course," Audrey said as they rode in the handcrafted carriage of oak and pine draped in wildflowers dripping confection aromas. They followed the formal procession back to South Castle to dance the night away under twinkling dragonflies. Piper had truly gone all out and made the castle a wonderland of enchanted natural beauties. Jun had shared some of the secrets her nightclub had employed to dazzle and delight their patrons. Brianna found some fun ideas hidden in the grimoire. She'd bewitched vines to grow at lightning speed and shape into impossible statues. With Theo's help, she'd managed to concoct a never-ending fountain of champagne punch. With everyone working together, the impromptu ceremony turned into the party of a lifetime—an immortal lifetime.

Tarian's caress brought her out of her trance. He stroked the wisps of hair that escaped her laced braid halo, narrowing the scope of her attention to him alone.

"Don't worry about those birds. They'll adapt," he said.

Audrey chuckled and shook her head. "I'm fine." She wasn't concerned about the hundred swallows Piper had imported and let loose, as they'd been introduced as husband and wife. It had been an amazing display of flight and population replenishment.

"I'm your husband now." He smiled widely. "Mrs. Audrey Ballard Gualtiero Prescott, I can tell when you're upset."

She kissed him. He was wonderful and knew just how to make her smile, ease her anxiety. He'd brought fun back into her life. She gazed into his warm eyes, still full of curiosity but much wiser. He wasn't the novice cadet she'd surveilled over two years ago. And she wasn't the hard-as-nails immortal fighter she used to be.

"I wish your mom could be here."

"Ah," Tarian sighed in understanding. "I'm looking forward to watching Chloe and Joe Jr. walk down the aisle as a flower girl and ring bearer."

Audrey smiled as the thought paraded in her mind's eye. "They'll be adorable."

Inside the grand ballroom of the castle, everyone danced.

They twirled and dipped, smiled and laughed. Even the ancient sober paintings that hung on the walls seemed less dreadful and more delightful. As if the hint of a smile suddenly appeared on the past royals' faces where a stern frown had been seen before.

The height difference between Marcus and Germaine was comical, but they had moves that entranced a crowd. Audrey and Tarian stopped dancing to watch. A circle formed, then they all clapped to the beat. Christopher joined them. The men were large, but they'd had hundreds of years to learn how to move gracefully.

Germaine's smile warmed Audrey's heart. The teenager wanted desperately to see the Entente of Nations and hopefully someday she would. Teresa and Patrick would find a cure eventually. But at least, for now, she was free to dance with giants, to skip in the sunshine, to laugh out loud with her new friends in the library, to enjoy her youth until she was ready to venture into adulthood where she'd seek justice for the innocent and steadfastly hunt the wicked.

The circle turned into a group event with each person or couple moving to the center to strut their dance moves, sing obnoxiously, or giggle shyly. Axon and Ralph had rhythm that blew all others away, as did Roberto and Esmay to Germaine's embarrassment. Piper and Nichola took their turn, and it was pure magic. Nichola's inner light radiated. After that infamous night, she'd not cried or spoken of Gregory. She also hadn't opened up to Tarian yet, but she had a mother and a best friend in Piper.

Eleanor and Queen Priscella conversed and smiled

politely. Audrey suspected Eleanor might actually throw down at the next party. She loved her villagers after all.

The party roared deep into the night. The stories told got more humorous and naughtier as more wine poured from crystal carafes. The royal siblings mingled with the Cerveau leaders, the Guardians with the Nerve Rebels. The entire city reveled.

Audrey tugged Tarian onto the balcony. They passed a kissing Marianne and Zella. Maybe their romance would last this time. Lace and tulle and sweet edelweiss cascaded over and down the railing. All the rails that encircled the castle were lavishly decorated. From the city below, the castle looked like a gigantic, decadent wedding cake. It sparkled and glowed and shed soft light onto the clear sky.

Music flowed out the windows and into the night. Partiers checkered the lawn. The celebration spilled over into the streets of Balefire and would last days. Piper had not only created a party to remember, but also a holiday of light and hope to be recreated annually.

"Piper is talented." Tarian's fingers traced the petals of the little white flowers.

"She is. She's already pushing a date on Gabe and Maria and encouraging Marcus to ask Brianna to marry him so she can do this again."

"Good thing she can vade back and forth. I think she's split in her homelands now."

Audrey nodded, her hollowness returning. Audrey's home

was the village, and she knew that, but she'd grown fond of the people in Balefire. She nestled her head in the center of Tarian's chest, listened to his beautiful beating heart, and collected his loving warmth.

They stared out at the horizon that could finally be seen now that the veil of shadows had been lifted. Then something surprising appeared. A starburst of fire flames glowed far away where the land met the sky. A prowling tiger of light.

Audrey squeezed Tarian. "He came."

Tarian kissed the top of her head. "Of course, he did. He loves you."

She looked up at the man she'd tried not to fall in love with but had failed miserably. An affable, brown-eyed boy somehow fit perfectly with a reserved, icy girl. For an eternity, she'd love him.

FIRST BORN TRILOGY

WHO HELPED AND WHAT HAPPENED?

First Born has been a unique journey along a very bumpy road. One I began several years ago. Book 1, *First Born*, was first self-published in December of 2015 with *First Awakened* launching soon after in March of 2016. The third and last book in the trilogy manifested slowly and in pieces that proved difficult to organize. Also, another book idea took root in my head. It was loud and wouldn't yield so the *First Born* trilogy got placed on the back burner. I wrote *Dog Girl*, my debut young adult contemporary romance. *Dog Girl* found an agent and a publisher. If you're interested it's out in the world under my pen name, Gabi Justice.

Meanwhile, the third book, *Last Chance*, began to come together. Before releasing *Last Chance*, I decided to query a few independent publishing houses that accepted self-published books. One loved it and offered to publish in 2022. So, in 2019, *First Born* and *First Awakened* were shelved and the waiting game began. Then the pandemic hit. The said publishing house went out of business. It was difficult and discouraging but all three books were complete, never published with said publisher, and I had my rights back, so what was I to do—relaunch the trilogy myself!

I'd learned a few things since 2015. The wild ride had brought me knowledge and industry friends. I am forever grateful to those who have helped shape the *First Born Trilogy*.

A big thank you to my SCBWI critique group: Jill Watson, Andrea Tripke, and Ann Marie Meyers for reading lengthy, monthly experts of *Last Chance* and other stories. Thank you to my friends at the Tampa Writer's Alliance critique group—over twenty-five fellow writers who thickened my skin. Special thanks to my agent Sharon Belcastro for constantly believing in me. You may not have played a key role in these books but within my writing marathon you take the lead.

Thank you to Allison Newell, Tarian Prescott's first fan; to Sandy McCain who helped edit my first drafts; Jim Robertson for my eye-catching covers; to Diane and Jenny at BookRhythm for the fabulous support and promotion. I will be forever thankful to have sat next to Tasha Vincent at the On Point Book Fair in Tampa. Your editorial input lifted my writing to a greater level. Thank you, April Schlee for your keen proofreading eye. Thank you to my insightful friends and beta readers Mark Charest and Darrel Polsley for finding those pesky typos and errors that slipped past, for letting me know when something was out of place, and for your constant encouragement and input. To Emcat designs for former book covers and beautiful map designs. To Marina Charalambides for bringing the characters to life with your drawings. Also, to the beta readers who probably wondered if this trilogy was ever going to be completely published: Mattea Carberry, Valerie Senske, Susan VanNort, Julie Carrigan, Mimi Daniels, and the Book Gremlins.

Since this journey has been a long and winding path, I've probably forgotten to mention someone. If I have, I'm truly sorry. Every little bit counts and I'm grateful.

Lastly, a giant thanks to my readers and fans that have written reviews, joined my newsletter, and parties, all in support of Tarian and Audrey. You have brought my characters and world to life.

JANELLE GABAY

Janelle lives with her husband, three dogs, and a cat in Florida. Two of her three children are out of college and in the workforce. The third is close behind. They are her pride and joy. She was born in Nebraska and grew up in the Philippines, Virginia, Alabama, Maine, and Florida as an Air Force Brat. *First Born* is her debut novel. She spends her time writing, taking care of her animals, going to hockey games or tennis matches, and traveling with her family. She is a graduate from the University of South Florida.

You can visit her online at www.janellegabaybooks.com
Twitter @JanelleGabay
Instagram @janellegabaybooks
janellegabaybooks@gmail.com
Follow on Goodreads
Facebook page Author Janelle Gabay @authorjanellegabay

www.ingramcontent.com/pod-product-compliance
Lightning Source LLC
Chambersburg PA
CBHW021726110726
47902CB00005B/1355